THE
GIRL
from
PROVENCE

BOOKS BY HELEN FRIPP

The French House
The Painter's Girl

HELEN FRIPP

THE
GIRL
from
PROVENCE

bookouture

Published by Bookouture in 2024

An imprint of Storyfire Ltd.
Carmelite House
50 Victoria Embankment
London EC4Y 0DZ

www.bookouture.com

ISBN: 978-1-83525-476-9
eBook ISBN: 978-1-83525-475-2

For my family, and everyone's, everywhere

Fix your course on a star and you'll navigate any storm.

— LEONARDO DA VINCI

CHAPTER 1

THE END OF INNOCENCE

VALLON-DOUX, SOUTH OF FRANCE, NOVEMBER 1942

Lilou and Freddie shared the bike down the hill, him pedalling too fast, her balancing on the saddle, the big baker's basket on the handlebars filled with honey from their farm. It was All Saints' Day, a festive, bright and cold November morning, sharp-focused and crisp. The dense oak forests that clung to the hills and valleys had dropped a crackling carpet of fiery leaves, and a feast of acorns and chestnuts for the wild boar. Jays flashed iridescent blue and autumn blush amongst the trees, and sunrise blazed on the mountains.

Her beautiful Provence, with its soaring peaks, vineyards, fragrant fields, mild air, and the sea that spread out like a glittering silk ball gown. The land, the mellow stone, the fountains and the people, so full of fun and grit, were in her soul. For some reason, today it all seemed extra precious, as though the breeze that caught her hair was bringing with it a change to everything she held dear.

'Slow down, the honey!' shouted Lilou as the jars rattled dangerously in the basket.

'I've done this a million times, just hold on tight!'

Her brother Freddie was a thrill-seeker and the combination of steep hill and two wheels was irresistible.

'Scout will never keep up,' said Lilou, screwing her eyes closed at the rushing road. She knew better than to give her brother orders; that would just make him go faster. But he'd do anything for Scout, their oversized sheepdog puppy, and he slowed down to an easier pace for their faithful companion, who was panting with the effort.

They were the first to arrive in the square, where the closed shutters gave the village an air of desertion. The leafless, pollarded plane trees were cut right back like upturned palms, spreading out gnarled fingers, architectural against the pristine blue sky. Lilou spotted her ginger tom's tail flick round a corner into a silent alley. She smiled to herself. Her errant cat, Casanova, had a habit of following them into town, although he would never run alongside them like Scout. A lone dog barked by the fountain and the baker turned his sign to open, waving to Lilou through the glass.

Lilou couldn't remember the last time she'd tasted a buttery croissant, delighted at a window display of mirror-glazed mousselines, or scooped a treat from neat rows of ruby *tartes aux framboises*. Not since the town council had been replaced by officials from the German and French alliance they called the Vichy government. Now any food you didn't grow yourself was rationed, and daily bread was scarce.

The Vichy delegation had seeped in from their wartime stronghold in the north of France, wearing cheap suits and waving official papers, and unceremoniously ousted the outraged local councillors. Monsieur le Maire and Madame Aveline had complained that they wouldn't have a clue how to run things and everyone had muttered in the Café des Amis when they changed road names to honour people Lilou had never heard of. But the villagers settled down soon enough

when they realised they could go about their daily lives as unfet-
tered as they had under the previous regime. Most of them had
always been poor and lived off the land, so the wartime short-
ages didn't make much difference. Vichy government directives
to confiscate bicycles, or to change daylight saving to make the
working day longer, were 'undelivered' by the postman, or
ignored by the officials and the police, who were country people
themselves.

War was happening in France, but at the same time it
seemed very far away from everyday village life up here in the
hills. Officialdom, paperwork and government were sneered at
as petit bourgeois concerns compared to the real world of
working the land, hunting and fishing. The only time the
authorities really crossed anyone's path was when they were
born, married or died, and that carried on apace, like it
always had.

Plus, they had Madame Aveline. She trod a clever line
between acquiescence and resistance, allowing the Vichy lot to
think they were running the town while still making sure
everyone had what they needed. So when she helpfully found a
sign-painter to change all the road signs that were named after
anyone deemed too revolutionary, the Vichy council were
appeased. They had no idea that the sign-painter was also the
local bicycle mechanic, who used his tools in garages, barns and
behind haystacks to ensure the town's main form of transport
kept running smoothly, despite the orders for everyone to hand
in their bicycles.

'Where are you off to? You said you'd help,' said Lilou to
Freddie's back. He kept walking in the direction of the boules
court, where the local boys gathered to smoke. Scout followed
on his heels, giving Freddie wet-nosed nuzzles from the sheer
joy of being with his master.

'Your brother's going to ruin that dog. The hound won't
want to spend any more summers alone in the mountains with

his sheep, and the wolves will recognise him for the pretender he is. You have to keep them a bit wild, you know. You don't want to be ostracised from the village as a Patou-spoiler. People talk,' complained the old shepherd from the butcher's stall.

Lilou tied her apron and threw a cloth she'd embroidered with bees over the trestle.

'What makes you think I have any say over anything he does?' said Lilou, glad that her old family friend Gabriel Rivière was here with her, unloading squashes, potatoes and apples from his Citroën van for the market.

They weren't really meant to gather in large groups, for market or for any other reason, but the word was that the council would turn a blind eye to the last market of the season. Now that Gabriel was here, she knew everything would be fine. No one crossed Gabriel, not even the Vichy lot. With his ebullience, sharp tongue and burly frame, he could bulldoze anyone round to his way of thinking, and no one dared provoke his fierce temper by crossing him.

Gradually, the square filled up with the usual stall-holders: the fish boys, the goat's cheese lady, the church committee with their home-made knits, Monsieur Soulier's spices, the fat butcher's best charcuterie, and bits and bobs from people's houses. Everyone did their best to bring an air of abundance, but the nuts stall was the only one whose baskets were overflowing, thanks to the season. It didn't really matter. Children zigzagged around the square playing tag and eliciting tuts from the elders, dogs barked, predictions for the farming weather were exchanged, and the place was buzzing like nothing bad had happened.

Few people had enough money to pay the premium Lilou charged for her lavender honey, but she gave a jar free to the Blanc brothers' mother. Her son was missing in action, and she hadn't smiled since the postman had delivered the official letter from the War Office.

A fight broke out over the single seabass on the fish stall, and Madame Aveline was forced to mediate. Gabriel Rivière cuffed the skinny Jumel boy around the ear for trying to steal an apple, but gave him two anyway. *You only had to ask.*

Madame Aveline had just clipped open her purse to hand a note to Lilou when a dark hush descended over the gathering, like chattering birds swooping down to roost. A shining black police car, a black Mariah, was bearing down on the fountain in the middle of the square, followed by a truck lined with German soldiers, each pointing a rifle to the sky.

The driver of the black Mariah, unfamiliar with the village's unspoken one-way system, took the wrong way round the fountain and clipped it, knocking a chip off the stone bowl that had survived hundreds of years until now. Lilou's tomcat narrowly missed being squashed by the speeding vehicle. He leapt out of the way and hissed at the car, squatting on his haunches. Inside the vehicle, two men in braided caps and black uniform looked straight ahead as they skirted the market. The soldiers in the truck that followed, lads not much older than Freddie, avoided eye contact, looking wary, nervous or embarrassed even.

Both vehicles came to a halt outside the town hall, and the Vichy officials stepped out to greet them with half-hearted Nazi salutes. The German officers snapped back smart salutes, slicing the air.

'What's happening?' said Lilou.

'I'll take two jars, dear,' said Madame Aveline, making a show of ignoring the Germans and handing over the money.

Lilou looked around desperately to try to understand. Gabriel weighed out some potatoes, slipped them into a bag and handed them to two old widows, who took their time counting out their centimes with shaking hands. The boys on the fish counter dipped out of sight and didn't stand up again, and the nut lady cracked a walnut and handed it to the tobacconist, who stared at it blankly in his palm.

It was like the hive had sent out a secret distress signal.

'Why is no one saying anything?' whispered Lilou, her heart pounding her ears in the silence.

'It's been lovely to see you dear.' Madame Aveline gave her a tight smile. 'If I were you, I'd pack up a little early today, the weather looks like it's on the turn. I think I saw you arrive with your brother? He can help you back up the hill. I suggest you find him as quickly as you can.'

Madame Aveline put the jars into her basket and proceeded smiling towards the soldiers, buttoning her coat as if that would stop a bullet.

As soon as the soldiers disappeared into the town hall, escorted by Madame Aveline, the stall-holders began to hastily pack up. No one had the appetite to shop or trade any more, and Lilou heard low murmurs about krauts and filthy Boches from some people, a purse-lipped *finally some law and order* from others. The change in the air she'd sensed earlier was brewing into a glowering storm.

Before she could pack the final honey jar back in her basket, the Jumel boy came skidding round the corner.

'You're needed!'

'What for?'

'A bee swarm. In *November*.' He blew out his cheeks for emphasis.

She had to see this. Swarms were usually a spring thing, but one of her hives *had* been acting strangely. She grabbed a box she could transport them in, and felt in her pocket for her trusty queen clip.

The boy led her to the statue outside the tailors' shop, where a small crowd had gathered, presided over by the abbé. One of the baker girls had fainted, and a Blanc boy was gallantly fanning her.

The abbé frowned. 'Superstitious heathens, the lot of you.

Here's Lilou. I'm sure there's an explanation, isn't there?' He smiled indulgently in her direction.

She studied the swarm. It was an unusual shape, like a teardrop.

'Our Lady of the Roses. It's a sign!' slurred the tobacconist, who was always worse for wear after lunch.

The abbé turned to the swarm and crossed himself. He always knew how to play the crowd. The bees had swarmed the statue of Sainte Roseline, their local saint, and today was the All Saints holiday. Even Lilou had to admit it was a delightful coincidence, even if it was November, which meant this swarm was probably in trouble. It was certainly a welcome counterpoint to the arrival of the soldiers.

If she could successfully bring the swarm home, their honey would be worth a fortune. With Papa dead and Maman struggling, the money would be a godsend.

Lilou scanned the swarm for the queen bee's long abdomen and glowing chestnut sheen.

'Where are you, your royal highness?' she whispered.

The silent crowd got bored with the wait, and began to chat amongst themselves, the murmur blending with the sound of the bees while Lilou watched for the cluster around their queen who would be moving in a tell-tale spiral royal progress. And there she was, the queen bee: a beauty who had led her court of worker-bees to Sainte Roseline, the most revered flower girl of the village.

A pink dab of paint on the queen's head placed her exactly for Lilou. Pink meant she'd marked her in 1941, last year's hatch. This swarm unquestionably belonged to her. She and her brother Freddie would have nurtured the eggs, given her a home, and watched as her hive grew, harvested the lavender-tinged honey made from their fragrant fields.

Lilou secured her queen in the clip, pausing to watch the sunlight illuminate her downy tiara, and released her into the box, where a jar of honey water was waiting. The queen led her procession of loyal workers to the food source. Nearly there. A few clever bees remained on top of the box and began the waggle-dance to guide any stragglers in, their wings charging the air with their mesmerising, transparent beat.

Once they were all safely in the box, Lilou bowed her head to Sainte Roseline for her good fortune. She might not be particularly religious, but the old country ways stayed with you.

'You're not such a sceptic when it suits you,' said the abbé.

'I believe in Mother Nature and all her mysteries. Who knows anything more than what's right in front of you?' she replied, picking up her box of buzzing treasure.

'You young ones are always questioning the status quo, and quite right too. But when you've lived a little, you'll understand the need for a spiritual life.'

What he didn't understand was that she had a spiritual life, in the purple lavender fields, the herb-strewn alpine foothills, in the byres and sheep pastures that filled her with wonder every day. Churches were dark and gloomy places she had no need of, even less after her father had died five years ago. She had only been thirteen and her rage against a careless, spiteful God would have frightened off any other abbé.

Her friend Joseph Monteux emerged from the tailor's shop to see what all the fuss was about. He kissed her on both cheeks. 'A swarm in November?'

'It can happen,' said Lilou. 'If they feel threatened, or something's wrong in the hive.'

Joseph frowned. 'That's how me and Maman feel now.'

'What do you mean?'

'Those soldiers who've barged into the town hall. They won't like me and Maman being here.'

'Don't be silly. As long as we ignore them and keep out of their way, we can just carry on as normal. They're probably just passing through,' said Lilou breezily.

'What I mean is, they won't mind *you*, but they will mind *us*.'

'Quite right too,' slurred the tobacconist.

Joseph turned to face him, but the abbé already had the drunkard by the collar.

'I swear to God, one more word like that from you, or any of you,' he addressed the crowd with blazing eyes, 'and I'll bring down eternal damnation on every one of your ignorant heads.'

The tobacconist was whimpering, but the abbé squeezed his collar tighter before he let go. The crowd fell silent, ashamed, but Lilou didn't like it. What was wrong with Joseph?

'Come on, you'll need a lift home with that box of stingers. I'll give you a lift as long as you promise they won't escape,' said Joseph.

'They've got their queen, their honey and me. They're not going anywhere.'

'Lucky them,' said Joseph, only half-joking.

Lilou busied herself sealing up the box. She'd known Joseph since their schooldays and he'd always worshipped her and she wished he wouldn't. She'd made her feelings more than clear, but he couldn't help himself and he was the last person in the world she'd ever want to hurt.

Joseph was shorter than her, a teddy bear of a young man with an already receding hairline of fair hair and intelligent, pale eyes that were reduced to pinpricks by his specs. His light skin burned in the southern sun and every boy and in their schooldays most of the girls could outrun him, but when he played the cello, everyone listened, and a charisma settled around him like an aura. And best of all, he was the funniest person she knew. No one could make Lilou laugh like Joseph.

His parents had made a fortune from their little tailor's shop in Vallon-Doux and although Lilou's grandma had taught her how to sew, it was at the Monteux tailor's shop that she'd learned how to make the fine garments she sewed for the society ladies in Paris. Any extra income for the farm was a godsend, even if it didn't come from the land.

On the way home in Joseph's Citroën, they bounced along the potholed road. Cars were still a rare enough sight in these parts, and small boys threw down sticks to form a noisy convoy behind them, hitching up oversized hand-me-down britches.

'Give us a lift!' shouted a boy with one shoe.

'Blow it out your exhaust pipe!' roared another.

'Filthy rich thieving Jew,' shouted another as he threw a stick at the windscreen.

'What did he say?' said Lilou. 'I know that cheeky little scut, I'll go straight to his maman…'

But Joseph had gone uncharacteristically quiet, and his knuckles were white with gripping the steering wheel so hard.

'There's no point. His parents probably taught him to say it,' he said.

Lilou held on to her box of bees for dear life. Of course she'd heard what was happening in Paris, and the north. War, politics, refugees. But that might as well be another country. Nothing like that ever happened here. Of course, disease struck crops, people got ill and neighbours had petty feuds, but nothing world-changing, big and dark. Like most people, she'd chosen to ignore what was happening and hope it would go away. And now that kid was spouting hate at one of the people she loved most in the world, and no one would tell him to stop.

CHAPTER 2

DISBELIEF

Joseph put his foot down and the Citroën left the boys behind in a plume of dust. As it settled behind them, he gave her a sideways glance.

'Heil, Kapitän, if I show you my prize begonias can you see your way to keeping the bridge open?' he simpered in Madame Aveline's Marseillaise drawl.

Lilou hitched up her imaginary bosom. 'I know all the best places to look for truffles, Commandant.'

'That salami looks delicious, Herr General,' said Joseph.

'You're disgusting, why do you always have to go too far?' giggled Lilou.

They rattled along through the lanes, their laughter whipped away on the crisp air, and everything seemed almost normal again.

Maybe it would still be all right. All the mothers had breathed a sigh of relief when the ceasefire was declared, and the south of France was safe, still under French rule, with their husbands and sons still home and working the fields and factories. As long as you kept going and worked hard, like the bees, the lavender would bloom, lambs would be born and grow, Lilou's creations would emerge from reams of cloth, food would appear on the table, and her hills, valleys and emerald rivers were all she needed.

Lilou agreed with Joseph not to mention the Germans to her mother so as not to upset her. He understood. He'd known her family forever.

Joseph crunched down the gravel track to the front door. She hoped her brother was already here. Gabriel had warned her to find him before he left the market, but she'd forgotten. 'Tell that brother of yours to keep out of the way,' he'd said darkly. 'This isn't a game.'

At the sound of the car, Maman came running out. Even though Lilou was twenty-one, she still never relaxed until she and Freddie were home.

Lilou got out of the car with her bees. 'A November swarm, Maman. Docile as anything.'

Joseph jumped out and kissed her maman warmly on both cheeks.

'Good afternoon, Madame Mistral. Your Lilou certainly is a chip off the old block. Rounded up the stingers in a jiffy, an oasis of calm amidst the madding crowd.'

Maman gave him a rare smile, a bitter-sweet reproach to Lilou's heart. Her beautiful mother used to smile like this when Papa was alive. That was before. Now her hands trembled so much she couldn't sew, and at night she muttered to dark shadows, which scared Lilou however much she told herself there was nothing there. She had always covered for her maman as best she could, by taking on most of the chores and making sure Freddie went to school and looked to all the world as if he was well cared for.

'Don't look so sad, I can't bear it,' said Joseph as Lilou walked him back to the car.

'I'm fine,' she said.

'You're a bad liar.'

'And you're a good friend.'

'My mother sent something,' he said, reaching into the boot and pulling out a package.

The latest copy of *Vogue*, featuring society beauty Marie-Madeleine Fourcade on the cover, wearing a dress she'd helped Joseph's mother sew for her.

'It's her, your mum's client! She looks so beautiful.'

'You look better in your dungarees than her in all that finery,' said Joseph.

'Don't be ridiculous, she's a goddess,' said Lilou.

And she was. The dress was a hip-skimming floor-length mink-coloured silk from the best mill in the Ardèche valley, cut on the bias, with spaghetti straps. Understated, daring and expensive, like its wearer. Joseph's mother had shown Lilou how to sew the seed pearls that edged the neckline and straps. Threading the needle never failed to give her a thrill of anticipation and, for the long hours it took to create something beautiful, the couture filled her every thought. During fittings, Marie-Madeline had whisked her away to Shanghai with stories of the Buddhists who had taught her how to meditate as a child. Lilou imagined this was how it must feel. Just her, and the task at hand, creating something beautiful, while thoughts and the world rushed outside in another place and time.

Lilou still couldn't believe that this beautiful creature made the effort to travel from her holiday home in Saint-Tropez especially to get her clothes made. Marie-Madeleine was a force of nature and she entertained them with her tales of flying lessons, running a radio show in Paris, and the deathly boring (in her words) round of parties, society balls and marriage markets. It sounded like Lilou's worst nightmare, and she thanked her lucky stars for her lavender fields, hills and freedom.

Her sewing room was her refuge, with its colour-wheel of

neat threads, folded piles of fabrics, her grandmother's mother-of-pearl thimble, the padded sewing box full of treasures collected over the years – buttons, trims, diamanté, feathers, pincushions and her old silk measuring tape. Where the small-holding was the lifeblood of the family, providing them with basic food and a little left over to sell or barter, her sewing bought them their luxuries. Like Lilou's most prized possession: the bike with the enormous basket that she'd bought from the baker. Speeding along the plateau where the woodpeckers drummed, then flying down the hill into the village, was heaven.

She'd left her bike in the village in all the rush! She hoped Freddie would remember to bring it home.

'Hello, Earth to Lilou! I had no idea a magazine could be so much more scintillating than a real-life person,' said Joseph, pulling up the fur collar on his expensive tweed coat ready for the drive back.

'Oh sorry!' Fashion magazines from Paris did transport her. It was easy to fall down a rabbit hole with all the expert cuts and exquisite stitching. 'I'll come and thank your maman next time I'm in the village.'

She kissed him distractedly on both cheeks and he gave her an extra squeeze.

'You know I'm here if you need any help with your maman. She's just fragile, that's all.'

'I know. Thank you. You're the only one who really under-stands how she is.'

Joseph's father was dead, but, where the rest of the village gossiped about her maman 'not being right', Joseph and his mother were a tower of strength to her and Freddie.

She waved goodbye, carefully picked up the swarm box and went off to the yard to find Freddie.

She was relieved to find him where he always was, in the

sheep pen with Scout, her bike carelessly dumped on the ground where he'd dropped it.

'You're not supposed to be in there, Freddie!' said Lilou.

Sheepdogs round here were called Patous. They were big and white and fierce and were supposed to work independently of humans to ward off the wolves in the high pastures. The shepherd in the market was right; Scout was in danger of becoming far too domesticated under Freddie's rule.

'I want him to learn to protect me, too. He can help me fight now the Germans are here.'

The dread she'd felt when she'd seen the teardrop swarm rose again.

'Just stay out of their way. They're not here to fight, the abbé and the mayor have both said so. It's a peacekeeping force.'

'You don't believe in God, but you believe that rubbish. Of course they're going to fight. All the boys in the *Garde Champêtre*, the country guard, are learning how to use Sten guns.'

A ewe bumped Scout with her horns and Freddie gave the dog an affectionate pat.

'He's a Patou through and through, he just knows he has to protect them. Look, he's letting the ewe prod him, gentle as one of the lambs. He's going to do us proud.'

'Not if you mollycoddle him and pet him. He's supposed to be up in the mountains on his own with his flock. C'mon, leave him be, I need you to find the Sainte Roseline swarm a good home. They'll buy you that bike you wanted if you take good enough care of them.'

Freddie ran his hands through his dark curls and whistled through his teeth. 'Nice, how?'

Her sweet little brother. Not so little now, nearly eighteen. The abbé called the two of them the angel and the devil. Everyone said they looked very alike, with their olive skin, dark eyebrows and navy eyes, but Lilou's hair was long and wavy, the colour of wheat, while Freddie had thick, dark curls like Papa's. Lilou did the buying at the market – she loved picking out the shiniest, freshest produce – while Freddie was supposed to do the carrying. But more often than not the basket was abandoned, and Freddie would be raising a riot, starting tomato fights with the other boys, or charming wild strawberries from the old widows who'd brought produce to sell from their kitchen gardens.

Freddie gave Scout a pat, let himself out of the nursery pen and stomped off towards the apiary with the miraculous brood of bees. Sweet Scout made no attempt to follow him, but took up his place guarding his ewes and lambs, his white matted fur blending with his charges'.

Lilou made chestnut soup, and roasted Gabriel's squashes and roots in honey and thyme. Maman was herself today, and she laid the table with their best tablecloth to celebrate All Saints' Day. She'd laid a crackling fire in the grate, and had even been to the kitchen garden to pick late roses to make a cheery centrepiece.

Freddie gallantly pulled out the chair for Maman and gestured for her to sit, pouring her a glass of their best Bandol.

She beamed at him. 'What do you want?'

'I'm just happy something's finally happening around here,' said Freddie.

'Don't tell me, you've persuaded some poor girl to fall for you with that ridiculous grin.'

'No, the Germans drove into town today, and me and the boys...'

Maman's eyes glazed and the spark disappeared. Her body was present, but her soul slipped away to hide in the shadows.

'No they didn't, don't be silly, Freddie,' said Lilou, putting a hand on Maman's shoulder to bring her back.

Freddie poked at the fire disconsolately. Lilou knew he hated it when Maman left them like this.

'It was inevitable,' said Maman, back from wherever it was she went. 'Freddie, you just keep out of the way and attend to your chores at the farm. That's how you can contribute to the war effort in Provence. Maréchal Pétain has done his best to protect our lads from conscription and war, and you and the boys – and you are only boys, remember that – will never defeat the Germans. We just need to keep our heads down and wait for better times.'

Before Papa died, Maman had been a schoolteacher, one of the best-educated women in the town. She and Papa would have fiery debates about politics and the world. Of course Maman knew what was going on beneath all their noses. There was so much unspoken in their little family; it was easier like that. Lilou was the optimistic one, who always looked on the bright side of life, enough for Maman and her. Freddie was the indulged son, and Lilou did everything she could for him when Maman couldn't. They all carried on as best they could, as if nothing at all was out of kilter since Papa's death had punched a hole in their world. Facing horrible truths was useless, and wouldn't put food on the table.

Queen bees hid underground and overwintered to emerge the following spring to hatch another colony, and that's what Lilou knew she had to do. But now she realised Maman had been protecting her, rather than the other way round. She'd cancelled their subscription to the *Le Petit Provençal* newspaper and told her to ignore village gossip as just gloom, doom and hysterics. In this, it was Lilou who had retreated from the world, not Maman.

For grace, Maman prayed to Saint Monica, the patron saint of mothers, to protect her beautiful children, and all the golden lads and lasses of Vallon-Doux, and a special prayer for Joseph. After that, Lilou didn't feel much like eating.

. . .

In the village the Germans took what they wanted, painted a black cross on the Hotel des Chasseurs and moved in. Rumour had it that the proprietors did very well out of their new German guests, who rewarded them for their assistance. The tobacconist said he'd seen truffles being delivered, and crates of champagne from Épernay. The officers were distant and didn't mix in much, but the young soldiers were friendly enough, and often hung around the square, looking bored.

Attitudes varied wildly and rumours flew. The Sunday after the soldiers had driven into town, Lilou lingered on the church steps after mass, listening intently to the gossip.

'Very well-behaved, polite young gentlemen,' was the verdict of the two widows whose heavy bags were carried home for them.

'It won't last. It's human nature. They have power over us and, at some point, you can be sure they'll abuse it,' said Colonel Manhès. 'The Boches can't be trusted, full stop.'

The chatter splintered and flowed. *If this is what it takes to keep my sons from being killed in some rat-infested trench, so be it... Madame Roustin gave them an entire season's wild mush-rooms and they paid her way over the odds... All right for some... It's just the way it is, we might as well get used to it.'*

There had always been rivalries, but in just one week the village had fractured right down the middle. Families argued behind closed doors, some wanting to keep the new status quo, others furious about how the town had rolled over. They didn't say it, but Lilou knew from the way that they went about their business – more considered, less open – that mainly people were afraid, never mind which way they swung.

The whole village was outside the church. Whether they believed or not, the wrath of the abbé was more than even the toughest of farmers were prepared to face.

A gaggle of boys ran out from Sunday school with sticks and pointed them at the soldiers, who were taking coffee in the square.

'Hands up!'

'Don't shoot!' The soldiers held their hands up, and the boys ack-acked at them as they obligingly pretended to be shot.

A loud, husky mewling suddenly had the whole congregation searching for the source. High up on the church spire was Lilou's cat, Casanova. He was a bruiser, and not easily scared, but he'd got himself stuck climbing the metal rungs on the precipitous spire and was frozen, miaowing pitifully. Lilou felt sick with vertigo just looking up. If he fell, he'd die.

'It's my cat!' said Lilou to Abbé Aloïsi. 'Is there a way up there?'

'There are steps and a hatch, but there's no way you're going up, you'll kill yourself. The last time anyone climbed those rungs was ten years ago when the steeplejack came to repair the lightning conductor, and he had his ropes with him.'

Country people were tough, and animals were ten a penny, treated dispassionately, as farm assets, but Lilou started to cry in front of the whole village. It happened every now and then, a hangover from Papa's death, taking her by surprise with an unresolved kind of grief.

'He was Papa's. He raised him from a kitten and I promised to take care of him and Maman and Freddie.'

The abbé put his arm round her. 'Come inside, don't watch. That cat's got a better chance of survival than any human.'

'May I assist? I climb the mountains at home,' said one of the Germans in perfect French. He tapped a winged insignia on his uniform. 'I have a head for heights.'

It was the German who'd helped the widows with their shopping, and had generally made himself useful around the village. He was taller than her, with kind eyes, but he looked so out of place standing there, with his fair hair, pale skin and alien looks.

She shook her head and the abbé stepped in.

'We look after *all* God's creatures, even the sinners,' he said pointedly. 'It's too dangerous and I won't allow it.'

Lilou was shocked that he dared to cross the German, but the man gave a polite nod and stepped away. He was hurt, Lilou saw it in his eyes.

The gathering on the steps turned their attention to what could be done, and there were as always two camps, one who couldn't bear the pitiful mewling and poor Lilou's distress, the other who deemed him a stupid moggy for getting himself into the situation and declared he'd have to get himself out of it. No one knew what to do, until one of the Sunday school boys whistled and sucked his teeth, pointing up to the spire.

The German who'd offered help was poking his head out of the hatch, coaxing Casanova to come to him. Casanova miaowed even louder, and scaled two more rungs, while the crowd gasped.

The man stretched out of the hatch, grabbed a rung, pulled himself out and clung to the side of the spire, which soared higher than any building in the village. Lilou wanted to screw her eyes tight shut until it was all over, but if she looked away, she was sure he'd die, as if her intense concentration could somehow magically stop him falling. The rungs were spindly and hand-sized, the spire tapered to nothing, the sky spun sickeningly as the German let go with one hand to loop a cloth bag over her pet. He slung it over his shoulder, Casanova protesting loudly inside. Still holding on with only one hand and one leg on the rungs, he took a bow, but the crowd were holding their breath too much to cheer.

Nobody said a word until he was safely inside the hatch.

'Daredevil idiot,' said the abbé under his breath. But Lilou was entranced. The faith in himself, the supple assurance with which he'd climbed, the act of kindness despite the obvious resentment from most of the village.

The abbé ushered Lilou into the church tower to collect her cat. The man rounded the spiral staircase, with a furious Casanova, still in the bag, protesting loudly at his prison.

'That was reckless of you,' said the abbé coldly.

'I miss my father, too,' he said simply, handing the bag to Lilou, who opened it to hug her pet. But Casanova had other ideas. He leapt out, gave the man a sharp scratch on the calf where his trouser leg was rolled up, and skittered off. Blood bloomed in two neat slashes. Casanova had dug in hard.

'Thank you, I'm so sorry. He's pretty wild and very stupid.' Lilou rummaged in her pocket for a hanky and gave it to him.

He dabbed his leg. 'We can't expect thanks,' he said. His eyes didn't look German. They were hazel, flecked, like the forest floor.

'What's his name?'

'Casanova.'

He raised his eyebrows. 'That's some name for a cat so lacking in charm.'

'Papa had an unusual sense of humour.'

This was almost flirting, and she remembered the abbé's presence.

'Thank you for risking your life to rescue my gangster cat... I hope your father is well... I've got to get back.'

'Any time.'

The abbé only gave him a tight nod. 'Close the door when you leave,' he ordered as he ushered Lilou away.

Joseph's laugh was infectious. 'Good old Casanova, he's got a temper on him, that cat.'

Casanova, and the German soldier she later found was

called Kristian and was a Luftwaffe pilot stationed among the soldiers, had become village legends within a week.

'Don't be so cruel, at least he wanted to help,' said Lilou.

The Monteux tailor's shop was like a second home to her – the long mahogany counter, with the glass drawers full of haberdashery, ticking, tapes, rickrack and more buttons than you'd ever need, was everything a seamstress could dream of. Fabrics arranged by hue, and every grade of thread lined the walls from floor to ceiling in a rainbow of colours. If she couldn't find what she wanted out here, there was always something special out the back, just for her.

Madame Monteux brought three reams of suiting wool for her to browse and put it on the table between her and Joseph, where she'd also laid out black tea with lemon slices. The proprietor of the German-requisitioned hotel had commissioned a new suit for himself, and that kind of work was rare nowadays, so it was nice to be back here, selecting cloth.

'Here you go, chérie. How is your maman?'

'A little brighter, thank you,' Lilou lied. Maman had been in bed since All Saints' Day.

Madame Monteux pushed a plate of rugelach cookies towards her.

'Eat, you're looking a little thin. You work too hard for such a young thing. I never see you going to dances with the others – you spend all your time either working with those bees or making beautiful things for other people. And if you don't mind my saying, that brother of yours is old enough to help a little more than he does.'

Lilou took a biscuit. They were just flour and water, but they looked like the almond and raisin confections Madame Monteux used to make before ingredients became scarce.

'Delicious!' she lied. 'I hate those dances, and I don't care about clothes, at least not for me. I'd rather be out on a moonlit night spotting hares than stuck in a sweaty church hall.'

'I bet you terrify those poor hares, looming up on them at night,' said Joseph.

His mother ruffled his thin hair. 'Ever the gallant,' she said.

'Oh shut up,' said Lilou to Joseph, slurping her tea. 'You know I'm more of a mountain herb than a flower.'

Lilou chose her cloth, a fine-woven tweed, threw it onto the counter to check it for flaws, then measured it against the metal rule on the counter, deftly folding to get the length she needed.

Clang. The sound of someone pushing at the door and causing the bell to ring wildly broke the peace. Lilou turned to see two German officers and three soldiers in the doorway, including Kristian from the church. He avoided her gaze.

Joseph put down his coffee cup and turned to face them. Madame Monteux crumpled into a chair next to him, white as a sheet.

One of the officers was fat, with a doll-like, smooth face.

Joseph got up. 'Can I help?'

'Stay exactly where you are and shut up,' he commanded in French.

For such a fat man, he moved surprisingly fast as he bore down on Joseph, gripping his face so hard his flesh spilled over the officer's thumbs. The man snapped out a folding ruler from his breast pocket and held it up to Joseph's face, noting down the measurements of his features in a little black book. First Joseph's forehead, then his nose, the width of his eyes. It was inhuman. Lilou felt sick. What the hell were they doing?

'Sit,' he said.

Joseph lowered himself slowly into his chair, looking wildly to his mother. The man pinched Madame Monteux's chin and tilted her face to the light, grimacing as he measured her face like she was a heifer at a market.

'You're hurting her, please...' begged Joseph. His voice caught in fear.

The second officer slapped him hard across the face. Joseph held his nose in disbelief, blood seeping through his fingers.

'Here,' said Lilou, tearing at the cloth to give to Joseph. 'You've hurt him,' she hissed at Doll-face.

'Leave him! Stay where you are, or you'll get the same. And don't worry, my dear. They don't feel pain like we do.'

Fear slithered up her spine like a snake, then struck her with hot anger at the injustice. Her mind raced through the rumours she'd heard and hadn't believed. How was this going to end? She clutched the cloth, bound it tight so they wouldn't see her hands trembling.

'It's all right, Lilou, they're just doing their job, let them,' whispered Madame Monteux, folding her hands in her lap and submitting to the indignity, pale as ice.

God, she'd been so naive. So all the rumours about this war, the Jewish people being persecuted and worse... they were all true. It was happening right in front of her.

Doll-face took his time making notes in his hideous black book, then closed it and set his sights on Lilou.

'Keep completely still. Shaking makes it take a lot longer,' he said, so close she smelled his cabbage breath. His lips were cruel and his pale eyes were malevolent as a goat's. He was feverish with the task, his fingers clammy as he gripped her chin. He licked his lips to savour the moment, leaving a slick of mucus where his tongue had been.

He slowly scrutinised her features and the world stopped turning, the air thickened and charged with his power over her. The molten hate she felt for him was liquid and every nerve ending fired revolt.

'Only the *Juden*, we have our orders, sir, we're not savages,' warned the other officer piously.

Doll-face stepped away from Lilou, and waved a hand at her friends like they were a bad smell.

'They are, the girl most definitely isn't,' he declared. 'Right, let's get this over with. Get the girl out, and take these filthy animals somewhere more fitting for their status.'

A soldier dragged her towards the door.

'I'll come and find you!' screamed Lilou.

'Hush, child. Just go,' said Madame Monteux, pale and frozen.

She looked wildly at Joseph, who was stricken and bloodied, then she was on the street.

'Get out of here if you don't want to make it worse. It's better for them if they come quietly,' brayed a young soldier.

Lilou vomited hot bile right there on the street, then ran off to find Madame Aveline. Surely she'd be able to do something?

CHAPTER 3

MARS

VALLON-DOUX, NOVEMBER 1942

Lilou ran blindly through the village and dragged a protesting Madame Aveline back to the tailor's shop. Too late – it was empty, and Joseph and his maman were gone. Lilou's tears blurred the gold-painted Monteux Tailors sign as they rattled the door-handle.

'It always jammed. You have to pull and wiggle.'

The words caught in Lilou's throat. That was what Madame Monteux had taught her and Joseph, and they had always giggled hopelessly like a couple of kids as she swung her hips to demonstrate.

Madame Aveline pushed the door and pulled up the blind. A torrent of light barged in to reveal the tawdry scene. The shop had been ransacked, the tea set they'd drunk from was smashed on the floor, the sliced lemons dried up on the tray.

'She always had it neat as a pin. She'll hate this,' said Lilou, knowing in her heart this disarray was the least of it.

Madame Aveline hugged her close. 'We shouldn't have come,' she whispered.

Madame Monteux's rainbow wall of precious silks was half empty and the eau de nil with the real gold thread she'd ordered from Paris was crumpled on the floor; a careless boot print had soiled its delicate hue. The glass drawers were pulled out and flung down so hard their fronts had cracked, the old gold lettering split. The ornate cash till was open and naked: everything was brutalised and desecrated.

Lilou picked up a bolt of wool and put it where she knew it should be, rolled up the eau de nil fabric and grabbed the sliding ladder to put it back at the top out of reach. Her hands were so clammy she left a mark on Madame's precious silk.

'*Putain,*' she swore.

'Leave it, Lilou. They want it like this, as a warning. It's no use you getting yourself into trouble on their behalf.'

'What's wrong with you all?' Lilou flung the fabric onto the top shelf and scooped a pile of buttons back into the drawer, gathered up bits of lace and feathers in a frenzy. 'No one says anything. The village is like a kettle that will never boil. It just hisses and spits and rattles, and I wish it would explode! What happened to them, where are they?!'

'They're with others, of their own kind. It's for the best, Lilou. People are afraid for their children, it's horrible, but we just need to carry on and bide our time.'

'Their own kind, what the hell are you talking about? They're *our* kind. They belong here, with us.'

'When you have your own children, you will understand. There are sacrifices... no one wants to send their son to war.'

Lilou thought of Freddie, but it was Joseph's broken glasses that made her see red. Why should he matter less? She snatched the glasses up. If no one else had the guts to confront them, she would. She flew past Madame Aveline and her protests, and made a beeline for the town hall.

The village was carrying on as normal, balancing songbirds on windowsills in their cages, polishing the windows of empty shopfronts. The baker waved, but she didn't wave back. When would they all do something?

At the town hall, she rapped on the door and it was opened by a *Milicien* in a black beret. Lilou recognised him as one of the local village boys. Now he was full of his own importance as a German lackey.

'Wait your turn,' he said when she demanded to see an officer.

'It can't wait. I want to see someone now!'

He pulled her inside, gripping her arm so hard she dropped Joseph's glasses. 'You can see me, any time.'

She dug her nails into his arms and twisted free. 'Don't touch me,' she hissed.

He backed off. 'Quite a sting you've got, bee girl.'

'What is going on here? Back to your post, soldier. And apologise to Mademoiselle Mistral immediately.'

It was Kristian, Casanova's rescuer. How did he know her name? The boy spat an apology at her and retreated.

Kristian bowed his head slightly. He was taller than her, unusual in Vallon-Doux.

'Is there something I can help you with, mademoiselle?' His voice was clipped.

She picked up the glasses. 'I need to get these to Joseph, the tailor's son. He can't see without them.'

He took the glasses, deftly clipping the lens back into place, a tiny gesture somehow done with tenderness and care.

'I'll see he gets them.' She knew he was lying.

'I'd prefer to give them to him myself,' she said.

The *Milice* boy let out a snort. 'You'll be lucky.'

'Silence!' snapped Kristian. 'Let me escort you out. This building is classified to civilians, and he should not have let you in.'

Out on the steps, he checked behind him. 'I can tell you

more, but not now. I tried to help him and his mother. I'm on patrol tonight, so I can find you after curfew at your farm.'

'Not there,' she said, thinking of her mother's reaction to a German patrol jeep bearing down their path at night. 'Meet me at the old tower at the chemin des Beliers up on the hill at eight p.m.'

What the hell was she doing? This man had watched while they hurt Joseph and he'd done nothing. But he'd also been kind that day in the square when he'd rescued Casanova, protected her from the *Milice* boy, and now he was her only hope for Joseph and Madame Monteux. She knew the old tower and the surrounding areas like the back of her hand, better than he did, and she could go there in advance and hide the old hunting rifle somewhere she could get at if she needed to. It was a risk, but a calculated one, and worth it for Joseph.

'I'll be there. I hate this war as much as you do. You can trust me, I promise,' he said, reading her thoughts. She believed him, and she had nothing to rely on but on her instincts.

'If you try anything, you'll regret it,' she said passionately.

He saluted her and waved goodbye with Joseph's glasses. The gesture was noted by the usual gathering in the square, and a fieldworker spat in his hand in disgust.

The baker girls beckoned her over. 'Sit down with us and have a coffee. We've got at least ten minutes before our shift.'

Lilou joined them, grateful for the chance to put the record straight.

'He's handsome and he's a *pilot,* not like the others.' Clémentine giggled, inviting more.

'He's a dirty Boche, like the rest of them,' said Lilou loudly. 'I told him to give Joseph his glasses.'

The girls' eyes curdled in fear, and they hastily changed the subject, but the fieldworker smiled and winked, and the table of men he was with pulled on their cigarettes approvingly.

. . .

A full frost moon shivered over the fields as Lilou pulled her coat tight around her. An owl call haunted the air and wild boar busied themselves in the oak thickets. In the distance belligerent cows lowed, and dog barks rang around the valley, hunting hounds enraged by the antics of the boars. Just a normal night, one that generations of Mistrals would have experienced for centuries as they ventured out from the family farmhouse after dark.

Everything was the same, but nothing felt familiar.

At the tower, Kristian's fair hair caught the moonlight, and he looked like a ghost standing tall in his dark overcoat. Lilou nodded at him and wordlessly took out the ancient key to the door, hoping he couldn't see her hand shaking.

She gestured him in and locked it behind them both. It was pitch black inside. Thank God she'd hidden the rusty old rifle at the top of the steps behind a hay bale. The knowledge steadied her nerves a little.

'Follow me up the stairs. You can feel your way, and there's a rail you can hold on to. We can talk at the top where there's some light,' said Lilou tersely.

When they reached the roofless platform, Lilou realised she'd been holding her breath, and she released it, a frosty plume lit by the moon. She kept a wary eye on the hay bale in the corner where the rifle was hidden. One false move and she wouldn't hesitate.

But Kristian was looking up at the night sky.

'Andromeda,' he said, almost to himself.

'And Draco, to the north. He opens his eyes in the summer,' Lilou added without thinking.

He looked at her in surprise.

'All us Mistrals know the stars, they were shepherds mainly, out on the hills at night,' she said with a shrug. She gazed up, afraid that her friends would be freezing, or worse, under these brittle, distant pinpricks.

'What happened to Joseph and Madame Monteux? Can I see them?'

Kristian thrust his hands into his pockets.

'The last I saw, they were on a train to Germany. More than that, I don't know.'

Lilou gasped. 'They've left France? Why? What will happen to them? Did Joseph get his glasses? And I need to get a letter to them, send supplies, keep track of where they are. Are they together?'

'They split the men from the women...' Kristian began, then stopped.

It was so much worse than anything she'd imagined could happen to her friends. Lilou felt her world shift.

'Don't hold anything back from me. I want to know what's happened to them, tell me everything.'

'I tried to help them, I even requested that they could stay together for the journey, but the guard refused.'

'Did Madame Monteux cry?'

'They were too afraid to cry. There were so many people on the platform, but it was completely silent. I'm so sorry, but I didn't want to draw attention to them.'

Lilou felt nauseous.

'So you did nothing.'

'I did what I could.'

'It's not enough! You stood there while they brutalised my friend, and his beautiful mother. How could you?'

He seemed to crumple a bit at that. 'I am witness to things I would rather not see. But better that I'm there to mitigate the worst as best I can, than be shot for insubordination. A dead man is no use to anyone.'

'The Monteux don't need witnesses; they need someone to help them.'

'I don't expect you to understand.'

Knowledge is power. Papa always told her that. She needed to know more.

'Apart from that filthy uniform you're wearing, who are you, why do you want to help? Why are you even telling me all this?'

He regarded her for a moment, checked the black night.

'I don't believe in any of what they're doing,' he said quietly. 'It's indefensible and wrong and I didn't ask to be here. I have two choices: stay and help from the inside, or die by court martial. I would give anything to be back on my mountain. It's winter, and the moon turns the snow to glitter—' He stopped, and continued more formally. 'I hope it gives you some comfort to know that I went back to the shop and packed a suitcase for Madame Monteux. I found all her warmest clothes, and a photograph of Joseph, and gave them to her. I wish she'd spat in my face rather than thanked me.'

'She would never do that,' said Lilou, as the realisation she might never see them again crept into her bones like a freezing night fog.

Nothing fitted. Joseph and Madame Monteux should be here, this man would look far more at home in a university quad in a stripy scarf than here in a Luftwaffe uniform, the people in the village she thought she knew were taking sides that should never exist. It was like planting seeds in all the wrong places and letting the weeds take over.

She had thought she didn't need to know about anything but the seasons, the quiver that meant a kestrel was about to swoop, the source further up the mountain in dry summers, country things. She hadn't really listened to Joseph when he'd told her that he and his maman were in danger. She'd ignored the talk from the big towns on the coast, the gathering of Jewish people in Nice and Marseille who'd walked there from the north in their furs, with their wealth sewn into the linings, it all seemed so far away. She didn't really believe the stories of jack-boots on Provençal tiles – men just liked to tell tall stories. She'd thought the boys who were taking to the hills were just playing at being soldiers, bored of working the land.

If she hadn't been so determinedly blind, maybe she could have seen. If she'd sensed the air around the Monteux the way she just *knew* when a disease was going to ruin that year's crop, she might have been able to see what was right in front of her and hide them away from danger.

Lilou sank onto the hay bale. This man was as trapped in the horror as she was.

'What if I got a train to where they are, vouched for them?'

He shook his head. 'It's not that simple. They keep lists of names, make inventories of valuables, that's all we see. I don't know what their final destination is...' His voice faded, but his face filled in the blanks.

'How would you feel if your family were on just such a list?' choked Lilou, her head like lead in her hands.

'I'd be as devastated as you are now,' he said gently.

At least he didn't try to talk. He just let it sit. He could kill her or rape her now, but he kept a respectful distance. He'd risked a lot to come and tell her this. Humanity was what the Monteux needed, the kindness of strangers.

'Who are your family?' Lilou asked.

'It's just me and my mum and my little sister.'

Not so different from Lilou's family. Or Joseph's. A pebble of light fizzed across the sky and petered out. At least they were all looking at the same stars.

'See how red that star is? It shines with a steadier light than the others.'

'It always comes in autumn,' said Lilou.

'That's because it's closest to the Earth at that time. Still 400 million kilometres away. It's Mars, the old planet of war. If I could send Hitler and his generals that far into space and watch them burn, I would.'

His words were tantamount to treason. She could report

him, have him arrested by his own kind. An eye for an eye, this man for Joseph. Indeed, she could reach for the rusty rifle from behind the hay bale. She somehow knew he'd take the bullet, that he wouldn't try to retaliate. But she also knew she couldn't do any such thing to someone who in other circumstances could be a kindred spirit with his knowledge of the stars and mountains, his maman and sister waiting at home.

Two headlights carved the night, and a powerful engine strained on the steep hill. A German patrol. No one else would dare break the curfew.

'It's not safe, I have to go,' said Lilou.

'Let me walk you home.'

'We both know it would be more dangerous for me to be seen with you than anything else. Wolves only attack if you show fear, and I'm more afraid of that patrol than any wild animals I might meet in my wood.'

'With good reason, and I'm sorry for that,' said Kristian.

There was only one road past the tower and the farm, so it would be easy to look out for the patrol vehicle, and she and Freddie had a million hiding places from playing there as kids. When the jeep headlights were well out of sight, Lilou unlocked the tower door.

'Thank you for Madame Monteux's suitcase,' she said, holding out her hand.

He shook it. 'I want this to be over, too,' he said. 'Would you meet me again?'

'Never,' she said.

'Of course. But if you ever need me to help, I will do what I can,' he said to her back. Only the owl could see her smile. She kept walking, the steady red glow of Kristian's war planet accompanying her home.

CHAPTER 4

USELESS HOPE

The shuttered tailor's shop was a closed, bruised eye on the street. No one talked about the Monteux family, and if she brought them up in conversation people shrank away, as if their names were cursed. Christmas came and went with its talk of redemption and goodwill. The German soldiers, including Kristian, even attended midnight mass and God allowed Doll-face to cross his threshold and kneel in prayer without retribution. In January news of more Jews being rounded up in Nice and Marseille had the whole village in uproar, but still they spent the winter like country people did, in their shuttered homes, a fire crackling in the grate, waiting for new shoots to bring them out again.

Kristian's red war planet shone steadily in the sky and Lilou hated it hanging there resolute, like a stain on the world. She tried to squash down how she'd felt when Kristian looked at her when he'd handed her Joseph's glasses, the spell of his voice on the night air at the tower.

All through the winter nights, the brief time she'd spent

with him – her cat's rescue from the church steeple, their meeting at the tower, his concern for her friends – came back to her in vivid colours like a story she'd never heard but already knew. A tall, fair man in a grey uniform speaking in German was so alien to everything she'd ever known, yet there was something about him that was so familiar. When the sun rose on the cold, short days, she made herself busy and told herself to stop. Ridiculous to have such thoughts about the enemy, whose comrades had taken her best friend in the world. If the abbé could read her guilty night-time dreams of him, he'd condemn her to eternal damnation, and he'd be right, too.

In the apiary, Lilou pulled out the Queen Roseline frame. Still going strong, despite the November swarm. It was two years since she'd crowned the queen bee in pink to signify 1941, five months since she and her workers had swarmed the saint's statue in the square, and five months since they'd taken Joseph – a lifetime away from the golden innocence before the Germans had rolled in. Please God someone kind on their side like Kristian was looking out for the Monteux. Surely the rumours of what happened to them when they got to Germany just couldn't be true? She chose to believe in the good of human nature and hope for the best, that Joseph and Madame Monteux would return, thinner and a little the worse for wear, but alive, and happy that their ordeal was over.

She studied Roseline's honeycomb palace, a world of perfectly honed hexagons in papery wax, as fine and beautiful as marble. Her seed-pearl eggs nestled in their sextets, the dark honey she and her court had worked so hard to store for overwintering glowed amber. At least here everything was as it should be.

It was the only thing in her life that hadn't changed since November, and sometimes she wished she could join them in their warm comb, so ordered and safe. They all knew what to do without question. But no one in the village knew what was for the best. Even though she'd decided to hope with her head, a nagging feeling wouldn't leave her heart alone. The uneasy peace they were experiencing since Joseph was taken was not a true peace, and it wouldn't last. How could it with such poison in the world? It had to end somehow.

But she and Freddie had agreed to forget everything just for one day. Today was his eighteenth birthday, and the Sainte Roseline honey had given Lilou enough money to be able to surprise him with the new bike she'd promised him.

The church struck 9 a.m. down in the valley, and Lilou squinted along the farm track. Punctual as ever, the abbé's rickety Renault that Papa used to say ran on the power of prayer alone pulled up. He never forgot Freddie's birthday, especially since Papa had gone.

Lilou waited by the front door while he parked up and waved. He skipped round to the passenger door to open it, and out stepped Marie-Madeleine Fourcade. Lilou couldn't think of a more unlikely combination of the society hostess from the cover of *Vogue* and the rebel parish priest.

It must have showed.

'I hope you're surprised in a good way?' said Marie-Madeleine.

Lilou gathered herself. Maman always told her she wore her heart on her sleeve.

'I didn't know you two knew each other,' she said, kissing Marie-Madeleine and the abbé on both cheeks.

The abbé's hug was warm and expansive as the southern sun. 'She might be the queen of Marseille society, but someone has to save her soul,' he blustered, pulling a long oblong gift-wrapped box out of his van.

'Marseille is a long way in a car with very little suspension, but I was lucky he was visiting – the trains are so unreliable these days,' added Marie-Madeleine.

Lilou swallowed a lump in her throat for Joseph. What she

meant was that the trains were either crawling with German soldiers, or being blown up by Resistance fighters.

It didn't make sense that the golden queen bee and this hard-working drone would have anything to do with each other, but everything was upside down nowadays.

Freddie burst out of the front door. 'What's in the box?'

'Good morning,' said the abbé.

'Oh yes, sorry,' said Freddie, kissing him three times and giving him a hug. 'Great to see you.'

'And happy birthday, my boy. Look at you, taller than me now and so much like your papa. Don't roll your eyes, I know that's what everyone says, but you have to allow us oldies our constant surprise at the tallness of the youth. Here you go since you clearly can't wait,' said the abbé, handing over the package with a broad smile.

Freddie opened the package, and Lilou's heart dropped to her boots. It was a gun.

'He already has a hunting rifle,' she said.

Freddie held it up and looked through the sights.

'Gently, my friend, it has a hair trigger. You're a man now and you need to act like one,' said the abbé. 'Let's take it to the field and I'll show you how it works.'

It didn't look like any hunting rifle Lilou had ever seen, and she didn't want the horrible thing anywhere near Maman or the farm.

'Now you're frowning,' said Marie-Madeleine. 'Just as well you're not a poker player. It's a Sten gun and you might well be pleased that you have it one of these days. You are very isolated out here.'

'Not isolated, just free. I know every nest, lair and den within a five-kilometre radius, and if anyone so much as cracks a twig I'll know about it.'

'I'm glad to hear it, but just the same it won't do any harm,' said Marie-Madeleine guardedly.

It was a bright February day but it was still biting cold, and Marie-Madeline pulled her expensive cashmere coat tighter.

'I'm so stupid. Us mountain people don't feel the cold and I wasn't thinking. Let's go in,' said Lilou. 'I can show you my sewing room where the magic happens. What's your latest fabulous commission? Good fabric's hard to come by since—' She stopped.

'Since the Monteux were taken and their shop trashed? The abbé told me all about it and it's a disgusting shame, those lovely people. That's partly why I'm here. Walk with me?'

'Do you know anything about them? I've been desperate to hear.'

'Sadly not. I'm so sorry, Lilou, there are so many disappeared. Only that we all *have* to do something about it for them, and everyone like them, and for France. Come on, the walk will keep me warm. Show me some of your lavender fields. I know they won't be in bloom yet, but they will be when summer comes, and it gives me hope.'

Marie-Madeleine held out her arm for Lilou to link. She was different from the bored party girl Lilou had met at so many fittings. She was dangerously thin, and her high cheekbones more prominent than ever, but there was a spark about her she hadn't seen before.

At a safe distance from the house, Marie-Madeleine stopped.

'I'm not going to beat about the bush. I work on instinct, and I know I can trust you. I'm recruiting for the Resistance. We need girls like you to carry messages. We're very near the drop zone here and you know every inch of this territory. Would you consider it? They're not going to stop until they've killed every Jew, and taken over every corner of France, and we have to stop them. Don't say yes lightly. There's no question that it's dangerous, but so's the alternative. We've got to the point where we have nothing to lose.'

So this was the reason for her unexpected friendship with her fiery abbé, the renewed vigour in her eye. Who'd have thought this distant society belle from another world would be fighting alongside the rebels in the hills? Marie-Madeleine's words were uncomfortable, like she was voicing something that had been swimming around in the back of Lilou's mind. Now, here was this frivolous, privileged person standing in front of her, risking everything. And why was she asking her, Lilou, a smallholder from the hills who hadn't even tried very hard at school?

Lilou looked back at the farmhouse, and thought of her mother. What if things were worse than she thought, that it was actually little people like her who were the only ones who could stop it? But her personal fight was for her home and her little family. She couldn't do it to her mother. If Lilou was found out, it would kill her maman. They needed her income to survive – and what if Freddie was implicated? She'd heard what happened to Resistance fighters, and she'd seen first-hand what some of the German officers were capable of.

'I'm flattered by your trust in me, but I have too many responsibilities here. Madame Aveline says it will all be over by the spring—'

Marie-Madeleine held up her hand. 'I never ask twice, and you are doing your bit by keeping house and home together here, I know.'

She reached into her handbag and briskly snapped on her gloves, clearly disappointed. Lilou swallowed down her discomfort. Marie-Madeleine wasn't used to people saying no, and Lilou felt guilty, but she was sure she could find someone in a better position than her to help.

'If there's anything I could do that wouldn't put me and my family under any kind of suspicion, I'd be glad...'

'But there is another way you could help,' Marie-Madeleine said straight away, 'and it carries very little risk. You have been sewing for me for years. What I need is secret compartments sewed into my clothes. I don't know anyone else who could do it as invisibly as you could. If I leave you a suitcase full, can you do it? It's essential the compartments won't be found, even under close inspection. I've picked the fullest skirts, the roomiest jackets I possess, so that you can make a double lining and sew the tiniest pockets inside. Each pocket only needs to fit a piece of fine silk about the size of a letter – we print our maps and documents on silk so that it blends in with whatever we're wearing. Your skill could mean life or death for lots of brave people.'

'Gladly. I want to help, it's just...'

'You *are* helping by doing this. Everyone has their own way to contribute and it's enough.'

Marie-Madeleine had always been good at second-guessing people. She'd tested Lilou for taking risks, but she must have already had this less difficult task lined up for her, and had brought the clothes ready. Lilou would be glad to help. And it was some comfort that she would be able to make a contribution using the skills that Madame Monteux had taught her.

The bells in the valley struck ten. The abbé was already waiting by his car in the yard, urgently pointing to his watch.

Marie-Madeleine handed over the suitcase. 'I'm sure I don't need to say it, but you haven't seen me since last summer, when you fitted my dress for the *Vogue* cover. Do you understand?'

'I do. I'll have your clothes ready in a week. And please, be careful,' said Lilou, afraid for her, her mind already racing about silk and pockets and the tiniest possible stitches.

'I always am. You look after that pretty face of yours and try not to stand out too much.'

Freddie saluted them as they sped away, and waved them off with the gun.

'Give me that, you don't need it,' said Lilou.

'I do according to the abbé. You might want to go on pretending, but I'm not going to sit here and let them walk all over us. There's also a rumour that the Boches are taking all working-age French men to labour camps. The abbé told me it could even be today, especially as I've just turned eighteen. There's a Resistance unit nearby. I can join them today, before they move to a different location.'

Lilou felt her whole world spin nauseatingly. 'Don't believe everything you hear, there are so many wild rumours and the abbé loves a bit of drama. We need you here, not dead in a field or in some godforsaken jail.'

'My friends are risking their lives to fight with everything they have, and I know how to look after myself. I can't stay here forever.'

'I know, just not yet. Please, don't leave us. You and Maman are all I have, and there's the fields, and the bees, and the sheep. We're helping to feed the village, keeping the home fires burning. It's important work. Heading off to the hills won't help us and if you went, I don't think Maman would survive. And Freddie...' Her voice caught in her throat with a fear she refused to name, not yet. 'I just don't think I can do it without you.'

Freddie checked the safety catch and put the gun in the box. 'Maman is worse today, isn't she? She didn't even remember my birthday.'

'But I did,' said Lilou.

'OK then, for now it's you and me against the world. But I'm keeping the gun, and I'll use it if I need to defend us.'

'OK, soldier.' Lilou clicked her heels and saluted. Would cheeriness make him stay?

'And I'm not staying for you, it's only because Scout would miss me.'

'I know that big hairy mutt is more important than me. Don't worry, I know my place.'

'Good, because you ruined everything that day you broke my catapult.'

'That was ten years ago, and you hit a sheep.'

'I just needed practice.'

'Don't do the same with that gun.'

'Make sure you don't break it.'

'Depends if you behave.'

'Shut up.'

'I win,' said Lilou, flicking him a loser sign. It had been the two of them for seven years now and they still had their rituals left over from when they were kids. 'Come to the barn with me, I've got something to show you.'

Bikes weren't easy to come by, but the village mechanic had done her proud for ten jars of Sainte Roseline's honey and a jacket remade from an outdated style.

Freddie took it out into the light.

'It's a beauty,' he said. Drop handlebars, steel frame and the thinnest tyres Lilou had ever seen. It was a sleek machine, like the ones they'd seen when the Tour de France passed through a lifetime ago.

'I'll make you a cycling jersey when I can get the fabric,' she said.

Freddie ran his hand over the metallic green paint, with not a mark on it, and sucked in his breath. 'Thank you. You work so hard for us,' he said.

I'm going to have to work even harder to stop you taking to the hills with that gun, thought Lilou. She'd already lost Joseph, she couldn't bear for Freddie to go. Everything was closing in so fast. Even Marie-Madeleine was giving up furs and parties for Resistance work, and if the abbé was giving guns to feckless boys... She couldn't think about it today. Better to sleep on it than face up to reality quite yet. And she needed to distract Freddie before he disappeared with dreams of Resistance camps.

'You don't deserve it.' Lilou thought fast. 'Now, we can take your birthday picnic to Pierrepont and jump in the swimming hole.'

'It's bloody freezing at this time of year.'

'So what? You know you'll feel fantastic afterwards, you wimp.'

'No one calls me a wimp and gets away with it.'

'Apart from me.'

'Lucky for you I'm in a good mood.'

Lilou put the picnic in her bike basket and they cycled across the plateau. It was the time of year for optimism, despite the bad news, and she could just *feel* everything waking up. Under the budding trees, the first crocuses were already making confetti, the ewes were plump with their babies and the skies were high and light. Up here, it still seemed that everything could be all right.

The swimming hole was a jewel. A clearing in the old oak forest that only the locals knew framed the swimming spot. Pale emerald, the glassy surface was ruffled only by the crystalline drips from the rocks above. Even in high summer it was icy as the snow-capped heights.

'Don't think, just jump,' said Lilou, still hot from the cycle ride. She stripped off to her costume and plunged in. The shock made her scream and laugh at the same time and Freddie bombed in, turning a somersault. The abbé was right, he was a man now. His shoulders were broad, muscles flexed beneath his skin and his boy's smooth figure was now transformed into angles.

'Fuck me that's freezing.'

'It's even colder like this,' yelled Lilou, spraying him.

'Or this,' said Freddie as he ducked her under.

Lilou screamed as she surfaced and front-crawled to the edge, closely followed by Freddie.

Back on the rocks wrapped in towels and both with a *chocolat chaud* in their shaking hands, they sipped in silence.

Lilou unwrapped the cheese and broke off some baguette and passed them to Freddie.

'No ham, I'm afraid, but the baguette's made with white flour. The baker girls saved it for you.'

Freddie bit into it hungrily. 'Nice. I haven't had white flour since those Boche arseholes rolled into town and requisitioned all the good stuff for themselves.'

'They're not all bad. Some of them are just lads, like you.' Like Kristian.

Freddie jumped up. 'When are you going to catch on? They're *all* bad. And the longer we let them stay here and boss us around, the worse they get. They sit in the square guzzling meat and wine and helping themselves to anything they want, while the rest of us go without. It doesn't matter how many big promises they make about preventing war and bringing fair governance. They're thugs and the more we give, the more they take. They dragged Joseph and his mother out of their shop and ransacked it. Isn't that enough of a red flag? I'm sorry, but they haven't gone to the other side of the rainbow. They're in a *camp*, being treated worse than animals if they're lucky enough to be alive. Can't you see what's happening right in front of your eyes? I can't bloody stand it!'

She was scared of Freddie's vehemence. She could look after herself, but he was likely to do something rash.

'I thought we were going to forget, just for today. I made a cake...'

'I just can't do it any more, I can't pretend. It's like I've had my balls chopped off. Sorry, sis,' said Freddie as he jumped onto his bike. 'I can't eat a birthday picnic when there's all this shit going on. I need to get the hell out before it's too late. I'll take my chances, rather than let them take me. I'm not working for those fuckers and I believe the abbé when he says they're coming for us today, even if you don't.' He scowled at her. 'He didn't want to worry Miss Head-in-the-Clouds, but you have to face the truth. I'm eighteen now, a sitting duck, waiting to be caught if I don't do something.'

Freddie sped off, and Lilou hastily gathered her stuff. She knew when Freddie was ready to do something stupid, and this was one of those times. He was faster and stronger than her and, no matter how fast she pedalled back over the plateau, it was impossible to catch up.

Back at the farm, Scout was howling like a mad thing and a German jeep was parked across the drive. Maman was on her knees in front of three soldiers. Freddie was in an armlock as he screamed obscenities at them. Doll-face was inspecting the Sten gun, which they'd carelessly left in the barn in their haste to leave for the picnic.

'Ah, the pretty young Jew-lover,' said Doll-face as she ran to Maman.

'Tell them. He's just a farm boy. We need him here,' said Maman as Lilou gently pulled her to her feet.

Lilou turned to face them. Kristian was one of the three, standing stock-still, arms behind his back, legs apart. He flickered a 'careful' at her with his eyes.

'Touch her and I'll kill you,' said Freddie, trying to writhe free. The soldier kneed him in the back and wrenched his arms tighter.

'Shut the fuck up, traitor. We'll do what the fuck we like with them when you're gone. If you come quietly, no one gets hurt.'

Freddie spat on the ground, but the fear in his eyes was unmistakable.

'Let my brother go. He's done nothing wrong. We've just been on a picnic for his birthday and now we need him on the farm.'

'It's his birthday, boys. Of course, sweetie, we'll make sure we give him a cake and a candle,' said Doll-face.

'Please, madame, mademoiselle, it's not as bad as it looks,' said Kristian. 'We're requisitioning him as part of the national programme for young men, to work for a temporary time as a labourer on a farm in Germany. He'll be with other French men his age—'

Doll-face stopped him with a wave of his hand. 'No use sugar-coating it. There will have to be some kind of punishment for possession of an automatic weapon. I don't think you can pass this off as a farm implement. Young men who think they can resist us need to be corrected and in our experience, unfortunately, the lesson needs to be a harsh one. I'm afraid, madame, you should have exercised more control over your offspring when you had the chance.' He smiled, feeding on Maman's misery.

'Leave him with me, sir, he won't leave the farm, will you, Freddie?' begged Maman.

Freddie opened his mouth to speak, but the soldier twisted his arms tighter and Freddie yelled in agony.

Doll-face waved her away. 'I can't listen to this bleating any more. Get him in the truck. Best to do these things quickly and cleanly, madame. You have a farm here. It's like taking a calf from its mother, she'll bellow for a while, but she'll get over it,' he added, delighted with his analogy. The soldier dragged Freddie off, escorted by Kristian.

'Freddie!' shouted Lilou, trying to push past Doll-face, who blocked their way.

'Make a fuss and he will suffer more than is strictly necessary. Let him go quietly and we'll show leniency for the boy.'

Lilou and Maman clung to each other and fixed their eyes on the truck as it retreated. The soldier held Freddie's head to his knees so he couldn't even look up at them. Maman whispered prayers and the old country traveller's charms under her breath.

'There we are, it's done,' said Doll-face efficiently. 'That wasn't so bad, was it?'

They couldn't even hug Freddie goodbye, and her soul flew with him and left her empty and aching and exposed to every hurt she'd tried to hide from.

If she'd let him go off with the abbé this morning, he'd have been free.

CHAPTER 5

DEATH OR GLORY

VALLON-DOUX, MARCH 1943

Marie-Madeleine Fourcade

Marie-Madeleine Fourcade instinctively checked the shadows. Nothing, but experience had taught her never to assume, even in a supposedly safe space. It was big enough to hide a battalion down here, surprisingly spacious for the crypt of a country church, with a few precious candles in the ornate candelabras, just enough light to create a low gloom. Abbé Aloïsi was busy battening down the tomb of some late eminent personage or other, the remains long gone and replaced with her war chest of coded books, maps and three million francs in bills. All indispensable to maintain a network of agitators and spies.

If she had believed in ghosts, the determined apparition that now loomed in the doorway, pale hair clinging to her slim shoulders, could easily be one. Luckily, Marie-Madeleine Fourcade prided herself on only dealing with the facts. Anything else was a waste of precious energy.

This particular ghost was flesh and blood, the country seamstress Lilou Mistral, wearing a look that was hauntingly familiar to her now. It was a mix of outrage, desperation and passion for everything that was gone. A lonely wish to be on the side of the angels in the face of atrocity, whatever it took. A loss of innocence Marie-Madeleine didn't have time to mourn.

Abbé Aloïsi regarded Lilou with a mix of pride and regret, the way he always did when he was handing one of his flock to Marie-Madeleine. 'I can vouch for my brave beekeeper. She's responsible, discreet and has a complete disrespect for authority,' he said indulgently. 'Dump her in a quagmire or at the top of a snowy mountain and she'll come out smelling of roses. She's a mountain girl through and through and knows every inch of the countryside within a fifty-kilometre radius.'

'With the face of an ingénue entirely above suspicion. The ideal recruit,' said Marie-Madeleine. 'You know everyone who joins the Resistance has already resigned themselves to death?'

The girl saluted with a defiant nod. Good. She needed to know she wasn't joining a noble court of knights and ladies. It was a dirty, unprincipled fight to the death, with capture and torture almost certain.

'I'm ready. Holing up and sewing compartments in clothes isn't enough, I see that now. I'll run whatever messages you need me to, just tell me and I'll do it. I have nothing left to lose,' said Lilou.

Such touching naivety. This girl had no idea how much she still had to lose. Marie-Madeleine nodded to the abbé. He handed over the locket containing the cyanide pills and gave her absolution for the mortal sin of taking her own life, if she needed to.

Lilou fastened the doomed locket round her neck with steady, deft fingers. Not a tremor in sight. Perhaps she thought she was indestructible, but, in Marie-Madeleine's experience, flesh was weak, even when the mind was strong.

'If you're caught, better to take the pills than sing like a canary. You may think you'll be brave, but nobody knows until they're in there with those sadists. We don't judge, just ask that you don't name anyone else. We work in tight cells. You will only know five operatives, including your friend Gabriel Rivière. He's one of our best. The garage mechanic is our radio expert, and the girl from the baker, the one with the red hair, transports messages in the bread.'

Lilou looked more shocked at that than the cyanide pills. But she'd learn she wasn't the only one with a bit of sass in the village. The baker girl did the simpering airhead act like a pro. She was the last person anyone would suspect.

'The abbé is the fulcrum of our cell. If you are caught, get a message to him by whatever means.'

Marie-Madeleine gave Lilou her detailed instructions for her role as a local guide. She'd be meeting the Resistance parachutists at the various drop zones near her home. Some of them would give her documents or packages to be delivered to locations they would inform her of, then disappear. Other agents would need her to guide them to wherever they needed to be next, and she'd need to ensure they weren't seen. Instructions for her missions would come via the abbé, or through the messages in the bread from the bakery girl.

Marie-Madeleine hoped this girl was reliable. According to the abbé, Lilou was known for her midnight wanderings to watch the moon, or listen to the owls or some such. God knew she herself would rather be sipping cocktails in the Crillon after lobster at La Coupole at that hour, but each to their own. It all played into her hands, and would serve Alliance well to have Lilou's intimate knowledge of the terrain. And a girl was always less detectable than a man. Men didn't believe women were up to the job.

Marie-Madeleine took out a silk map from one of the hidden compartments Lilou had made in her last good tweed suit, and unfolded it.

'Could you find this in the dark, Lilou?' she said, pointing to the upcoming landing spot.

The girl grabbed a candelabra and illuminated the stars painted on the vaulted ceiling. She sketched out a shape amongst them.

'Follow Andromeda, then left at the north star, just beyond old Veuve Lièvre's place. And don't worry about her, she'd never breathe a word.'

'And if it's cloudy?'

'I'll reconnoitre during the day, but take a different route back at night, just in case anyone's seen me.'

'That's the spirit, never assume you're safe,' said Marie-Madeleine, confidence growing in her new recruit.

'You least of all,' said Lilou.

'How so?'

'I don't have a target on my back, yet. The abbé's already told me how you're constantly on the move, how many narrow escapes you've had. It's a long way from that bored society hostess I used to sew for. Thank you for all you've done.'

That nearly broke her, more than any gun at her head. She busied herself with the job at hand, and gave Lilou the final thing she would need. The manuscript.

The Little Prince, by Antoine de Saint-Exupéry. Tonio to his friends. He had a way with words, which was of no particular concern to her. It was useful though, as the prose contained planet numbers and plenty of different characters. A little sentimental and childish in her opinion, but good for code. It was also unpublished, so unlikely to be discovered, and the Brits had an exact copy back in London at the SOE, the Special Operations Executive, or, as Churchill called it, the Bureau of Ungentlemanly Conduct. A network of British *Rosbifs* who provided supplies, information and money to support Alliance and other groups in their work to resist the Boche. In return, Alliance gathered information on the Germans' movements in

France and sent it back to Blighty. Simple really, but incredibly dangerous.

The girl was immediately absorbed by Tonio's scrawlings. Marie-Madeleine prayed to the abbé's God that her romantic nature wouldn't get her into trouble.

'It's sweet,' she whispered. 'There are so many levels to the childish messages. It makes me feel like I've lost the ability to just see the simple truth.'

'This isn't a reading club. Be careless with it and you'll get us all shot. I suggest you keep it in a safe, undiscoverable place somewhere in your house or land. The key number for our messages consists of the page, paragraph and the word number. It's laborious, but it will give you the precise coordinates of the date, and intended landing zone for your rendezvous. The Lysanders only fly once or twice a month, without navigation or lights to avoid detection. They depend on good weather, and the light of the full moon.'

'I'll know when that is, without your codes. They're the nights when the moon makes shadows and everything comes alive in a different way to when the sun shines.'

'Whatever it takes, just don't get caught,' said Marie-Madeleine briskly.

The girl fingered her cyanide locket. 'I'd rather die than let them win,' she said.

Good. The girl had the right attitude at least.

'You'll go to the baker the day before every full moon and Sandrine the redhead from the baker will serve you. Inside the bread you'll find your code, and you'll take it from there. The abbé here will find a way of getting any other essential information to you, should missions be aborted, or if there is any danger of discovery. We also expect you to relay anything you hear or see that you think is important.'

'The set of tubes in the steeple is almost as good a communicator as prayer, and you'll be familiar with that,' said Abbé Aloïsi wryly.

'A radio hidden in the steeple?' Lilou put her hands together. 'Amen to that,' she said.

'It's been a while since I heard those words on your lips,' said the abbé. 'Seriously though, I know you will be, but I'm going to say it anyway. Please be careful, and use me as a link and sounding board whenever you need to. Best to keep to Sundays and high days to avoid suspicion though. Everyone around here knows you avoid this place as much as Madame Aveline will allow you to get away with.'

The girl had a quiet, skittish stillness about her, like a deer in a forest clearing. Marie-Madeleine put out of her mind what they did to beautiful young operatives like her if they were caught; she couldn't allow herself to care too much about individuals. She was still raw from the latest raid where she had learned how it felt to be an ant when a boot kicked the nest wide open. In a single day last month, three major Alliance sectors had been wiped out across Toulouse, Pau and Nice. If they were still alive, God only knew what they were going through.

'I know not to run back to the lair when I'm being pursued. We southerners are tougher than you Paris drones think. This is my territory and I know it like you know the Paris metro. I want my brother home safe, justice for families like Joseph's, and I'll do anything to protect Provence and my mountains. It's in my blood.'

That's the spirit. The *Service du Travail Obligatoire* scheme, sanctioned by their own government, provided slave labour like Lilou's little brother to the Germans, and it was the best recruiting sergeant for Alliance to date. It was one thing sending soldiers to fight, it was another when brothers, husbands, sons and friends were wrenched from their families in front of their eyes.

'We all take an animal name. At Alliance you're not a person, you're a number, and a codename. We take personality out of the equation. It's better for everyone like that. Do you have a preference?'

'Patou.' She didn't miss a beat. Everyone had their favourite. 'It's what we call a mountain dog here. They stay up in the hills throughout the summer with the sheep on their own. That's what I intend to do until this is over, and guard whatever is left to us,' she said.

'We all have our reasons, keep them with you, and you'll find strength in them,' said Abbé Aloïsi. He hugged the girl and it hurt something inside Marie-Madeleine.

She'd been on the move so long she barely remembered which town she was in, never mind having a warm hug from someone she'd known forever. She couldn't even hug her own children, who were in grave danger every time she went anywhere near them. The last time she'd seen them was months ago, and even then only when she arranged for them to be paraded past the window of a house she was hiding in. They'd looked so lost and bewildered and it had buried her alive.

Marie-Madeleine looked at her watch. 'You have your orders. The abbé and I don't have much time,' she said to Lilou.

'I won't let you down.'

Most likely she would, but who knew, she might be one of the few who made it. Lilou left, her footstep on the stairs fleet as a wild thing.

The baby kicked. Little sprite was growing stronger and more insistent, like his father. It took her by surprise, and she stumbled. What the hell kind of world was she bringing her lover's baby into?

The abbé put his arm round her. 'Even you can't save everyone. You need rest and sleep. Stay, just tonight. You must be six months by now. To everything there is a season – you've loved and wept and fought and mourned. But you need time to heal, even if just for a night.'

'Oh stop it. I'm not one of your mountain lambs. I'm pregnant, not ill, for goodness' sake. I have to move on tonight, there's too much at stake, including your ethereal mountain spirit. She's an absolute vision, but she seems to have no clue about the effect she has on everyone around her. Now, I have messages for you to transmit. You're sure they don't suspect? That radio's been up there a little too long for my liking.'

'I've got eyes all around the village, and there have been no detector vans up this way. Apart from that piece of work they call Doll-face, the other German lads aren't too bad, and they all come to church. In fact, there's one who's clearly infatuated with Lilou, a pilot they've dumped with the battalion by the name of Kristian. I just don't know how he couldn't have seen the radio.'

'What? Why was I not informed of this immediately?'

'Sometimes you have to work on instinct. He climbed the steeple in an absolute frenzy to rescue Lilou's errant cat, which was perfectly capable of looking after itself. He gave her the stupid thing back with a pathetic look on his face and it swiped him and drew blood.'

'I bet you were happy about that.'

The abbé raised his eyes to the heavens. 'And some say they have no reason to believe.'

'Seriously, what if he blurted to his fellow warmongers?'

'I believe it's better where he knows it is. That way he can help protect it. I've seen a lot in the parish, good and bad. And that man seems to be one of the good ones.'

'Well it's on your head. If you get caught...'

'I know. But there are many taking far greater risks, including you.'

'It's my choice.'

They all knew the risks and it was up to each of them to

deal with it in their own way. But inside she was churning, hanging on a string. The abbé was one of the only ones who knew she was pregnant, and his kindness slammed her into a wall. There was a time when her handsome Léon Faye had brought her oranges from his sorties in Morocco, her favourite Schiaparelli perfume from Paris. They'd danced under the stars on the tower at the Chateau de la Napoule, and made love on the beach and ruined the gown Lilou had sewn for her as the waves crept and whispered under the smiling moon. Now he was a thousand kilometres away, risking his life making sorties between London and France. She'd begged him not to. But then again, he'd asked the same of her. Now here she was, carrying his baby in a body that was like a skeleton and hardly up to the job, on the move most days to stay ahead of capture, regularly saying goodbye to the cream of men and women that France had to offer.

What a fucking mess.

The priest knew not to press her further. Neither of them could risk her breaking down. She gave him his messages to transmit and left for her rendezvous, grateful that her suit was a good two sizes too big now and hid her secret child, who she already loved more than anything in the universe.

CHAPTER 6

THE AVIATOR

BAY OF AGAY, MAY 1943

Tonio de Saint-Exupéry

The Lysander was a responsive little plane, gratifyingly dependent on the wits and savvy of the pilot. Quite the thing to be rolling around in at night, carving a swathe through Orion's belt, the thin, high-altitude air quickening the senses of Tonio's battered old carcass.

The Yanks might have deployed all the latest tech in their shiny Lockheed P-38 Lightnings, but the craft were oppressive at 30,000 feet and the cabin pressure would weigh heavy on a man twenty years his junior, never mind a 42-year-old pilot who was dragging round a body that had endured one too many high-speed liaisons with the desert. The Brits' little Lysanders were far more civilised affairs, ones a man could take complete command of, take charge of his own destiny. If death was to come, it would be Tonio's own doing.

The full moon smiled its phosphorous grin, picking out

crests on the sea below with an opaline glow. A luminous night that belied the horror of Hitler's war.

Tonio steadied the throttle and unscrewed the thermos. Whisky-laced strong black coffee packed by his engineer. Nectar. He took a fortifying swig and set it back into the holder. Everything in its place; the thrum of the Bristol Mercury 9-cylinder engine, gyro horizon a reassuring parallel to the sea, a silvered cloud slung across the moon, ethereal enough to entertain Greek gods in all their capriciousness. This was his place in the world.

No chance of being assailed from below. The view was clear and not a battleship in sight. The strafers could appear from nowhere like birds out of the horizon at dawn, spitting fire and bombs. He stayed on high alert, confident he could drop and fly low, loop the jalopy back on itself at a moment's notice and lose them if needed. Flying was still a relatively new phenomenon, and those Boche lads may be younger than him but he had the advantage of twenty years of flying on his side. There were few people in the world who could boast that, and most of these losers were torn from their mothers still wet behind the ears, given ten weeks' tuition, then chucked into the air, dispensable as gnats.

Still on course, he retrieved a crumpled piece of paper he'd dropped on the floor, fished a stubby pencil out of his pocket and hastily sketched a German battleship, which transformed into an elephant in front of his eyes. *Lumbering behemoth with a dark heart*, he scribbled, then thought better of it and screwed up the slip of paper, discarding it carelessly on the floor.

Checking the position of the moon, and with the fading star of Mintaka at his back, he bore down towards the coast. The map sat untouched on the rear seat. No need to consult it. He knew the bay of St Raphaël like the back of his hand, from happier times where he'd taken up wide-eyed passengers on hot summer's days to swing around the bay and marvel at the sparkling expanse. The makeshift landing field the agent had described and pinpointed on the map he also knew; it was part of his sister's estate at Agay. The familiar clump of three umbrella pines just beyond the big house would be his guide if he flew low enough.

The Esterel coast glowed red, even at this time of night, and Tonio thought his heart would burst to see France again. Two years in exile in New York getting fat, hopelessly trying to shepherd his faithless, fragile and wayward wife from her worst excesses. He still proudly didn't speak that infernal language, English, even after all that time.

Here he was, back in the homeland, where he was destined to be, in the air, defending his beloved France.

He took a wide curve in. The Boche had anti-aircraft bristling along the entire coast, so he overflew Le Muy, where he dropped a package of documents, hoping he'd been accurate enough not to wake some unsuspecting farmer with the package crashing through his terracotta roof, and doubled back to the Bay of Agay over land.

Flying at 1,500 feet, it was easy to spot the L-shaped landing lights he was looking for, a makeshift affair of brave men holding torches on sticks, simple but effective. He flashed the code in Morse and prepared to land, coming in lower than he needed to over the umbrella pines just to give the landing crew a bit of a jolt. That one always got hearts racing and he liked to make an entrance.

The responsive little ship bumped across the corn stubble and came to a halt just short of a stone shed that had placed itself presumptuously in the way of his trajectory. Nothing could faze him when he was in command of his cockpit, but the relief of being back in France nearly floored him as he stumbled out and onto the soil of the Var.

The torch bearers melted away into the night and, instead, out of the shadows stepped a girl who could only be a product of this exact place. Heavy, arched eyebrows, dark soulful eyes, tanned skin and a face chiselled into stark beauty by poverty and hardship. A mountain girl, judging by her ruddy cheeks and untamed air. He was tall, over six foot two, and he was used to towering over nearly everyone he met, but this girl could give him a run for his money; she was only a few inches smaller than him, willowy and athletic where he was stout and stiff.

She looked him up and down, surprised. It was a look that often greeted him when he stepped out of an aircraft. People expected the great aristocratic aviator and man of letters Antoine de Saint-Exupéry to shimmy out of his cockpit in a dashing flying suit, a gust of wind catching his immaculate scarf as he climbed down. The truth was, he'd rolled out of bed in the late afternoon and dressed in haste, and the flying suits were always a little too small for his big frame. His receding hair was dishevelled, his socks didn't match, and he was probably still wearing his pyjama top and hadn't noticed.

'A warm welcome to the man who fell to Earth.' She delivered the pre-planned greeting in a whisper, a suitably poetic choice for his return to France. Someone at the bureau had clearly read one of his books.

He handed her a playing card from the deck he always carried.

She fixed her intelligent eyes on his. 'Ace of clubs?' she said in a broad southern accent that filled him with nostalgia.

'One is always the beginning of a mountain number. I think I'm right?' he said.

She handed it back. There was a self-possessed quality about her that made him feel safe. 'That's classified information,' she answered.

'Quite right, soldier,' he said. 'Lead the way.'

It was like following a fallow deer, and his great clodhoppers felt heavier than ever in her wake.

'I've met you, before all of... this. You were one of Marie-

Madeleine's entourage at a party I didn't want to go to. I'm her seamstress, and she persuaded me to join the party after her fitting and I felt so out of place. You were pacing, looking longingly up at the skies, and I was there on sufferance. I hate parties, but now I've thought back to that moment so many times and wished those times back. We had no idea what we had.'

'You're Marie-Madeleine's pet seamstress! I remember you. She loved to have "projects", people she thought she could improve. But you were having none of it, looking surly amongst all that glitter and bluster, refusing to be impressed. Good for you.'

'Not *refusing*. I just wasn't. Impressed I mean. I only agreed to go because my best friend Joseph was playing in the band. He was Jewish. They've taken him.'

'*Is* Jewish,' corrected Tonio. 'Don't give up hope.'

An owl called. The girl didn't answer, and he wished he could comfort her in some way. She looked so alone pacing along amongst the trees, a canvas satchel over her shoulder, walking so sure-footed and determined. In the old days he'd regale whole rooms with stories of being lost in the desert, hallucinating, ready to welcome death, which seemed sweeter than hope at times. Hope meant striving, he meant to tell her. He instead respected her silence, which melded with this strange twilight just before dawn. She was striving, everybody was, and no one knew how things would turn out.

At the edge of the clearing, she pointed to the house. He didn't have the heart to tell her he could have found his way with his eyes closed.

'Sterling effort, mountain girl.' He smiled.

'It's Lilou, Lilou Mistral,' the girl answered.

'A good Provençal name, mademoiselle. Vive la France.' It was good to say the words now that he was finally home.

'And the Resistance,' replied Lilou. And she was gone,

untamed by him, and, he could tell, anyone else that might attempt it.

The house was in darkness and a lone dog barked a warning. That would be his sister's Labrador, Coco, and she was swiftly silenced. They were expecting him.

Nelly was at the door to greet him, his beautiful, statuesque fixer, and lover. She was a duchess, and if you were to draw your idea of how one should look, you'd draw her. Tall, confident and bronzed, her fair hair in a perfect chignon that was never out of place, she looked like an aristocrat and fucked like the world was about to end. Which maybe it was. He felt a stab of desire and a recoil of remorse for his wife. Not that his wife knew the meaning of the word remorse. They'd cheated on each other so many times it was a joke. And Nelly, Countess Hélène de Vogüé, was the flipside to Consuelo's coin. If Consuelo was all Latin-American volcano fire, Nelly was air, and he adored and needed them both in order to survive.

They kissed, and pulled apart. Tonight wasn't a lovers' tryst, it was war. She led him through to the shuttered drawing room, the enormous space dimly lit by a single candle. His sister was nowhere to be seen. Marie-Madeleine was sitting, hugely pregnant, at a table, feverishly making notes with Tonio's old mate, and Marie-Madeleine's lover, Léon, who was reading out a series of numbers.

There was a time when she'd have swept over to him, sparkling, to welcome him into the party, pressing a crystal champagne coupe on him, with a whispered, 'You'll need this darling, the place is a crashing bore, so buckle up.'

Tonight, she only looked up distractedly and waved, though they hadn't seen each other in years.

He saluted. 'Your orders, Madame la comandante?'

A man receiving the numbers and tapping them into a radio turned round and paced over to shake his hand.

'Jean Moulin. I'm honoured, sir,' he said.

Tonio knew he was to meet high-ranking Resistance officials, but not the man himself, the president of the National
Council of the Resistance, 'All mine, Jean Moulin. Without
you, we'd all be dead.'

'Many of us already are. All the more reason to keep going.
We don't have much time. Once the messages are sent, we're
moving on. We need you at Le Muy airfield in two days' time to
transport an agent back to the base at Alghero. In the meantime,
you'll stay here with your sister and I'm sure you'll find a way to
hide the aircraft in the field till then. It's a tight take-off, but if
anyone can do it it's you.'

'Just need a couple of stones at the end of the field to give
the old girl a bit of momentum and I'll be up in the clouds
before the Boche take their morning shit, sir.'

That put a cracked smile on their weary faces. The least he
could do.

With the radio operator otherwise engaged, Marie-
Madeleine took a break, and Léon helped her to her feet. Tonio
was afraid she'd snap, she was so thin, and the bump she was
carrying seemed in danger of toppling her over.

They hugged.

'Congratulations to you both,' he said to Marie-Madeleine
and Léon. No need to ask if it was Léon's and not her
husband's. Anyone who knew them would understand.

'Pretty difficult to run carrying this little bundle, but it's a
brilliant disguise,' she said bravely. 'Talking of little ones, we
have a favour to ask. We have to keep moving, and we seem to
have taken on a little more ballast than we can fly with,' she
added.

'You were always a brilliant aviatrix, how so?' said Tonio.
He'd let Marie-Madeleine take the controls of his little red
C630 Simoun many a time. She was more competent than most
men he'd flown with, and she was better company than ever if

they hit a storm or high winds. They both knew that danger heightened the senses in the most delightful way.

'A little boy. A refugee from the rue Ferrachat, Roman Stavinsky's son.'

'My old friend from Lyon?' Roman Stavinsky was a brilliant scientist, a stalwart Resistance member and totally eccentric. Top scores on every count.

'We've got the boy because his parents have been arrested. They're being held at Hotel Terminus.'

Marie-Madeleine shook her head. They both knew the significance. The head of the local Gestapo, Klaus Barbie, had installed himself in the Hotel Terminus and was using it as his own personal torture palace. Ruthlessly efficient and sadistic in equal measures, he was so brutal they called him the Butcher of Lyon.

'Friends of his parents brought him to us. They found him cowering in the family hiding place under the floorboards. His parents acted as decoys when Klaus Barbie turned up with the Gestapo. They were leading lights in the Resistance and good people. The little mite hasn't uttered a word since.'

'I know how good they were. The last time I saw that kid, he was just a babe-in-arms, and his parents doted on him. I gave them an early version of *The Little Prince* for a christening present. It was a very happy house, full of books and music and laughter, and now he's been wrenched from everything, poor little man. Is he here?'

'Yes, with your sister. But he can't stay, it would put her whole family in danger. He's been travelling with us for days, but it's no life for a little one, and frightening, for one who's already afraid. He came to us clutching a toy aeroplane and the *Little Prince* manuscript you gave his parents all those years ago, so we thought you might be able to cheer him up a bit.'

She rang a bell, and a maid ushered in a kid with enormous

cheeks and the roundest, most solemn eyes he'd ever seen, fringed by a pelt of glossy dark hair. He was like his parents all right. If he'd set his artist's eye to combine the best of both of them, he'd choose the same features: his mother's melting, intelligent black eyes, his father's dimples and olive skin. God only knew what this boy had witnessed, and what kind of hell his parents were suffering now.

The boy regarded Tonio with a mix of reproach and fear, so he gently knelt to his height, and held out a deck of cards. 'Pick one, show the others, but don't show me.'

The boy looked past him to some distant point, mute.

'OK, you pick one,' he said to the maid. She held it up to the gathered crowd, then put it back in the pack.

He shuffled and showed them the jack of diamonds. The whole room gasped, and there was a flicker of recognition in the boy's blackberry eyes. He held the pack of cards out to him again and the boy slipped out a card and put it in his pocket. He was about seven years old, Tonio guessed. Judging by the scars on his knees and the defiant look in his eye, a tearaway, like he'd been. Good for him if he didn't want to speak.

Tonio held out the pack for him to replace the card, shuffled, and showed him the one he'd picked. The boy shrugged, but Tonio saw the corners of his mouth twitch. The way he held on to himself, a forcefield around him that no one could cross, was worse than if the little guy had bawled and wailed. He himself had never left his mother's side at their chateau in La Môle, but he'd been a devil too. It was every little boy's inalienable right.

'It's supper time now, Eliot. Can't you say anything to Monsieur de Saint-Exupéry before we go? You know what a famous pilot he is. Don't you want to ask about flying over mountains and deserts?'

The boy met his eyes at that, tempted, but Tonio had the sense that if Eliot allowed himself to speak he'd cry, and that he didn't want to let himself down.

'No need to say a word, if you don't feel like it. Boys have more interesting things to do in my experience, like flying, or climbing, or calculating the distance between an anthill and a dome of spilt honey.'

He fished out a scrap of paper and his stubby pencil, made a quick sketch and handed it to Eliot.

'Here. What do you think of this?'

Eliot took the drawing. It was of him and Tonio in a biplane, with a dog in the back, ears flapping, hair and scarves streaming in the breeze. He smiled, but his eyes were sad and resigned as a dying star. This war had to be won at all costs for him, his parents, and every child who was suffering like him.

'I hope you'll come up with me soon,' said Tonio as the maid ushered him out.

'Who's going to look after that child?' he asked when they were out of earshot. 'Ask me to fly over a Boche airfield at a thousand feet, charm hostages from a petty dictator with a machine gun at my head, or pull a comrade out of a burning wreckage with my bare hands, and I'm at your unflinching service. But I can barely look after myself, never mind a broken fledgling in need of his mother.'

Marie-Madeleine put her hands protectively on her belly. 'Darling Tonio, we were never going to ask you! You've still got your pyjama top on under that flying suit and whisky on your breath, the poor boy can't live on charm and drawings alone. We'll think of something. In the meantime I have some documents for the agent at Le Muy airfield when you go.'

Tonio was used to the finer things in life, and he recognised an expensive silk blouse when he saw it, so, when Marie-Madeleine pulled out a silk map from such a thin fabric, he was amazed.

'Good God, where did that exquisite diagram come from?'

'My little seamstress. She's an absolute find – all my clothes contain the most undetectable secret compartments.'

The penny dropped. 'And my guide tonight. There's something intriguing about her, a toughness, and soul.'

She studied the map intently, then flung her hands in the air. 'That's it! Lilou! We can assign Eliot to her! She lives in the middle of nowhere in a cosy little farmhouse. I can't think of anywhere better for him to hide out, and I'd trust her with my life. I can't tell you why, but we need to keep in France until July 1944, and keep him safe.'

'Aren't you assuming a lot? You can't just *assign* him, surely?' said Nelly, ever practical.

'As the head of Alliance in the region, my word is final. She'll have no choice. We have an hour before we need to move, so that's settled.'

Marie-Madeleine turned her attention back to the map, tracing it with her finger, then addressed Tonio.

'Lilou got here by train, and she's used to walking long distances, but we can't risk the boy on a treacherous journey over land and up into the hills. You could fly him there when you go to Le Muy. I'll arrange for her to be there to meet him.'

'It will be my honour, patronne.'

This war was full of contradictions, assignments, missions. But what on earth was going on with this kid? Why couldn't they just spirit him out of harm's way, to Switzerland, away from the occupation? What was this mysterious July 1944 date? Tonio knew better than to ask. All information was on a need-to-know basis and, if Marie-Madeleine deemed it essential for him to know more, she'd tell him.

Léon put a protective arm round Marie-Madeleine. 'Orders given, my love. Now, you've promised to hide out for our little one. I need you to be in one place for at least a month.'

'You worry too much,' said Marie-Madeleine briskly. Nevertheless, she allowed Léon to guide her to a sofa where she could put her swollen feet up, and to bring her the pile of papers that still needed attending to.

Tonio drew a picture of the three of them in a cloud, their little newborn a cherub with wings and an Alliance medal on its chest. He handed it over, and was rewarded by warm hugs and thanks from his old friends. Marie-Madeleine handed him his instructions.

He pocketed the silk map. 'Orders understood, madame. Proud to be your operative.'

'Thank you, Tonio. Look after yourself. Even you aren't indestructible, and surely you've had more than your quota of miraculous near misses than other men are awarded in three lifetimes.'

'I'd rather die for France than of humiliating old age,' he said. The truth was, the edifice of his body was already crumbling. He hugged his brave friends and left to go and find his sister. Some refuge, at least for tonight, before he and Eliot made a dangerous journey together.

CHAPTER 7

PRECIOUS CARGO

VALLON-DOUX, JUNE 1943

Lilou

June was Lilou's favourite month. It was hot and new, still pristine, and filled with screeching swifts bursting from every
rooftop. Geraniums glowed crimson on windowsills, stag beetles
dive-bombed candle-lit dinners, and the air was sweet with
lavender and gorse. But this wasn't any normal June. Half the
men in the village were gone – disappeared into the maquis,
rounded up by the Germans, as Freddie had been, or joined up
to the forces despite the tears of the women in their life. An air
of sadness and suspicion pervaded everything human, but
nature was as exuberant and cruel and careless as it had always
been.

It was a good year for the bees, and the Sainte Roseline
brood had swelled and swarmed until it was impossible to tell
which frame she'd spawned. A satisfying line of workers buzzed
their unerring path to the lavender fields, setting out light and
quick from the hives and returning laden and lazy from their

heady forage in the fragrant, sugared heat. Lucky them, to have nothing more to worry about.

For Lilou, everything was disintegrating. The day after they'd taken Freddie, Maman had taken his rucksack, filled it with stones, and left. She returned in the evening, put the rucksack down, and went to her room without a word. The next morning she'd done it again, and now, a month later, she did exactly the same every day. Locals reported seeing her on the route to Claviers, heedless of rushing traffic or passers-by, never wavering from her path. She hardly ate, and it was a superhuman tramp of at least twenty-four kilometres at pace, going backwards and forwards like a demented bee on a flight path that would weaken it to death in the summer heat, her beautiful dark hair streaked with sudden grey. She started in the morning, still dressed in yesterday's clothes, and didn't stop until the sun rested on the evening mountains and burned them orange.

'Leave her, she needs to grieve,' Madame Aveline had advised. But now it had gone beyond that. In the village they started calling her The Ghost, and crossed themselves as she passed, unseeing. Every evening Lilou waited by the path in the twilight until she arrived home exhausted. Even after all that exertion, she still couldn't settle, and Lilou could hear her pacing the best part of the night, too.

Maman was now so fragile that Lilou was afraid she'd walk herself to death in the heat. Lilou had to stop it somehow.

It was dawn, the mountains only just turning from violet to orange, but, as usual, Maman had already left. Pulling her bicycle out of the shed, Lilou set off and cycled down the road until she spotted her, pacing doggedly, sweat patches already forming under her arms.

'Maman!'

She quickened her pace.

'Maman, stop, please.'

Lilou caught up with her, but Maman kept going, shoulders

sagging under the weight of the rucksack, tracking right down the middle of the road. Lilou slowed to her pace at the bend to talk to her, but then a German army truck screeched round the corner. Lilou screamed and dodged just in time, and the truck swerved to avoid Maman, careering into the ditch. Maman didn't flinch. She just kept walking.

'Maman! Where the hell are you going?!' said Lilou, dusting herself off and picking up her bike to follow her again.

'*Halt!*' said a German accent. A soldier was standing by the stricken truck. 'Stop, right there.'

She threw him a finger and got on her bike. The soldier cocked his gun. 'I said, *halt!*'

She stopped. If she stayed, at least they wouldn't go after Maman. God knows what she'd do or say if they caught up with her.

He marched over, still pointing his gun. 'Does that madwoman want to die? And you? Bicycles are not permitted, mademoiselle. You know the rules.'

'They're not our rules,' she said.

'It's a good thing we're here to protect you. Cycling with your skirts over your knees and all that long blond hair flying attracts the wrong kind of attention.'

'Private Schmidt! Back in the truck and get it out of the ditch, now. I'll have you disciplined for dangerous driving, and you'll treat Mademoiselle Mistral with respect.' It was Kristian, furious.

Schmidt's face twisted at the reprimand in front of a French woman. 'She's the one whose cocky little brother we took. He cried like a baby when we punished him,' he spat. Lilou felt sick.

'Keep a civil tongue in your head. Get out of my sight now,' commanded Kristian.

The soldier stomped off, backed out of the ditch and scooted past them, burning rubber as he took the bend.

Lilou got on her bike. 'Don't expect me to thank you. None of you should be here in the first place.'

'He didn't cry,' Kristian said gently.

'What?' choked Lilou.

'I personally supervised his passage, and there was no punishment of any of the group who were put on the train that day. I wanted you to know.'

'Is he going to the same place as Joseph?'

'N-no,' Kristian replied. 'He will be sent to work in Germany, on the land. He might be lucky and end up on a farm like yours, with someone like my family who I know would care for him.'

'Or he might not be lucky,' said Lilou.

'We don't all agree with what's going on.'

'But you're still here.'

He didn't reply.

'I've heard about your maman. They talk about her in the square.'

'Since Freddie was taken...' Her voice wavered.

'You don't need to explain. I'll try and look out for her. I think the boys are a little afraid of her, but they do all have mothers, even if they don't act like they do sometimes. I'm sorry. How are you managing on the farm?'

'I'm not. Isn't that the point of what the Boche are doing?'

'Let me help,' Kristian said.

The mistral wind bent the trees and blew her hair across her face, a reminder of all the Mistrals who'd worked this land, their pride in their name and traditions.

'I can manage. You can help by staying away from us.'

Help from a German, even one like Kristian, was completely out of the question.

When she got home, she looked at herself in the mirror, fair hair tumbling over her shoulders, a pair of scissors in her hand.

It was just her and Maman now up on the farm, and she

didn't need Schmidt's kind of attention. She chopped the whole lot off and chucked it in the bin. A boyish Lilou stared back. She wondered what Kristian would think. Would he still look at her like he had something urgent to confess?

The full moon was late in coming that June. Tonight, there was just a sliver missing, and she realised with a jolt that it would soon be time for her second Alliance assignment.

The abbé told her to go to the bakery straight after church on Sunday, and, as she left the morning service, the mistral wind was blowing an unseasonal chill, scattering the leaves on the church steps like confetti.

She put a protective hand on her cyanide locket as she swung open the bakery door, and the redhead stopped her sweeping for a millisecond as she clocked the gesture.

'Lilou, the last loaf, saved for you,' she said breezily. Apart from the miserable little brown *miche* she wrapped for her, the shelves were completely bare.

'I'll take the last one,' a German voice said from the doorway. It was Doll-face. Lilou froze. There was a message hidden in the bread, her next assignment.

The redhead didn't miss a beat. 'This one's reserved, I'm afraid, monsieur.' She took out her notepad. 'I'll take your order and bake it for you right now. We still have dough from the white flour you bought for us, and this one's made with the lowest-grade old husks. Not really up to your exacting standards. I'll deliver as soon as it's ready.'

Her co-worker tutted in *I bet you will* disgust.

'Nevertheless, you know we must come first...'

'Kapitän Weber, *there* you are!' Madame Aveline swept in. 'Didn't you receive our invitation to join us for the fete breakfast? Or perhaps you did, and I should feel offended! It's one of the most important days in our town calendar, you know. The mayor and I have pastries and baguettes and my home-made jam waiting for you and we've used all our rations for the month to entertain you and the boys in a fitting manner!'

Lilou forced a smile. 'No one has ever been known to refuse an invitation from Madame Aveline and live to tell the tale. But I'll happily swap you for a white baguette and leave you to your fate.'

'Lilou Mistral.' Madame turned to her in anger. 'Take the *miche* and leave the officers to the food they've paid for.' She crooked her arm for Doll-face, who simply stared at it. 'I'm afraid some people are still unaware of the new hierarchy, but they have to be told.'

'Here,' said the redhead to Lilou. 'You're lucky to get it, and don't forget to say thank you.'

'Thank you,' said Lilou as meekly as her hot fury at having to simper to this murderer would allow.

Madame Aveline looked down at her still-crooked arm and smiled again. 'Kapitän Weber? As the highest-ranking official here I hope you're not going to refuse me?'

Clearly murdering bullies love to be so flattered, because he allowed himself to be ushered out in a cloud of lily-of-the-valley perfume and entreaties about having someone eloquent to make a speech at the fete. Was Madame in on this, part of the Resistance? It was impossible to tell nowadays, but Lilou didn't care either way. She grabbed the *miche* and left.

Out in the square, the village was getting ready for the *fête de transhumance* that celebrated the animals being led to higher pastures with their Patou dogs for protection. If you ignored the German soldiers at the café tables smoking and sipping coffee in the sunshine, you'd think it was no different from any other year. But it was like the chip on the fountain the Gestapo had made when they drove in. Unmistakably there, and the gash it had left looked vulnerable and new and broken. Lilou didn't dare look in the direction of the café in case she caught Kristian's eye. She hurried up the hill with her *miche*.

At home, Scout rushed up the path to greet her. He'd grown enormous, as big as a bear, his cloud of creamy fur flying everywhere as she ruffled it.

'Stop licking, boy,' she spluttered, overwhelmed by his great tongue and wet muzzle.

He seemed to sense it was nearly time to leave for the cool hills, and he stalked her all the way to the house, and sat outside the front door to guard her as if she were a sheep. Freddie would have loved that. Scout was the last she had of Freddie, and she was dreading him leaving them for the summer with their animals, but he had his work to do, the same as everyone else.

Lilou set the *miche* on the kitchen table and broke it open carefully, saying a silent prayer of thanks for Madame's interventions. Sure enough, a piece of paper was tucked inside. Holding it up to the light, she made a note of the numbers on the code grid as the abbé had shown her. Double-checking she'd got it right before she tore up the pieces and pocketed it to hide it in the compost (a fire would attract attention should there be a spot-check on such a hot day), Lilou heaved the dresser and ratcheted up the floorboard.

She pulled out *The Little Prince,* by Antoine de Saint-Exupéry. Such humanity, wisdom and innocence was in short supply in these times, and she practically knew the charming book off by heart. She was sure one day after all this it would be published; such work deserved a life outside of all this. Now was it unknown to all but a few operatives, whose only interest in it was to use it for deciphering code.

Picking out the words from the manuscript, she deciphered that the rendezvous was in two days' time, on the full moon. She knew the exact spot, near Bargème, where the *transhumance* would pause before it scattered to individual pastures. Perfect timing. No one would question a Mistral girl for driving her animals to summer pastures at this time of year, especially with the men of the house gone.

Lilou spent the next day preparing the flock, and packed a small bedding roll and supplies for the journey. She told Maman she'd be back, but was met with a blank stare. Lilou felt a guilty relief at the thought of being out on the open road for a while. Maman would have to be all right without her.

On Wednesday, the saint's day for Saint Remy de Provence, she and Scout waited. He pricked up his ears, and a few moments later Lilou's human ears heard them too. The cowbells, bellows and bleating of hundreds of animals sweating up the hill at first light. It was a sight she'd loved since she could remember, holding Papa's hand to wait for them to come. Today the drove was different as it rounded the corner. In place of the usual gaggle of weather-worn shepherds and farm workers were women of all ages, pacing up the hill with their flocks, whooping and calling orders to their dogs in a tide of undulating woolly coats of flaxen white, straw and cream. As they approached the gate, Lilou waited for the signal from the lead drover, old Madame Isnard, who was spry and apple-cheeked as her orchard.

Madame Isnard raised her hand, and Scout drove the flock to join them, nudging the stragglers into line. With so many inexperienced hands on the drove, it was chaotic, and the dogs seemed to sense it, and were frenzied with their charges if they so much as glanced sideways. Things were always unpredictable in the countryside, but these were the people that Lilou had grown up with, all going in one direction with a common purpose, and she took strength from that as they all paced upward, high enough for the breeze to freshen and cool them all.

At Bargème, in a cloud of dust, over three thousand animals descended on the hill town, bells ringing, baas, neighs, moos, barks and a sea of sheep flowed into waiting pens, and the Patou were rewarded with water and fresh rabbits.

At the local market, stalls strung with bunting sold everything from leather belts to thick jumpers to pickles, and small boys begged non-existent candyfloss from skinny mothers who looked like they hadn't eaten in weeks. Somehow she hadn't expected them to have got this far but, of course, soldiers in German uniform sauntered around like they owned the place, shown around by *Milices*, taking whatever they wanted without paying.

Lilou headed for Monsieur and Madame Pascal's goat's cheese stall. In her happier days, Maman had declared that they bred the happiest, glossiest chestnut-coated Alpine goats in the whole of the Alpes-Maritimes. Five of their best were now chewing the cud in a pen behind the stall.

'Lilou!' Madame Pascal hobbled out from behind her stall and kissed her warmly. 'Look at you, all grown up, and beautiful! Where's that wayward brother of yours?'

'Taken,' said Lilou. 'By the Germans.'

Madame Pascal hugged her, and Monsieur Pascal spat and crossed himself. 'Dirty Boche,' he said loudly, his deafness making him shout.

'What did you say?' a passing German soldier said officiously.

Monsieur Pascal looked him straight in the eye. 'Dirty Boche.' Monsieur Pascal was not known for his even temper.

Lilou felt her hackles rise.

'Apologise to your superiors, old man,' said the soldier.

The space around the stall emptied, collective eyes averted, loud conversations struck up to try to cover up the situation.

'I'll apologise when you grow up and learn some manners.

Don't your mothers teach you anything but how to suck cock in Germany?'

Sensing the aggro, Monsieur Pascal's Patou barked wildly, and the soldier cocked his gun.

'Tell it to shut up.'

'Go, boy,' shouted Monsieur Pascal, always up for a fight.

The dog lunged, and the soldier shot. Blood exploded and spattered the stall, children screamed, and the thousands of gathered animals let out a chorus of panic. Lilou closed her eyes to fight back nausea. She remembered Monsieur Pascal's dog when he was a puppy. He wouldn't have known anything, she comforted herself.

'More guts in a French dog than we thought,' said the soldier casually. His fellow squaddies laughed, and they sauntered off.

Monsieur Pascal didn't flinch, and stared them down till they were gone, only the redness of his face giving him away. Mothers hushed their children so as not to draw attention to themselves, and only when the men were out of earshot did people mutter about Kraut hooligans frightening the ewes. No one retaliated, and Lilou thought passionately that this silence only served to unite the underdogs. She felt the rage and impotence of the oppressed, and poured her anger into a silent curse on the full moon after them, like her grandmother had taught her. Whatever mission Alliance had for tonight, she was ready.

Before evening fell, Lilou bid her goodnights to the gathering and headed for the Mistral summer shepherd's hut. It was set well away from the crowds, but when she left for the rendezvous at midnight, a dark shawl pulled around her fair hair, she still took a moment to stand and listen.

The rustle in the hedge was a family of boars, the owl was unlikely to call if it was disturbed by humans, the cicadas were going strong. The moon was huge and bright, the opposite of a poacher's moon. For lovers, such a moon silvered the fields and bathed everything in magic. Now, it was a spotlight that threatened to give her away. Tonight, her country girl's ears were not just useful for observing the comings and goings of her beloved Provençal nocturnal wildlife; it was a matter of life and death.

Lilou scanned the village lights below, spotted two bright torches, a good distance away, heading up the track that led to her hut. She froze. The church bell struck midnight, the allotted time for the Lysander landing. She listened for a propeller, or the sound of an engine. Nothing but a nightjar in the trees. Down the track, the torches veered off towards the Pascals' goat farm. Please God, no retaliation tonight.

She edged closer to the clearing, on high alert. A branch snapped, leaves cracked. Unmistakably a human footstep. Lilou ducked, peered through the thicket, and there they were. Two boys Freddie had raised mischief with, now men, crouching, searching the skies.

'It's a good moon for the wolves,' she whispered.

'Better to watch for the sheep,' replied Xavier to confirm their mission code. She stood and showed herself. They put their hands on their hearts by way of greeting, and she followed them as they checked their watches. She found herself mourning the lively boys who were now these silent men, both on high alert, toting useless farmers' rifles. They might be dead before the next full moon.

The Lysander engine split the air as it came into view, and the boys stepped into the clearing to make the L-shape with their torches to help the plane land. When it came to a halt a safe distance from the trees and the pilot cut the engine, Lilou could breathe again. So far, so good. Freddie's friends melted away without a word and her heart flew with them, *please God, stay safe.*

A svelte figure in a flying suit and goggles clambered out of the cockpit and jumped lightly to the ground. Marie-Madeleine! She blew Lilou a kiss, put her fingers to her lips and turned to the plane.

'Friend. All clear!' she hissed.

Lilou was shocked to see a terrified little boy being guided down the ladder on the side of the plane till he was close enough to the ground for him to take the leap.

'There we go,' said Marie-Madeleine, jumping him to his feet and brushing the grass off his trousers. The boy stared at her wildly. His cheeks were round and rosy, a straight black fringe encroached on serious dark eyes, and he was dressed in a warm jumper and old-fashioned corduroy trousers that were too short for him, a satchel across his chest.

Marie-Madeline pushed the boy forward. He clung to her.

'This is Eliot. We need you to take him until further instructions. Eliot, say hello to Lilou.'

The boy stood stock-still, head still bowed.

'You can't pull this routine every time. You have to be brave. As we've told you, Lilou will be your guardian,' she said, not unkindly, but a little impatiently. She looked beseechingly at Lilou and mouthed, 'Help.'

Lilou racked her brains. Before she even considered the question of how to take care of him and where to hide him... what on earth did you say to a small boy who was being handed to her from a plane in the middle of the night?

'Hello, do you like dogs?'

The boy looked up at that.

'He's waiting at the hut, his name's Scout, and he's very used to looking after boys.'

The boy went to speak, caught himself and stared at the floor again to hide a tear that threatened to give him away.

Marie-Madeleine patted him on the head. 'There, there, he's had a rough time of it. Chin up, little soldier. Lilou lives on a farm and she has bees, and sheep, and you'll have a marvellous time until we come and get you again. On you go.' She gave him an encouraging push. 'I'm afraid his parents were taken in terrible circumstances and he still has nightmares. He needs fresh air, love and understanding. I'm sure you're the girl for the job. Thank you, Lilou. Our instructions are to leave immediately, the abbé can tell you more, and there's a letter here that explains everything.' She handed over an envelope. 'We're grateful to have you on board, operative Mistral.'

'Wait... your baby?' she blurted, before realising it might not be good news.

Marie-Madeleine looked down at her flat stomach and protruding hip-bones. 'Oh that, two weeks ago. Louis. He's safe now, but unfortunately he can't be with me.' It was only a momentary chink in the armour, but in the bright moonlight Lilou saw the dark flare in her eye where she hid her hurt.

'Goodbye then, Eliot. Be good for Mademoiselle Mistral.'

The boy didn't answer, so she kissed his head awkwardly, saluted Lilou and nimbly climbed back up the ladder into the Lysander.

'Well,' said Lilou to the boy. 'It's you and me now, and we'll make a very good team, I promise.'

She wanted to hug him tight and tell him everything would be all right, but that would be a lie, and he wasn't ready for such familiarity. She pocketed the letter, dreading to see what had happened to this kid. What the hell was she going to do with a boy who was so afraid that he couldn't speak, and had witnessed horrors that no one should ever have to see? Kristian had said that perhaps Freddie was lucky and had landed with someone kind. And Joseph, did he have a guardian angel who was looking out for him? She doubted it. But there was one thing she could be certain of. This smidgen of a heartsick boy needed her, and she'd guard him as fiercely as she prayed someone was guarding Freddie and Joseph, and, if the whole world did the same, there might be some hope.

CHAPTER 8

OUT OF THE MOUTHS OF BABES

BARGÈME, VAR, JUNE 1943

Lilou

Eliot took two paces for her every one as she rushed him on in silence, desperate to get him back to the shepherd's hut and relative safety. He trembled at every animal noise, and was as spooked as a restive foal in the darkness, wary of her whispered reassurances.

At the hut, Lilou made a sheepskin nest for Eliot, and a pillow of straw stuffed in a sack, just like Papa had for her and Freddie when she was little. The boy lay there, eyes wide open, fighting sleep, still fully clothed, shoes and all. When she'd told him to take off his jumper, shoes and satchel, he'd shaken his head vigorously and clutched his bag tight. He still hadn't said a word.

'Can't sleep? I'll build a fire and you can light the match if you like?' said Lilou. Eliot kept his eyes firmly on the ceiling, but nodded.

She set the wood and kindling, humming an old mountain tune to soothe him and fill the silence.

'Here,' she said, holding out the matches. 'Strike it and hold it right there till the kindling takes.'

His hands were shaking, and it took him three strikes, but he concentrated hard on holding it in the kindling as she'd shown him, and his thick eyebrows un-furrowed a little when the flames leapt in his eyes, a glow on his soft, olive skin.

Lilou drew up a chair to the fire for him. 'My maman used to tell me that all the stories in the world were made in flames, and the warmth you feel is the protection of all your relations, past and future.'

His silence seemed to dam a torrent of suffering, and Lilou could do nothing but wait for the balm of sleep for this boy who had been made to swallow all the violence and prejudice of supposed grown-ups who were meant to protect him.

'Everything will feel better in the morning, I promise you're safe with me,' she whispered. His eyelids drooped drowsily, but he hugged his satchel like his life depended on it.

'Tomorrow I'll introduce you to my dog Scout, who protects sheep for his work. He'll be given a new assignment in the morning – you. I think you'll like him.'

He flicked his eyes to meet hers briefly. Finally, sleep got the better of him and his head lolled. Lilou left him to drift deeper into sleep, dwarfed and lonely in the big armchair. When his hands fell from his satchel and he was floppy with dreams, she gently lifted him onto the sheepskins and tucked him in with his bag, carefully taking off his shoes and arranging them neatly where he could see them. She understood that all he had in the world were the clothes he stood up in and whatever was so precious in the bag, and it would be important for him to have everything close by when he woke.

She was exhausted, but there was still enough oil in the

lamp to read the letter Marie-Madeleine had given her, so she peeled it open as quietly as she could.

The details were typed in stark, *Croix-Rouge* official letters.

Displaced Minor

Name: Eliot Stavinsky.

Age: 7.

Parents: Transported, possibly deceased, under orders of Klaus Barbie.

Next of kin: None known.

Status: Clear and present danger to life. Whereabouts to be concealed at all costs.

Marie-Madeleine had scrawled a note beneath in a rushed hand:

Poor mite saw his parents beaten and dragged away. I couldn't think of anyone else, please love him on behalf of all our lost and missing children. Destroy this letter. With love and eternal hope, MMF

Lilou screwed the letter up and chucked it as hard as she could into the fire. Why the fuck should he suffer for this madness? Who hurts a kid's parents right in front of them? Klaus Barbie was renowned for his brutality and sadism, for feeding on fear and horror. God only knew what Eliot had witnessed; no wonder he was mute. She looked at him sleeping peacefully. His hands were bunched up to his face and his eyebrows arched in seemingly permanent curiosity. Were they his mother's or his father's? He was almost pretty with his round, dark eyes, perfect olive skin and straight, glossy bowl-cut hair, which, now his maman was gone, had grown too long over his eyes. Did he resemble her? How did his maman feel at the moment she knew she could no longer protect him?

He slept long after the sun rose, and Lilou slipped out to whistle for Scout, who came bounding to her as if he'd been waiting his whole life for the call.

'Whoa boy, not so fast,' she whispered into his fur as she hugged him. 'You have a job to do.'

She told him to heel as they went into the hut, but guarding sheep is thirsty work, and Scout took noisy slurps of water from his bowl before she could stop him. Eliot's eyes blinked open, and he looked around him in silent terror.

'It's me, Lilou, remember? And this is Scout. I'm sorry he woke you with such bad manners,' she said.

Eliot sat up and Scout dashed over and nosed him right in the face.

'Stop!' said Eliot, giggling. His voice was low and husky for a seven-year-old and the morning sun streamed right into Lilou's heart.

'How many slices of bacon would you like?' she asked. She'd only bought enough food for one, so she'd have to go without, but she was glad to be able to do something for him.

Eliot addressed Scout. 'That's the problem with adults, they always ask the wrong questions.'

Scout nudged him sympathetically, both conspiring against her.

'What question does Scout think I *should* ask?' said Lilou.

'Not how many slices, but do I eat bacon? I'm sorry to say that the answer is no. Scout knows that,' he said emphatically. 'Though I thank you.'

He had a curious, formal way of speaking that melted Lilou's heart. Of course, Joseph and his family didn't eat pork, and they were Jewish too. She kicked herself. How could she have been so insensitive?

'All right, how about some toast? We could build another fire and use the fork to toast the bread ourselves.'

He nodded obediently, and helped her light the fire with serious efficiency, doing exactly as she'd told him last night.

'One slice or two?'

Eliot ruffled Scout's ears, pulled his satchel over his shoulder and patted it close to him. 'That's the trouble with adults, Scout. They spy on you and don't ask you how brown you like your toast, only how many slices you want.'

This was starting to sound strangely familiar. Lilou cut two slices of bread anyway. In her experience, boys were permanently hungry.

'Funny that you flew here,' she said.

'I would have preferred to arrive by bird than plane,' he confided in Scout, who pricked up his ears by way of reply.

'There's only one boy I know who travels by bird, and he comes from an asteroid,' Lilou said casually.

'You know him too?' said Eliot, impressed, forgetting he was only speaking to Scout.

Lilou nodded. 'Antoine de Saint-Exupéry is a great man. I've met him in his aeroplane,' she said.

Eliot held his satchel closer, suspicious. It made absolute sense. Tonio de Saint-Exupéry was liaising with Marie-Madeleine the night of her first mission in the Bay of Agay, so he must have met Eliot. From the little she'd seen of him, giving this terrified boy a book to lose himself in was just the sort of kind, understanding gesture he'd make. And now Eliot must have a copy of the same book that Lilou used to decipher the code, *The Little Prince*; and he was clinging to it for dear life.

'*The Little Prince* is one of my favourite books. I have a special copy, which hasn't even been printed yet,' Lilou said breezily.

'Me too!' said Eliot. Then, retreating slightly, 'He only gives them to special people who would understand.' He looked at her sideways, testing.

'Then maybe I'm not a spy,' said Lilou casually, poking the fire and handing him a toasting fork.

He took it and held it up to the fire. 'Where are the lambs that Scout guards?' he said.

'Do you want me to show you?'

'Is it safe to go out?' said Eliot.

Lilou sent one of her grandma's curses out to all the German soldiers she'd seen parading around yesterday's fete. What seven-year-old child should need to ask that?

'Of course, you're with me and Scout now and we're in the mountains, which is a bit like being on a planet above the Earth.'

'We can't see any sky or stars below us, but I suppose we *are* high up,' said Eliot, kindly making allowances for Lilou's ignorance.

'And you have Scout to protect you now, and he never lets anyone hurt his lambs,' said Lilou.

Scout yawned, and Eliot fell silent. Lilou didn't push any further. A lamb had to get to trust you before it would follow. Lilou spread the toast with the butter she'd churned herself, and opened a precious jar of Sainte Roseline honey. Eliot devoured the toast in seconds, and eyed Lilou's hungrily.

'I've already had my breakfast,' she lied, handing him her portion.

'I'll need strength to walk back to Lyon. It must be a long way from here,' he said.

Lilou smiled but said nothing. He was never going back to Lyon, not in any timeframe he was able to conceive of.

Eliot saved his last corner of toast for Scout, who took it primly, lips pulled delicately over gnashers. Good old Scout. If Lilou had offered it, he'd have practically bitten her hand off.

They walked across the meadows to the sheep pasture, Scout running ahead to make sure all was in order. Eliot watched, entranced, as Scout did his work, the early-morning sun warmed them, and meadow sage reached up in purple spires above the tall grass to catch the rays, celandine glowing dots of phosphorescent yellow as far as she could see.

'Do you want to catch up with Scout? You can run ahead if you like,' said Lilou.

Eliot shook his head solemnly. 'No, I'm fine,' he said, his shiny lace-up town shoes slippery and hot on the uneven ground. No chance today of this little boy making a run for it barefoot like she and Freddie used to in the high meadows, just for the sheer joy.

When they reached the pasture, Eliot took a pen and notepad out of his bag. He flicked through to find a clean page, and Lilou saw his drawings were of angry faces, stars of David and Nazi insignia, punctuated by neat rows of numbers.

'Can I go in?' he asked.

'Yes, you can help Scout if you like,' said Lilou, opening the gate a chink for them to slip through.

Eliot moved amongst the sheep slowly, making notes in tally marks of four lines, then a cross for every five, his fringe dropping over his eyes as he looked in concentration, lips mouthing the numbers. Scout rounded up a few stragglers and the flock shifted. Eliot threw down his pencil, tears welling.

'They keep moving. How am I supposed to count them?'

'I can tell you how many if you like.'

'No! I need to count them myself, then I'll know how many there are to look after and I can tell Monsieur de Saint-Exupéry how many I've saved for him.'

'You don't need to look after them, Scout is here to do that.'

'I DO! Otherwise they'll all be killed.'

'Not here, they won't. Listen, there are fifty-one. Write that down, and you can keep them safe in your notebook.'

That calmed him, and he settled down cross-legged to begin his work of making sure that each one was noted.

He didn't speak again that day, just kept counting the lambs over and over to make sure each sheep and lamb in the pasture was accounted for, telling them he needed to be sure, for Monsieur de Saint-Exupéry. Even Scout couldn't distract him, and she understood. In the pages of Tonio's book, and his own notebook, he was safe in a world he could control.

CHAPTER 9

SWEET DREAMS

BARGÈME, VAR, JULY 1943

Lilou

The sun rose, of course, the dawn chorus exuberant as ever. Lilou took a moment to listen, to pretend it was the same as any morning she'd known, just to remember how it felt.

She glanced over to the little nook where she'd tucked Eliot up last night with his satchel and sat with him till he could no longer fight sleep. Scout had made himself into an enormous furry pillow and Eliot was pale in deep sleep, nestled cosily into his canine guardian. Scout's eyes were already on her as she stirred and smiled good morning, but he didn't move a muscle. Instead, he acknowledged her with a blink and put his head gently back on his paws with a resigned look.

'That's it, Scout, he belongs to you now,' whispered Lilou.

Scout flattened his ears and licked his chops, Eliot's cap of dark hair glossy against the dog's grubby white shag. What on earth would his maman think of her neatly dressed little boy using a dog as a pillow?

Lilou's mind raced. She couldn't stay here with him where they'd easily be discovered. How could she tear him away from Scout, who'd have to stay in the hills to guard his flock? And what about when she got Eliot back to the farm? Lilou couldn't stay with him all day, there was too much to do just to survive, and he couldn't join her on her chores in case he was seen. He'd need new clothes, and food, and... what else did a small boy need? Where could she hide him without him suffering even more loneliness and fear if she had to leave him alone?

For the first time, Lilou felt a stab of resentment for Marie-Madeleine. Lilou had promised to take care of Eliot and of course she would never ever break that promise. But why her? Why a girl running a farm in Provence all on her own?

But even as she had the thought Lilou chided herself. Why anyone? Why not her?

First things first. She needed to get him back to the farm undetected, and for that she'd need transport so she could hide him. Not many people she knew had cars, but the drove leader, Madame Isnard, had a horse and cart. She'd always been kind, so perhaps the old lady would look after Lilou's sheep alongside her own flock in return for an attractive barter, and lend out her cart?

Scout snuffled, and Eliot woke. Giving Scout a distracted pat, he propped himself up, fastened his satchel over his shoulder from under his pillow, pulled out his notebook and began to write feverishly.

'It must be something important if you're writing before breakfast,' said Lilou.

'I'm trying to remember.'

'What?'

He put his hand over the writing to shield it from her. 'None of your bloody business. I promised Papa I'd remember and it's all jumbled up.'

He threw his pencil on the floor, trying not to cry. Whatever it was obviously meant a lot. She picked up the pencil.

'Sometimes it's easier to remember if you do something else. Why don't you try another thing?'

Eliot sighed and took the pencil back. 'I'll try.' He started writing again, focused and absorbed.

'Does that feel better?'

'It's my itinerary.'

'That's a big word for a small boy.'

'Papa had one every day.'

'I see. What's on your itinerary?'

'If I remember the numbers, then I can rescue Maman and Papa.'

Lilou put food down for Scout. 'What are the numbers for?'

'To kill the dirty fucking Boche,' he said evenly.

'Eliot, you can't swear like that!' *Good for him,* she thought silently even as she said it.

'Why not? It's what Papa said when they took him, then they hit him and Maman cried.'

God, he needed a hug and someone to erase his memory of what he'd seen. But it was too soon for a hug, she just knew, and no one could ever help him unsee. Perhaps with time she could help him to trust, though.

'I have an itinerary today, too,' she said. 'I have to go to the village to get us a horse and cart, and then we'll go on a journey to my farm where you'll have your own room, and Scout can stay with you in it. You can meet the bees, and see fields of purple lavender, and there's a vegetable plot and you can help tend to it all every day if you like.'

'I would be delighted to help,' said Eliot huskily, adding those items to his list.

'I'm going to lock the door, so if you hear anyone knocking, you are to stay completely quiet and not let them know you are here. Can you do that?'

'I did it when they took Maman and Papa,' he said quietly.

'Good,' said Lilou, longing to scoop up this jumble of anguish in her arms. 'Nothing can happen to you while Scout is here, and I won't be long.'

Lilou hurried down the track to the village, and, as she reached the outskirts, the church on the hill rang out a slow death knell. She found Madame Isnard in her field, making repairs to her sheepfold, her stiff joints labouring as she expertly held up a plank and hammered in the nails.

'Morning! Let me hold that up for you,' said Lilou.

Madame Isnard stayed focused on the job. 'Lovely day for it. Put your hand there.'

Lilou secured the plank for her. 'Who's the bell for?'

Madame Isnard whacked the nail extra hard. 'That old fool Pascal. Never knew when to keep his mouth shut.'

Lilou's heart dropped to her boots. 'How?'

'The Boche found his place in the middle of the night. They dragged him out half naked and shot him in front of Madame Pascal.' Madame Isnard crossed herself with her free hand and spat on the floor. '*Salauds,*' she cursed.

Lilou crossed herself out of respect, even though she didn't believe, horrified for Madame Pascal and afraid for Eliot alone at the hut.

'Hold it still!' barked Madame Isnard.

When the plank was fixed, they embraced; they didn't need words. Her hands dug into Lilou's ribs.

'You're skinny as a runt. There's a few jars of confit duck hidden at the hut, I buried it in the back garden. Those Kraut kids wouldn't know a flower bed from a shit heap even if you rubbed their faces in it. Let me give you some for you and your poor maman.'

'Thank you, I can manage, Madame Isnard, and you need it for yourself. But I do have a barter for you. It's just me and Maman

at home, and Scout's such a good guard dog. I want to take him
back with me. I had the idea that I could merge my flock with
yours – they're all branded, so we wouldn't mix them up – and you
could use my pastures. You know how sweet the grass is up there.'

Madame Isnard looked up at the hills. 'Sweet and tender as
your maman used to be when she scrumped my apple trees. She
was a tearaway that one. I've heard about her, not right in the
head...'

Country people didn't mince their words.

Lilou leapt to her maman's defence. 'She just feels more
deeply than most, and when they took Freddie...'

Madame Isnard put her arm on Lilou's. 'We all have our
crosses to bear. A few more sheep is no hardship, and I could
use some extra pastures. Take the cart and the old horse. On
you go, I won't ask any questions,' she said, squinting at her
shrewdly.

As Lilou speeded Madam Isnard's old nag and rickety cart
back up the hill, the slow bell for Monsieur Pascal blackened
the sweet summer air like a disease at a christening.

Lilou took the old byways back down to the plateau. She hid
Eliot in a crate covered in blankets, and strapped it down tight.
She also loaded the cart with as many reasons as she could think
of for needing it, should she be asked. A few straggly hay bales,
an old hand-plough that was lying in the yard, a pile of sheepskins that Freddie had left for the fete. It was a hot day, so she
slung a white tarp over the top as a shade, and told Eliot that
Scout would guard him.

'It'll be an adventure, like being inside a secret den and
getting transported through the land,' she said.

'It's all right, you don't have to pretend. There was a place
under the floorboards where I had to go at home. Maman said it

was fun, but it wasn't. That was all dark and scary, too,' he said helpfully as he climbed in.

'The difference is, you won't have to endure it for long, and then we'll be back on the farm and that will be your new home.'

'I don't want a new home. I want my old one, with Maman and Papa.'

Poor mite.

It could never be his old home with his maman and papa, but Lilou moved Eliot into Freddie's old room. The first thing he did was take something out of his satchel and put it on his bedside table. Lilou was relieved that he felt comfortable enough to unpack something from his precious bag. It was a strange-looking brass instrument with a curved ruler, a mini-telescope and little round fold-out mirrors.

'That looks like some kind of science experiment, no wonder your satchel was so heavy,' she said.

'Papa gave it to me. It's a sextant and he used it for his work sometimes.' He stared very hard at it and shook his head. 'I promised him I'd remember the numbers that go with it, but we didn't have much time to practise before they took him.'

His temporary delight at his own room threatened to dissipate, so Lilou distracted his attention with the ephemera of Freddie's childhood, which he'd kept far beyond using them. There was an old model of a biplane and a well-used miniature farm that Papa had made, complete with a sheep, a pig and a metal tractor they'd bought on a trip to Fréjus. Eliot told her formally that the farm was 'very kind, however too babyish', but Freddie's unused set of encyclopaedias finally found a willing reader, and kept Eliot fascinated for hours.

The nights were hard for him. It was then that the terrors arrived, the numbers he was meant to remember eluded him, and the only comfort to be found was in the pages of his own copy of *The Little Prince*. His copy was different from hers, with an extra chapter about a dragon; it was a christening present he'd grown up with and knew off by heart, Eliot told her. And what different purposes it served for the two of them. Eliot used it to escape to, for comfort, but for Lilou it served as a code-breaking document. It was a relief to see that Eliot's copy was a different version from her own. If his book fell into the wrong hands, none of the coordinates would work because the extra chapter would throw everything out. She wondered how many other versions were out there. Tonio de Saint-Exupéry must have been working on the final version for years, between unfeasibly walking away from crashes in the desert and penning his famous books about his flying career.

With this in mind, she was sure that Marie-Madeleine wouldn't mind if Lilou read Eliot's version of *The Little Prince* to him every night. It was the only thing that would settle him, and Lilou had to read it to him over and over again, until he could no longer fight sleep.

As the weeks went on, Lilou found herself looking forward to opening the door a chink just before she went to bed, Scout half awake at the creak of the door, dominating the bed, with Eliot curled around him fast asleep. He was her serious, bookish, eccentric orphan from a different world, and more precious to her as every day passed.

Even Maman had one of her rare lucid moments when she came home one evening to find Eliot sitting at the dinner table, with Scout at his feet.

'Goodness me, who's this beautiful boy sitting at my table?' She ruffled his shiny mop. 'And you've got Scout very well under control. He doesn't take to everyone.' She beamed.

Lilou had told Eliot about Maman, that she lived in her own world but was the kindest person in the world, like a fairy godmother, and, if he was lucky and she spoke to him, he must be very polite.

Eliot gave her a rare smile and bowed. 'I'm Eliot Stavinsky. I quite like it here, but would prefer to live on a planet in space. In the meantime, I'm enchanted,' he said.

'That's lovely. And *enchanted*, well, well.' Maman returned his bow.

'It's my pleasure,' said Eliot, tucking into his bread and honey.

'Eat up, Freddie,' Maman said, her eyes blurring.

They established a fragile routine that could fall apart at any moment. Lilou didn't dare let Eliot out too far around the farm – you never knew who was watching nowadays. He spent his days drawing feverishly, and the more time he had to himself the more he drew the same thing over and over again. A dragon, jumbles of numbers, sketches from *The Little Prince* book.

Lilou told the bees everything and they always listened, a warm thrum from inside the hives melding with her thoughts and keeping her words safe. She sometimes whispered to them about the German soldier who'd rescued her cat and who knew about the stars. Should she trust him? Was it all right to feel a kinship with the enemy, to believe what he said about helping from the inside?

The bees didn't judge, though they should for even having such thoughts. What kind of dreamland was she in when she hardly knew him?

Visitors were rare nowadays so, one sweltering summer's day when she heard a vehicle crunching down the track, her hackles rose. She ran to meet it, no time to check if Eliot was in his room. *Stay where you are, little man.*

At the front of the house, she froze as Doll-face and a squad of young soldiers jumped down from the truck. Kristian climbed down behind them, eyes flashing a warning.

'What a shame,' said Doll-face. 'All that lovely hair, gone! You look more like a prisoner than a girl now.'

That's exactly what I am, thought Lilou, trying to give him a relaxed smile.

Doll-face waved at his men to move inside. 'We just need to carry out a routine inspection. A brief look around, nothing to be concerned about.' He licked his lips, savouring the moment. 'Boys, search the place from top to bottom.'

They marched past her as her mind raced.

'Wait! You can't just go in...'

'If you have nothing to hide, there's absolutely nothing to worry about. Your friend Madame Isnard thought we might find something though.' He flicked the pages of a notebook for effect. 'Ah yes, here it is. Out-of-character behaviour. The madwoman, your maman, I think? She told her that Freddie is home, which is of course impossible.' He pocketed the notebook and smiled. 'One of our best informants, that old woman. How do you put it in French? She has a sixth sense.'

Lilou forced herself to stay composed. 'Madame Isnard? She's had her eye on this farm since Papa died. You're right about her, she can play anyone like a violin. Now she's got you to do her dirty work.'

That knocked the smug smile off the bastard's face.

'Please,' she said. 'After you. Wipe those big boots on the way in.'

Lilou's chest was so tight she could hardly breathe, and Scout was barking like a mad thing in Eliot's room as the soldier's jackboots clattered across the flagstones and up the stairs. She ran up after them.

On the landing, Schmidt, the arrogant soldier who'd nearly knocked her off her bike, stopped outside Eliot's closed door. 'Get that dog out of there and shut him up.'

'It's best I just leave him in there out of the way. He's a guard dog, very suspicious of strangers, and I'm not sure I could calm him now,' she said, trying to sound helpful rather than terrified.

Schmidt waved an arm at his colleagues. 'Search the other rooms.' The soldiers fanned out into the other bedrooms, emptying drawers and pulling the handles off the rickety wardrobe doors. Scout pounded Eliot's door as he jumped up against it, ready to ravage the threat he sensed on the other side.

'This is nonsense, just delay tactics. Schmidt, take the men downstairs and search immediately, I'll deal with this animal,' Kristian commanded.

'Sir,' said Schmidt. The men hotfooted it downstairs. Kristian unholstered his gun and pointed it at Eliot's room.

'Open the door. You will be responsible for controlling the animal, and for the consequences if it attacks.'

She hesitated, so Kristian kicked it open. Scout went for him, but Kristian stood his ground. Scout stopped short, snarling.

'Ruhig, Hund, alles ist gut, Freund, shhh,' he said gently.

Scout subsided and Kristian grabbed his collar, dragged him inside and closed the door behind them. Eliot was sitting on the bed completely still, clutching his satchel.

'Are you going to shoot me?' he whispered.

Kristian put his finger on his lips, turned on his heel and left, striding past Lilou without a glance in her direction.

'Nothing here. The outbuildings, quick!'

Lilou could have collapsed in relief. *Thank you, Kristian.*

The soldiers mustered and fanned out through the grounds. Doll-face poked around in the shed and pocketed a jar of honey. They ransacked the haystack, frightened the cow, and helped themselves to the apple store, then sauntered back to the jeep while Kristian sat frowning, gripping the steering wheel.

He wound down the window and yelled, 'Get in, complete waste of time.'

The other men filed into the truck, but Doll-face turned to Lilou.

'I haven't forgotten how friendly you were with those dirty Jews. I'm a sentimental old bastard, and I'd hate to see that pretty face of yours in trouble. Let this be a warning.'

'I'm just managing as best I can,' said Lilou.

'That's the spirit,' he said. 'It's for the greater good. We're not savages, just civilised people tasked with keeping up law and order.'

He stepped primly up into the jeep to show her just how polite they were, and they left in a cloud of dust, knocking the gatepost as they left.

'Tell your informant to go hang herself,' she mouthed as she waved them off, baring her teeth in a smile.

As soon as they'd left, she rushed up to Eliot's room. He was curled up in a ball, humming the tune he always sang when he was afraid, a wet patch on his new fleece pyjamas.

'It's all right, they've gone and you were very brave,' said Lilou.

Eliot buried his face in Scout's fur. Lilou was furious with herself. Eliot should never have had to endure this, and she'd already taken too many risks. She couldn't trust anyone apart from herself, not even poor Maman. She'd have to move him somewhere less obvious, away from the house.

'Come on, they've gone now and they're not coming back, I promise. I'll draw you a nice bath, and it's sunny outside so we can go and see what the bees are doing. If you don't want to speak to me today, you can talk to them instead. There's a tradition that only beekeepers know, called Telling the Bees. They like to know what's happening on the farm, and they don't understand words, just feelings. If your feelings are bad, they'll turn them into honey and make them sweet again.'

'Do you talk to the bees?' Eliot said to Scout.

'He does. I can tell because he blinked,' said Lilou.

The bees were at their busiest this time in the morning, collecting nectar, tidying up the entrance, making forays to the lavender. Eliot was mesmerised as the sun began to melt away the morning's horrors a little. Scout settled in the shade of an olive tree, and Lilou busied herself with labelling some jars.

'I want to go home,' Eliot confided to the bees. 'I hate soldiers. They have guns instead of hearts and they can't feel anything even when Maman cries.' He waited, but the bees just went about their business.

Lilou spent the afternoon moving Eliot into the hay barn. It was easy to pile the hay up in front of the anteroom, and the entrance from the other side was pretty much invisible unless you knew it was there. She moved in everything from Freddie's room that Eliot loved, including the model farm, which he secretly liked, the encyclopaedias and the biplane. They drew pictures of space, and Lilou sewed some yellow stars to hang from the ceiling. It was his own little domain, far away from the evils of the world.

At bedtime he refused his pyjamas and insisted on going to bed fully clothed, as he had the first night up in the hills. They were back to square one.

'I might need this,' he said firmly, checking his sextant, manuscript and notebook were all in his satchel before strapping it over his shoulder and getting into bed.

'At least take your shoes off.'

He shook his head. 'If I need to run away, I have to be ready.'

Lilou read him *The Little Prince* for hours and, when his eyelids drooped, she hummed him as much of his favourite tune as she could remember. But she could never get it quite right.

'It's *wrong*. Only Maman can sing it right,' he said, eyes snapping open.

Lilou fell asleep with him in her arms, Scout snoring at the end of the bed. How the hell was she going to keep her scared little astronaut safe, so far from home?

The next morning, a chink of early sunlight coaxed Lilou awake. It was July-hot, even at this early hour. Carefully extricating her arm from Eliot's head still heavy with sleep, she pointed at Scout to stay and quietly opened the door.

'Tell her not to go,' said Eliot to Scout. 'I don't like it in here, it's dark.'

'I'm just going to get you some breakfast, and I'll be back.'

He sank back into his pillow, resigned. She couldn't hide him in here all day – a boy needed sunlight and fresh air and playmates to grow; but that would have to be another time, outside of his stay with her. Her job was to keep him alive, and they'd take it day by day.

As she crossed the courtyard the bells rang out 5.30 a.m. from the village. The mountains were pink with sunrise, a chorus of birds were babbling up, and the bees were already heading out to the lavender to forage. Scout started barking, and Lilou searched for Casanova, who would be slinking back from his night-time adventures to annoy his canine nemesis. But it wasn't Casanova, it was Kristian, leaning on the farm gate.

He lifted his hand to wave. 'I come in peace,' he said.

Lilou marched over. 'You've already searched the property.'

'Exactly. That's why I'm here.' He took a box out of his bag. 'I have something for the little boy.' He opened it, a telescope, a beautiful brass one, aged with use. 'I saw his sextant and recognised a fellow astronomer, and he looked so terrified, I thought this might cheer him up.'

'I can't take it. Thank you for yesterday, but he's already so afraid. You should go before he sees you. He can barely sleep as it is.'

Scout came bounding out, quickly followed by Eliot. Scout inexplicably downgraded his guard-dog status by licking Kristian's hand.

'Oh it's you. Scout likes you, he stopped barking,' said Eliot.

'He knows he can trust me,' said Kristian, more to Lilou than Eliot.

'But you're a fucking German,' said Eliot.

'Yes, I suppose I am. But my heart is French.'

'Germans don't have hearts.'

'This one does.'

'What do you think, Scout?' said Eliot.

Kristian ruffled Scout's fur, and got a lick in return.

'Is that a telescope?' said Eliot.

'Who wants to know?' replied Kristian.

'Just somebody who knows how to use one,' said Eliot, giggling. 'Is there a tripod with it? Can you help me use it? I'm looking for a planet that I can live on.'

'There are no habitable planets to my knowledge, but if you tell me the coordinates I can help you look for it.'

Next thing she knew, he'd be showing Kristian his manuscript of *The Little Prince*, and that was too close for comfort.

'Eliot, you're taking up too much of his time. Now run to the kitchen and get yourself some milk, there's a jug in the pantry. I'll be in after Kristian has gone.'

'Come on Scout. Lilou is a spoilsport and no one minds anyone just *borrowing* a telescope.'

Eliot stomped off towards the kitchen, Scout close at his heels.

As soon as he was out of earshot, Lilou rounded on Kristian. 'What are you trying to do?' she said fiercely.

Kristian stood his ground. 'He's terrified and you need my help,' he said softly. 'I can't unsee him, so here we are. He's kind of my responsibility too now. You're under suspicion, and I can bring you information to keep you safe, and by extension the little boy.'

'Why would you do this?'

'Because it's in my power to do it, and because I hope that someone would do the same for my family. My sister and mother are alone in the mountains back home. Because I want to do something right in all this wrong. I don't know who the boy is, and I don't care. The less I know the better. All I see is a frightened kid and someone trying to protect him, and that's the simple truth.'

Lilou searched the countryside for help, a sign. Two magpies, a four-leafed clover, a ladybird flying past. None came, but she already knew she could trust him and that somehow Eliot needed him.

Lilou hadn't realised how lonely she'd been till Kristian started visiting. Any reluctance she'd once felt melted away whenever she thought about how he could have had Eliot taken away and killed. Instead he had covered for him.

The war formed an unlikely cocoon around the three of them, each with their own lives somewhere else. Kristian was a reconnaissance pilot, primarily. His job was to take aerial photographs of enemy territory, but he was billeted here with the army unit in between sorties. Apart from that, they never talked about what he did – somehow when they were together only the moment they were in mattered; the rest was out of bounds.

Kristian was amazed by Eliot's knowledge of navigating by the stars. His papa taught him, he said. The summer days were long, and some nights Lilou let Eliot stay up late for the dark skies, and Kristian and Eliot would talk endlessly about the constellations that Lilou knew the shape of, but that they knew the names of, including lots of useless facts about distances from the Earth and points of magnitude. Eliot always slept better afterwards.

One night, Eliot begged for Kristian to read him to sleep from his *Little Prince* manuscript, and Lilou didn't have the heart to refuse him. Better to let him read, and for Eliot to sleep. Besides, she told herself that Eliot's manuscript was different from hers so effectively it wasn't a code key to Kristian. To him, it was just a lovely story.

A few short visits became a habit. Kristian never stayed more than half an hour, that would be too dangerous, but he always had something for Eliot. A butterfly wing, a peacock feather from the big estate, chocolate he'd saved from his rations. He showed Eliot how to make a catapult and how to climb trees without falling out.

It was wonderful to see Eliot in the sunshine and, while Kristian was there, there was no worry about being discovered. Kristian cared as much about the living world as Lilou did, his forest-green eyes fixed on the world around him. He'd know what bird of prey was being mobbed by jays by its wing shape, he could identify the kik of a woodpecker, notice the change in wind direction when the mistral was due. She loved that he knew. If her countrymen were rugged oaks and Mediterranean olives, he was a larch: tall and golden and far from home.

Kristian's grandmother was French and he'd spent summers with her as a child, which explained his perfect accent. There were times when she even forgot he was German.

They told each other their stories in snatched moments, in the minutes after Eliot was asleep, or while he was climbing a tree or playing with Scout.

Kristian told her that he had been studying astronomy at university when he was conscripted and given jackboots and a lecture on the superiority of the Aryans. A country boy who was a top student and spoke perfect French, he was afforded officer status for his knowledge of navigation, moon phases, their effect on the tides for planned landings. It was a knowledge he came to hate – he never wanted to use his precious education for death and destruction. Lilou found her maman's old *Larousse Encyclopaedia of Astronomy* to set him and Eliot riddles to solve. She loved watching him search for the answer, eyes fixed dreamily on an imaginary dome of stars.

A week before the August full moon, Kristian turned up carrying a big box for Eliot. Inside was a gramophone, the wind-up kind with a big brass horn. He picked the shellac 78 off the turntable, holding the edges with his palms.

'Look,' he said, grinning from ear to ear.

Lilou read the label. '"Dream a Little Dream of Me".' Eliot's lullaby, the one she could never quite get right for him. She showed it to him: 'See, here.' She ran her fingers along the words.

Eliot clapped. 'Can I wind it? Maman and Papa had the same.'

They played it ten times over, singing along, Lilou spinning and twirling Eliot to the melody until the moon was high and the church in the valley struck nine.

'You have to get into bed, and we'll play it once more, to sing you to sleep,' she said.

'Dance,' he said to Kristian and Lilou. 'You have to put your arm round her, and hold up her hand. That's what Papa and Maman did to sing me to sleep.'

Kristian wound the gramophone and put his arm round Lilou's waist, and they swayed to the music, giggling along with Eliot. They played it again, and Eliot began to drift off as Scout looked on cynically and the music wished Eliot sweet dreams till the sun rose.

The record ended, and Eliot was fast asleep. They set the needle back at the beginning again and let the record play on, dancing long after the music stopped, clinging to each other in the darkness, intent on guarding the curious child who'd flown to them clutching a book that created the only world he could feel safe in.

The moon wrapped them both in her cool rays, a sliver away from full. A warning. A friend was what she needed, not this. Lilou stopped the record.

'You have to stop coming, the skies are all wrong.'

'Surely you don't believe in all of that?'

No, she didn't, but the full moon would be in a few days' time and, with it, her next assignment. Why had she let things get this far?

Because she wanted to. In a different world, on a different planet it would be possible, but not now, not here. She'd made her pledge to Marie-Madeleine, who'd warned her that attachments were poison, that she should keep herself to herself as much as possible. She hadn't even bothered to mention that attachments to Germans were unbelievably risky; that was too glaringly obvious.

'I just need some time to myself, it's not right. I know you'll think I'm a superstitious peasant with all your calculations and studies of the stars, but we Mistrals have always listened to the skies and they're never wrong,' she lied. 'Give me a week, until the moon begins to wane. I think we both need to pause before we go too far.'

First and foremost she was a Resistance operative, and full moons were sacrosanct, the only time it was safe for the Lysanders to land without lights. She'd already taken too many risks, allowed a German Luftwaffe pilot into her life, and now she was dancing with him under the stars a week before her next mission. What the hell was she thinking?

CHAPTER 10

THE SUPERSTITIOUS MOON

VALLON-DOUX, AUGUST 1943

Kristian

'You should have seen his ugly face twist when we found him out. He put up quite a fight when we dragged him out, and his wife was squealing like a pig when we took her brats—'

'Enough!' Kristian threw down the book he'd been pretending to read to try to shut him out. That sadistic little bastard, Schmidt, needed to be disciplined.

'Shut up, Private, or I'll have you court-martialled. You know the directive: efficiency and respect. We work to win hearts and minds in France, even within these four walls. It's arrogant little shits like you who'll lose us this war.'

They'd all been lied to in their youth about the aesthetic beauty of the Aryan ideal, a race of gods, a world without hereditary disease or crime. He didn't understand then that the dream only included a chosen few. He'd dreamed their dreams in the lofty heights of the Black Forest of his childhood, revelled in the strength of his lengthening limbs as he grew, increasingly ready for the noble fight. But then he grew up. There were no gods, just monsters who believed in hate and bigotry. Their ideology was completely deluded and he was ashamed of ever having believed the school's indoctrination. When he went to study amongst the spires of Heidelberg and travelled with his mind amongst the stars and planets, he laughed at the thugs stupid enough to think the Nazis had a chance at political power. Now here he was in this beautiful sunlit place, witnessing a catalogue of ugly, banal, everyday brutality in its name.

'Oh come on, it's just a bit of fun,' Schmidt scoffed, readjusting his hat in the mirror and admiring his ratty features. 'These people don't have hearts or minds.'

'You will obey your superiors, you arrogant little arsehole. We have a job to do, and we do it with respect. Any more of that kind of talk and you'll be back in Germany lifting stones like the troglodyte that you are. Do you understand?'

'Sir,' said Schmidt sulkily, then sauntered across the mess to offer young Schulz a cigarette, and they set up a bored game of stone, paper, scissors to pass the time. Seriously, did they have to keep sending him these warped kids who were indoctrinated with hate and delusions of grandeur?

He looked around the billet, the well-appointed village hotel they'd commandeered with the help of the town council. Private Fischer was absorbed in a game of patience. He was harmless, just a kid really. Lieutenant Abereind was sitting opposite him, writing his diary. He was an aesthete who loved touring the sights, and treated the place like he was on holiday, avoiding anything nasty or distasteful as much as he could. Not a bad person, but totally unsuited to the job. Kapitän Weber was another matter – clever, every inch the officer and gentleman when he wanted to be, but a dangerous sadist when roused or drunk, which he was now, even at this hour. He was a real Jekyll and Hyde: the perfect Nazi recruit. Kristian made it his business to be at Weber's side on any mission he could to temper his worst instincts, treading a fine line so as not to reveal his own motives, which were to put a stop to the horror.

'Over here, lad, let's keep you out of trouble, just learn to play the game, and you'll be all right,' said Weber to Schmidt, his protégé.

He rewarded the loose cannon with a brandy and cigar, and they luxuriated in the ornate armchairs they'd taken from the tailor's shop.

Schmidt took a long toke on the cigar and sank back like a pig in shit. While the boys were fighting a brutal war on the eastern front, his *Gruppe* spent their time whispering with small-time gangsters and collaborators intent on settling old feuds with neighbours, dealing on the black market and lining their own pockets.

Kristian had led a double life, witnessing his fellow men brutalise and loot, for so long now he hardly knew who he was any more. The only time he felt there was anything left to strive for was on the farm with Lilou and Eliot. Lilou's cropped hair made her even more beautiful, emphasising her high cheekbones and dark eyes the colour of the deep sea; as secretive, too. He loved the way she followed Eliot so tenderly with her eyes, never let him out of her sight, and spent hours thinking up things to delight and amuse him, from drawing the patterns he saw in the hives to cartwheel competitions in the hay meadow. She had learned the constellations just by osmosis and was equally at home with a shovel as a needle. Her intimate knowledge of everything that surrounded her was in her blood, just as his Bavarian mountains and forests were in his, and in that they were wrought from the same stuff. Eliot was obviously Jewish, but that was unspoken between them to protect him. He was the cleverest, most eccentric child, with a thirst for knowledge and a longing for home. He never mentioned it, but constantly humming his maman's song, always wanting to talk about the stars like he did with his papa, gave him away, however brave he was trying to be. Kristian understood that all too well.

Apart from them, everything was a kind of nightmare, but he was here, and he could make a difference from the inside, and that was the important thing.

Back in Germany he'd used his position to warn Jewish families of impending raids, connected them with people skilled at forging false papers so they could escape. Now he was here, he was determined that no one would touch a hair on Eliot's head, that the abbé's ill-concealed radio in the steeple would remain undetected, and that he'd keep this battalion in check. If he'd known about the raid on the tailor's shop, he might have been able to warn them, but the Kapitän, suspicious of a defector in their ranks, had told no one and had sprung it on them the moment before they entered the shop.

Biding his time was more use here than being shot as a traitor and leaving them to do their worst. Plus, there was his own family to consider. If he deserted, what would happen to them? He'd heard of families back home who'd been ostracised, or worse, disappeared, for any sign of dissent on the part of their husband, son or brother out on the front lines.

Schwarz came in with an official-stamped letter and handed it to Weber. He stubbed his cigar out on the carpet, burning a careless hole, and opened it.

'Meyer.'

'Sir,' said Kristian.

'You're needed at the air base on the coast. Reconnaissance and intelligence as far as Germany, then return with a passenger to facilitate his ingress into France. Pack up your bags, there'll be a car here first thing in the morning. Oh, and don't forget your condoms. Nothing too irksome, a couple of reconnaissance flights, then you're free to fuck and frolic to your heart's content.' He winked at Schmidt. 'There are plenty of military brothels down there. Don't forget to give her one for the boys,' he slurred.

'I've just reprimanded a private for that kind of talk,' said Kristian. Drunken bastard must have been on the sauce since breakfast.

Weber put his hand over his mouth. 'Oops, sorry, college boy. Just the way it is, whether you like it or not.' He handed Kristian a document. 'Here are your orders.'

When Weber was drunk Kristian knew from experience that the sooner he left, the sooner he'd shut up, so he took his leave and went to pack.

He checked the document. The car was arriving at 0500 hours and it was nearly midnight. No time to see Eliot or Lilou before he went, and anyway, she'd asked him to stay away. He looked out of his window; it was a clear night, a late-rising moon. For such a practical person who wasn't afraid to scoop up swarming bees with her bare hands, Lilou was being uncharacteristically superstitious. She did have encyclopaedic knowledge of everything to do with the farm and the plateau, so maybe there was something in it – the spoken knowledge, passed down generations of people who'd lived deep in the countryside, had to rub off on her. In the old days, lives would have depended on it. Whatever it was, he'd take exactly what his soulful farm girl could give and ask no questions. The less he knew the better. But if he could make amends by protecting Eliot, he'd give his life if he had to. He knew Lilou would too.

It was good to be on an airfield again, the moon already high and waxing, just a sliver missing from full. He was assigned a Messerschmitt Bf 11, well within his comfort zone. He'd trained in one of these in the early days when he cared about the war, and what it lacked in manoeuvrability it made up for in speed, so his mission to Peenemünde Island, the top-secret base of a

German rocket research and development centre, was quick. The route had been plotted to avoid enemy territory as far as possible, and he logged and photographed friendly infrastructure with all the accuracy he was known for. In fact, he'd rather have undertaken a more dangerous mission. The laser focus required was the only time he could forget, and he found himself on the short journey wondering which of the canopy of stars was Eliot's favourite, and which of them were the planets belonging to the beguiling cast of characters the kid knew off by heart from his precious *Little Prince* book.

He touched down at Peenemünde at 0530 hours, the first time he'd been back in Germany in three years, but there was no opportunity to get out and touch the once-hallowed turf of his homeland. The task was a quick touchdown, on the runway just long enough to refuel, load supplies and take a passenger on board before heading back to France.

Kristian stared out of the cockpit at the dawn, the rising sun a misty semicircle in the early-morning haze. There was a time when every sunrise had brought with it a surge of possibility for his young heart. Not now. Whatever happened in this war, Germany would never be the same again.

While the ground crew made all the final checks, a man jumped into the seat behind him. Kristian turned round to greet him and the man took off his oxygen mask, raising one eyebrow with a triumphant grin.

Kristian stayed deadpan. 'You owe me ten Deutschmarks. Pay up or get out of my cockpit.'

'Oh yes sorry, here you go.' The man put his hand in his pocket and came out empty-handed, middle finger in the air.

Kristian hugged him hard. The last time he'd seen Felix was when they'd both been disciplined for causing a public disturbance diving off the old bridge at Heidelberg one halcyon summer's day. Felix had managed to swim to shore, but Kristian had been caught by the *polizei*, and he'd been hauled up in

front of the university authorities and fined for both their misdemeanours. The next day, they'd been conscripted and mustered.
The top scholars from Heidelberg university, athletic and
clever; they were sent out wreathed in glory.

While Kristian had been assigned to the Luftwaffe, Felix, a
talented scientist, was working on V-1 rocket technology, and he
had been so excited to be selected for a project that had unlim-
ited resources and possibilities. They'd grown up together in
their mountain village, raised hell in the forests, excelled at all
the mountain sports, and spurred each other on at school,
competing to win all the science prizes.

'I hope you know how to fly this thing, you were always
crap at driving,' said Felix, strapping in.

'Just don't touch anything and try not to shit yourself when
we get too high for you to bale. And I won't ask what strings you
had to pull to get into my jump seat.'

Felix saluted. 'I'd have to kill you if I told you. Everything's
arranged. I've got us both billeted in a chateau right on the coast
for the night, and I intend to do everything to forget before they
lock me up in the lab again.'

Air traffic control cleared them for take-off and Kristian
powered up and pulled the throttle, his heart soaring to be with
his friend again as he gained altitude. Felix turned pale.

'I've forgotten what all these buttons are for, but don't worry
– if it all goes pear-shaped, it's been nice knowing you,' said
Kristian.

'I see your sense of humour is sophisticated as ever.'

Kristian cut the throttle and let the aircraft plummet. 'Don't
make me angry, Müller.'

Felix managed a croaked *arsehole* through the communication system.

At this very moment, a Felix fix was exactly what Kristian
needed. His oldest and dearest friend, from a time when they
had the whole world at their feet, a time before everything good

and right had been twisted, before the youth of the world had been sacrificed at the altar of greed and bigotry.

Back in France, Felix was true to his word. He had done them proud and pulled off a bit of a coup, a chance for them to spend some precious time together during a twenty-four-hour leave from his work on Peenemünde. Kristian didn't know how Felix had found out that it would be him piloting the transfer from the island, but he had always been a resourceful charmer, and good at getting his own way. The Chateau de la Napoule was stunning, a world away from what was happening. But he still had work to do. Kristian laid out the charts in front of him.

His job was to ascertain optimum conditions for German bombers to make a pre-emptive strike on the Allied air force before they could make a rumoured attack on Peenemünde. It was crucial to strike first, and protect the place where Felix worked on the top-secret V-1 and V-2 rockets alongside hundreds of other scientists. Kristian made his calculations. The full moon would be tomorrow night, and would rise early. That would make it dangerous for the mission from Peenemünde, he calculated. Better to delay until the next day, when a late-rising moon would give them a cloak of invisibility on the out, and light their way home on the return.

After a double-check, Kristian took his calculations to mission command for them to radio through to intelligence. Work done on paper, at a desk, far away from any human lives that might be destroyed as a result. But it was French lives or German lives. Either way, families would lose their sons.

When he was done, he went off to find Felix. He found him in his bunk, reading a chemistry exercise book, just for fun.

'Come on, let's get out, I've recce'd a cove a walk from here. You've only got one day before you get back to whatever it is you're doing on that godforsaken island, and we have unfinished business,' said Kristian.

'The triple off the cliffs? You know I hate heights.'

'Then you lose.'

'Never!'

Felix jumped out of bed and pulled on his clothes. On the way to the cove, they bought two bottles of best burgundy, an eye-wateringly expensive jar of beluga caviar, a dressed lobster and a white baguette.

'This is the life, eh?' said Felix.

It was true, you could live like a king on German wages in France, though it felt like exploitation when the locals couldn't even think of buying such luxuries. Kristian told himself it was just one day, a special occasion with his best friend, and they might all be dead tomorrow.

The cove was deserted, so they stripped off to their trunks and ran straight into the sea, which was warm as a bath. They front-crawled, racing to the end of the cove, the water sparkling and blue as an Aryan ideal. At the big rock they surfaced and sculled, looking back onto the red stone of the Esterel cliffs to assess the possibilities.

'If we jump out far enough, we should easily do it,' said Kristian.

'Easy,' said Felix a little uncertainly. 'Race you back to shore.'

They cut through the water, catching the sun, revelling in the vitality of their stroke, and Kristian allowed himself to imagine that this was just a normal day with his friend, no war raging, no one suffering, no injustice. On the beach, they tore into the lobster, washed it down with swigs of burgundy and lay back on their towels, heady from the wine.

Felix lit up a fag and took a long draw. 'It's a shitshow isn't it? All those dreams, all that study, just to make superweapons that kill people we've never met in the most efficient and devastating way ever in the history of mankind. But it's awe-inspiring at the same time. The V-1 and V-2 rockets I'm working on break the sound barrier, enter the stratosphere and arrive with pinpoint accuracy on the cities they're aimed at. We've already test-launched one and it was incredible – the world's first spaceship, five storeys high, each one fuelled by 800 litres of petrol. The blast-off was like something out of those heroic legends we used to obsess about. Seriously, you'd have loved it. From a scientist's point of view, it's probably the most exciting thing I'll ever get to work on. Hitler's wetting his pants about them, and they'll probably win us the war. How fucked up is that? Endless knowledge for us to harness for good; beauty for the taking, and this is what we do with it.'

Kristian lit his cigarette off Felix's and passed it back. 'A war run by petty gangsters and bigots.'

Felix sat up. 'We're still doing it though.'

Kristian hugged his knees. 'I'm helping where I can.' He took another swig of wine and passed it back to his friend.

'There's a camp on the island where we're based. They're Polish. All ages, families, children, women. Some of the men go there and do whatever they want with the women. They could be my sister or my mother. What happens to people? It's fucked up. A few of us have got together to help the families escape, but we can't save them all. You know they say we're losing now, even when they hope the V-2s will turn the tide? There's so much bullshit out there, it's hard to know what to believe. All we can do is stay in our lane and try and make sure the right people come out of this alive, and the evil psychos are sent to whatever hell is.'

Kristian nodded. Whatever the end, it wasn't going to be pretty.

'Remember when I made that sledge and we ran away to find the world at the end of the mountain?'

Felix took another swig. 'Worst sledge in the history of the

Black Forest. We can't have got more than five kilometres. But you knew the way by the stars, even then.'

'We were seven years old, but it seems like yesterday,' said Kristian. Eliot's age, with not a care in the world. 'Just as well, or we'd have ended up in avalanche territory. And you were the master fire-starter. Without that, our parents said we'd probably have died of hypothermia.'

'A whole night before they found us, but what a night. Do you remember how many stars we counted before we got scared? It must have been at least a million.'

'I've never known a scientist with such a propensity to exaggerate,' said Kristian.

'Your dick's the size of a wiener, and that's entirely accurate.'

'Grow up.'

'I'd rather not,' said Felix. 'Triple or die.'

They scrambled up the cliffs and Kristian was first. He only managed two somersaults on the way down, but the adrenalin rush was exhilarating as he sculled in the bay, waiting for his friend.

'Come on, don't die though,' he shouted to Felix. 'You have to jump right out.'

Kristian looked up at his friend, his childhood partner-in-crime teetering on a ledge, suspended in the air for a moment, before he jumped elegantly, tucked and somersaulted, perilously close to where the cliff jutted. He missed it by a hair's breadth, turned a triple and judged it just right, cutting the water with a dive that barely made a splash. He'd always been a more perfect specimen than Kristian, cleverer, stronger, more quick-witted.

'That was a bellyflop if I ever saw one.'

'It was a perfect ten and you know it.'

They finished off the wine and spent the afternoon swimming and throwing stones.

'If it wasn't for the rockets, I'd refuse to go back to that hell-hole, but it's the opportunity of a lifetime, resources to develop the most amazing things, and the war has to end somehow. That's how I justify it anyway,' said Felix, who was due to fly back to the Luftwaffe base at Peenemünde that night.

'Pray to a God I don't believe in any more it'll be all over soon,' said Kristian, who was itching to be back at Vallon-Doux to check on Lilou and Eliot.

When Felix had left, Kristian felt something he hadn't felt since he was a child. Homesickness. That gut-wrenching longing for the familiar, the lonely strangeness of being displaced. He felt it for Eliot, for everyone in this war. He finished the second bottle of burgundy to anaesthetise himself, and fell into a deep sleep as he jolted back down the road in the back of the truck to Vallon-Doux. The August red full moon rose at precisely the hour he had predicted.

When the truck jolted back into the little village, taking the wrong way round the fountain no matter how many times Madame Aveline had told them they should go in the other direction, he was dead beat. Strangely, Vallon-Doux felt like home now, even though he hadn't yet been billeted here a year. But saying goodbye to Felix was harder than he'd imagined. In war, every farewell could be your last.

He woke up the next day with a hangover from hell and Kapitän Weber rapping on his door.

'Wake up, they've annihilated the whole bloody base.'

Kristian dragged himself up and opened the door.

'Here,' said Kapitän Weber, waving a radio transcription in his face. 'The intelligence you sent. Intercepted. The Allied air force – the Yanks, the Brits and the bloody free French – knew the whole squadron was grounded for the full moon and they sent in over five hundred Allied aircraft to destroy the research facility. A hundred and eighty of our best V-2 rocket scientists are gone, German civilians, and twelve night fighters. And the idiots wiped out half the prison camp in the process, which wouldn't matter if we didn't need the valuable slave labour.'

'Which scientists?' asked Kristian, blood congealing in his veins.

'That is not the question to be asking. A pivotal V-1 and V-2 development plant is decimated, and intelligence tells us that the information you radioed was intercepted and passed to the enemy. They've traced it to this village. One of our key informants is arriving in five minutes with important intelligence. Get your arse out of bed, make yourself presentable and you will be responsible for intelligence gathering and analysis. The locals will have to be taught a severe lesson.'

Kristian grabbed the piece of paper, and scanned through the list of names. There it was: Felix Müller, Killed In Action.

He imagined the army envoy with a letter of condolence in his bag, winding up the old mountain path through the pines to his friend's house, his mother opening the door and falling to her knees. Did he burn? Suffocate? How quickly did the end come? He'd never see his friend again.

He dressed in a daze, fastened the top button of his grey uniform so tight it nearly choked him, and felt numb. His footsteps echoed on the stairs from somewhere far away. When he reached the breakfast room, the mayor's wife, Madame Aveline, was impatiently drumming her fingers on the table. She was one of the first people who had made herself known to them when they'd rolled into town; it was she who'd organised their accommodation, introduced them to the purveyors of luxury goods and given them intelligence on the major players in the vicinity.

She was a charming, persuasive woman who seemed to know everyone and everything there was to know about the village and its goings-on, somehow managing to maintain the respect of her fellow villagers and the German occupiers alike.

She stood, holding her hand out for him to take with a warm smile.

'Kristian, my darling boy, you look like you've seen a ghost. Kapitän Weber told me it would be you who would receive the sensitive information I have to give. I know who shared your information. It's not easy, but I tell you for her own good as well as to help you charming gentlemen. I hear you took a lot of casualties, I'm so sorry.'

'Thank you,' replied Kristian, his voice catching unexpectedly for Felix, and wondering which innocent villager she was going to drag through the dirt now. She was a talker, and he was glad that she just jabbered on. He'd try to remember Felix on his sunlit dive, as the perfect specimen he was, rather than dwell on the moment he died.

'Now, down to business,' said Madame Aveline. 'I hope you don't mind but I've taken the liberty of ordering some coffee and breakfast for us. I hear you only arrived back from manoeuvres late last night.'

The maid brought in coffee, and croissants he knew he wouldn't touch. He braced himself for the usual useless narrative of overheard conversations and speculation based on petty rivalries.

'I have news for you of underhand dealings from some very unexpected quarters, and to think that she's directly responsible for the death of so many gives me the strength to tell you what I know with a clear conscience. Firstly I'd like to say that I hope you will look kindly upon her misdemeanours, as I'm sure she will have been influenced by outside forces. I have known the whole family for a very long time, and this young lady since she first appeared at Sunday school as a child and put a frog in the collection box.'

Couldn't these people just get to the point?

'So exactly what information do you have for us?' he asked.

'Kapitän Weber has been very generous, so I won't hold

back,' said Madame Aveline, dabbing her forehead with a hand-kerchief in the heat.

She was clearly enjoying the suspense, and he could barely concentrate. He'd write to Felix's mother and tell him about the day they had at the beach, how happy he'd been, that he wouldn't have known much...

'I have duties to carry out, I'm going to have to hurry you,' said Kristian.

'Very well, I'll get straight to the point. I have good reason to suspect that Lilou Mistral is running messages for the Resistance. She's always wandered around at night, but she was seen on the full moon leaving the farm, and I have it on good authority that she's meeting Lysander landings, carrying information, and guiding enemy British to safe houses.'

Kristian was careful not to allow his face to change. 'And what reason do you have for suspecting this? This is a serious allegation. Do you have concrete evidence?'

'Not exactly, but Madame Isnard says—'

'That woman is already discredited and has wasted valuable army time. Do you have any personal insight into this matter? Any first-hand evidence?'

'Not exactly, but there are so many clues and that girl's always had a mind of her own, I wouldn't put it past her—'

'If we followed up every citizen who came here with a hunch or an unfounded suspicion, from jilted lovers to jealous neighbours, we'd spend all our valuable time and resources on that, and none of it on conducting a war effort.'

'With all due respect, I don't appreciate the implication that I come here with idle gossip,' said Madame Aveline.

He was going too far. He took a breath. 'Of course, you are a valuable ally to us, and I apologise if I was blunt. I merely mean to look at facts in the cold light of day.' He gave a joyless smile now. 'Leave it with me, I will personally investigate, and we welcome any intelligence you bring to us. I would appreciate it if you would keep this sensitive intelligence strictly confidential, which will mitigate any risk of her being pre-warned of any suspicions. I know I can depend on your discretion.'

'Of course, Air Commodore Meyer. I will leave it with you, and I hope you know by now that you can rely on my discretion unquestionably.'

She left. Kristian returned to his room and sank his head in his hands to try to think straight. Lilou had spun him quite a yarn with her talk of superstitions and full moons. It all made sense now. She was carrying out dangerous missions against the Germans, and her latest sortie had resulted in the violent death of his most beloved friend in all the world.

CHAPTER 11

A LIFETIME IN A MOMENT

PARIS, ONE MONTH EARLIER: JULY 1943

Marie-Madeleine

Marie-Madeleine woke clawing at the air. She opened her eyes wider till the Nazis in the shadows focused into the solid, inanimate furniture of her Paris apartment. Just a bad dream. But so vivid that the feeling of dread in her stomach refused to fade with the morning light. Léon Faye, her Léon, codename Eagle, had stepped out of a Lysander, a red moon high in the sky, and drifts of pink heather carpeting the fields as far as the eye could see. The faceless landing closed in on Eagle, and the moon picked out the swastikas on their lapels. A tall man with a child-like face smooth as a doll's grimaced. 'It's him,' he confirmed to the group. 'The top man. Delightful,' he said, before kicking Eagle in the stomach. He doubled over and the figures closed in, stamping on his handsome face as one of them pulled out the Eliot Papers from his greatcoat. They'd hit the jackpot. She was somewhere there, watching in the shadows, helpless.

The dread stayed with her all morning while she dressed,

followed her to the metro where the real Eagle was waiting, dogged her while they entered the same carriage without acknowledging each other.

The metro was packed despite the occupation, and Marie-Madeleine instinctively made herself invisible, eyes down, doing her best to fade into the crowd. She relaxed a little. Here he was, wearing a drab office-drone suit with lapels much wider than her set would ever consider. It was a disguise, designed to make him ordinary, but whatever he wore he couldn't help but be striking. With his cold, pale eagle's eyes that missed nothing, his aquiline, almost beaky nose and patrician demeanour, he just looked like he was in charge. They allowed themselves a fleeting glance, a millisecond of greeting, and everything was right with the world again. With her, his cold authority turned to cool appreciation and a respect for her intelligence that few men had the grace to acknowledge. Despite her worries, she'd learned to live for the exact moment she was in, and it was delightful to be back in the capital, with Eagle by her side. For a second, she allowed herself to imagine it was just another day, travelling between parties in opulent drawing rooms and achingly fashionable cafés.

Impossible.

To pass the time, she checked her lipstick in her compact mirror. A gaunt woman with a tight blond bun and hollowed-out eyes stared back. It had been a terrible year and it showed. So many agents lost, so much bright potential ground into the dirt by the filthy Boche.

She touched up her lipstick and snapped her false-bottomed handbag shut, staring blankly at the row of faces opposite her. One of them stood out. Sweat prickled her forehead and she visualised the pearl-handled pistol she had in her handbag. On high alert, she prodded Eagle in the back and he followed her gaze. A stocky man in a studiedly elegant suit, with swept-back hair and a brown moustache, was reading yesterday's *Paris-Soir*, right in front of her. It was Kapitän Weber, the sadistic bastard Lilou called Doll-face. He knew her from a narrow escape she'd made when a collaborator had informed on her whereabouts.

She arranged her features into a blank again. Thank God her hair had been dark brown when she'd met him, and he'd only seen her wearing thick-rimmed spectacles. In the last two years she'd been a nurse, a nun, a secretary, a grocer, a teacher and God knew what else – she'd lost count of the number of personas she'd adopted. Nevertheless, he scrutinised her intensely, and she watched his vague flicker of recognition begin to search his internal lexicon of faces, then turn to utter amazement.

A yank started her to her feet and Eagle folded his arm round her. 'Quick, chérie, we're getting out a stop earlier.'

He shoved her through the closing doors and they fell onto the Opéra platform just as the train took off. Weber's round face was pressed hard against the glass, eyes fixed on her. Damn it to hell. He'd recognised her.

'Move, or he'll pull the emergency brake!' whispered Eagle, ushering her through the crowd at breakneck speed. She found her feet, the way she had a hundred times in the last two years, staying only just a step ahead of her pursuers, a familiar buzz of adrenalin and sharp-focused tunnel vision kicking in. Fight or flight. She was ready for both.

They slowed, separated, tracked through the densest part of the crush, took separate exits after the turnstiles, fell in step on the boulevard des Capucines, turned down rue Louis le Grand, doubled back and stopped to look in the window of l'Émeraude. Marie-Madeleine took out her compact mirror and pretended to touch up her powder while she checked behind them in all directions.

She readjusted her hatpin, the sign for the all-clear.

'Christ, that was a close call,' said Eagle. 'One of these days your luck will run out.'

'You make your own luck, darling,' said Marie-Madeleine. 'And mine is to have you at my side.' She tapped her handbag. 'Come on, HQ are waiting for these papers.'

Eagle glowered. He was angry at her seemingly laissez-faire attitude to her own safety, but danger only honed her senses and trust in herself.

Her mother had always said she kept a cool head, too cool sometimes. At least for a society girl bored by the endless parties and all the suitors who came her way, who, she must admit, she'd sometimes been cruel to. But it suited her well for her new life, which was terrifying, tragic and exhilarating at the same time. She had asked herself many times in the dark hours of the early morning why. Many of her society friends were happy collaborators, creaming what profits they could from the occupation. But for her, the answer was always clear. Justice, country, her people. Her agents were the cream of the country, many already sacrificed to the flames of Nazi hell, and she'd do anything to keep them safe and operating. The drive inside her was a fire that nothing could extinguish, not separation from her children, not fear of capture and torture, nothing. She owed it to every one of them, and there were too many already, who had made the ultimate sacrifice, to be cold, efficient and anesthetised to danger.

But Eagle, air force colonel, decorated war hero, her deputy and chief strategist, was also the father of their beautiful boy, their illicit child, and he loved her too much to stand by and watch her face down death over and over again. As soon as they reached the safety of the Intelligence Bureau, he flew into a towering rage.

'You have been ordered to go to England for your own safety. Every other Alliance leader has only lasted six months before capture and torture – you've been doing the job for two and a half years. It's only a matter of time.'

'I won't talk, no matter what the Nazi filth do to me, if that's what you're worried about.'

'It's not all about the bleeding crowd. I'm worried about *you*. Someone has to take care of the boss, and that person is me.'

'How hard are you going to try?' Marie-Madeleine closed the door to the office and slipped off her coat, let it fall to the floor to reveal her silk blouse and pencil skirt.

'This hard,' he said, pulling her close.

His kiss had visited her dreams every night they'd been apart.

The radio in the corner crackled now, interrupting the drone of BBC news bulletins with an alert in French. *Ici Londres! Before we begin, please listen to this personal message. Be careful, the animals are ill with the plague in the south of France.*

They jumped apart. Eagle grabbed the briefcase and hastily retrieved the code book. They got to work immediately, working in harmony without thinking about it, Marie-Madeleine scrawling down the message word for word, Eagle decoding. They barely needed to decipher the BBC message. They already knew that the Third Wave of Alliance was almost decimated, and she was dying of grief at all the losses. She steeled herself. All the more reason to focus on the job at hand.

They handed the messages to the radio man, who found a frequency and began to transmit immediately.

Abort mission. Return to civilian posts. The plague is raging.

No response from the Nice, Toulouse, Marseille or Pau transmitters.

Would *anyone* hear it? She only needed one person on the ground to get it. Her people were trained to find ways to get around

the Nazis to get the abort message out. A flare at the right moment.
A woman in a red hat sitting in La Caravelle café in the port of
Marseille reading *Le Petit Provençal* newspaper at table two...

Eagle put his hand on hers and she realised she was shaking.
Their eyes met, words were pointless.

'Someone will hear it.'

Her guts twisted and she tried to hope that the transmitters
were shut down to avoid detection. More likely her agents had
already been rounded up.

'All we can do is keep going,' said Eagle.

Yes, for her Ark operatives – the radio men who were on the
front line, most likely to be detected and captured. For the
agents putting obstacles in the Nazis' way, from dynamiting
railway lines to double-crossing from the inside. For the police
who turned a blind eye, and the girls, like Lilou Mistral, who
ran messages, guided British agents from parachute drops and
met full-moon Lysander landings in the dead of night.

Each of them had an animal name to protect their identity.
And so many had been lost. Jean Moulin, charismatic founder
of the National Council of the Resistance: tortured, transported
and executed. A mortal blow to the whole movement. General
Deletraint, the head of the Secret Army. Gone. Aristocratic
Saluki – and his brave wife, Firefly, crawling through barbed
wire with three children, and pregnant again. The list was
endless. Their worst enemies were twofold: overconfidence, and
treachery. There were also too many double agents, like the one
whose information had led to her near miss with Doll-face.
They were a cancer to her precious organisation.

The radio tubes crackled again. *Patou, under surveillance
STOP Vallon-Doux Gestapo informed of clandestine activities
STOP Immediate evacuation advised STOP*

Her beautiful Lilou Mistral, who'd taken the code alias
Patou, the name of the mountain sheepdog who stays up in the
hills alone to guard its lambs. Appropriate for the girl who was

protecting little Eliot Stavinsky. They were in severe peril on that remote farm of hers.

'Get me Abbé Aloïsi, Vallon-Doux parish church. Now. Cut me off at eight seconds.'

The radio operator consulted his transmission charts and found a frequency.

Patou and puppy in danger STOP Gibbet closing in STOP Removal from kennel essential STOP

The radio operator clicked off. Her heart was still pounding. If Patou had any idea of what she was protecting and why, it would punch a hole in her cosy backwater bubble. The little kid was the key to the blueprints of a deadly weapon. If those blueprints fell into enemy hands, it could be the turning point of the war.

Eliot's father was a brilliant scientist, and a complete eccentric who loved a puzzle. He had imbued his son with crucial knowledge as to the whereabouts of the weapon blueprints, maybe correctly thinking that little Eliot would be the last place anyone would come looking.

But the child alone didn't hold all the knowledge. There were key documents – the Eliot Papers – which would help the child remember his part of the puzzle and unlock the location. Celestial navigation was the key: a very particular time and date in July 1944 plus a particular alignment of the moon and stars. It was essential the child was kept safe until that date, and that the Eliot Papers were kept equally safe, away from the boy until the crucial moment came. At present, only she and Eagle knew the whereabouts of the documents. Now somehow the net seemed to be closing in on them.

Maybe it was just a coincidence, and Lilou was being watched for her Resistance activities. Either way, she'd get word to the abbé that it was crucial to arrange whatever was needed to keep them safe.

In the meantime, it was essential that the British maintained their support of Alliance. Without the Brits, their Lysander operations, money and intelligence, the French organisation were all lost. Security breaches and double agents made the British jumpy, as did rumours of splits. As far as the British were concerned, Alliance was already an 'unofficial' organisation that operated outside of the usual military protocols. It was risky business.

Marie-Madeleine barely had time to send up a silent prayer for Eliot and Lilou before she and Eagle were pulled into an emergency meeting with intelligence.

It was essential that she used this gathering of the top brass of the French Resistance to secure two things. One: unity, two: persuade them she herself must make a trip to Britain to secure continued support from the British War Office. Eliot and the blueprints would be her carrot.

The most important operatives in her Ark were all here around the table. Dangerous, but essential to be together in one room to arrange things, then disperse. There were guards in disguise everywhere, surrounding the building. Two were guarding the door, with nothing more than powerful biceps and alert senses as armaments. Others were dressed as labourers, mending the fence, ready with hammers in case of a Nazi attack. A female agent was cooing over a pram across the way, visible through the window. If she picked up the baby, it meant Nazis were coming her way. Shadowy figures walked nonchalantly by on the street outside. Eagle had organised everything splendidly.

They got down to business and covered a lot of ground in as little time as possible. Mahout even laid out reports of a plot to neutralise, ideally assassinate, Hitler by his own people. *Please, God, let it be true.*

Other highly sensitive intelligence was communicated to

THE GIRL FROM PROVENCE 133

agents with photographic memories, then destroyed. The Eliot Papers were discussed. At this point Marie-Madeleine took the opportunity to upbraid any agents who'd been too careless. She couldn't abide sloppiness, and she led by example with her meticulous handling of documents and information, never ever straying from protocol. Even after two and a half years, some of the big beasts round the table were still surprised at her courage and attention to detail. Even now, some of them would never accept that a woman was up to the job. Screw them. The fact was, she was in charge, and they'd have to swallow it.

Debates raged about who to back – de Gaulle in the UK, who would lead a provisional government, or Giraud in Algiers, who was commander-in-chief of the Free French army. Or both. In some corners anti-British sentiment reigned, which risked cutting off their lifeline to supplies and intelligence. Tensions were running high, and, with all the defeats and losses of their great leaders, Marie-Madeleine could see that Alliance and the Resistance were in danger of falling apart, fragmenting into warring factions with conflicting aims.

Not on her watch. Marie-Madeleine stood and tapped her coffee cup for quiet. The hubbub died down.

'Gentlemen, now is the time for unity. I am glad to see you all here round the table today. Many of you have escaped capture, or indeed endured it. But it's not enough just to survive. We owe victory to every single operative who has sacrificed themselves to our cause. Which of you actors in this tragedy will see this through? None of us can know. The one certainty in all this is that all those who have already gone beyond recall or vanished into our enemy's trap do not have the privilege of asking themselves that question. If we fall apart now, we have failed ourselves and everyone else.'

'What about the British in all this?' said Cricket, the agent whose family was in Gestapo custody and who she'd persuaded not to give himself up in their place. The tears of rage were unmistakable in his eyes, and Marie-Madeleine knew he was vehemently against British involvement. Poor sod – but this was no time for individualism.

'In Britain, the Gaullists are part of the Allied machinery, and in that case they come under Allied command,' said Marie-Madeleine. 'Our aim must be to acquire the same status and as such we can continue our work as before, but ensure it is to everybody's benefit.' She looked him straight in the eye. 'We all have deep sympathy for the great sacrifices you continue to make for the greater good.'

'We sacrifice so much, we talk endlessly about it, but our French compatriots don't give us any official help,' said Colonel Morraglia. 'What about our network's militarisation papers? At least if that was concluded, our agents would have some kind of protection.' He sighed.

'It's a painfully slow process,' Eagle admitted. 'That's the one reason we are sending our top agent, Marie-Madeleine, to London.'

It was her turn to blink back her grief. He was right of course. She *had* to go to London, though she felt like she was abandoning her post. Things couldn't go on if the lines of communications with Britain were not assured – without their financial help and without proper status for agents and their families, for Lilou, the abbé and all of them, they couldn't continue. Bravery, intelligence, a wing and a prayer had got them this far. Now Alliance needed to be recognised and on an official footing.

The meeting disintegrated into a melee of arguments and counter-arguments. *How the hell do you stop a French man from talking?* thought Marie-Madeleine wryly. But stop they must.

She stood. 'Gentlemen, this meeting is concluded. While I empathise with individual perspectives, unity and action is key. I therefore ask Eagle to present the motion he's drafted. I command you all to sign. If you're not with us, you're against us.'

The hubbub blew up again and she slammed her fist on the table.

'Sign, or operate out of my jurisdiction.'

Eagle tabled the document, and after some wrangling over the wording each man signed with his alias. With death lurking just beyond the door, they agreed on the pledges she was to take to the British – to remain united, and continue with intelligence activities to the benefit of Allied troops to the end of hostilities, whatever it took.

Eagle shot her a conspiratorial look of admiration for her marshalling of the troops, but she'd always known from the moment she took the job that failure was never an option.

The meeting finished with a new security plan that centred around contact henceforth coming only from the top down – the reverse of current practice with its incessant comings and goings, which had resulted in the network leaking like a sieve.

All Marie-Madeleine wanted to do was escape to make final arrangements for her Lysander trip to London, and even snatch some final moments in Paris with Eagle, but out in the corridor she was assailed by members of the group petitioning her with individual matters. She dealt with them as efficiently as she could, and saved a scathing dressing-down for Cricket, despite his troubles, when he asked for the reinstatement of his slug of a driver, who she suspected of double-dealing.

There was one more matter she had to conclude. This day had started with nightmares about her darling Eagle being caught in a field of heather while transporting the Eliot Papers. If any of these people knew how it had haunted her all day, how it had felt so vivid and real, they'd think she was mad. Perhaps the prospect of leaving France was making her fret for her homeland, but she couldn't leave without making sure.

She found her logistics agent in the office chatting to a typist in the poky office.

'Tell me, which of our landing sites are surrounded by heather?'

He thought about it and shook his head. 'None that I can recall, madame.'

'You're absolutely sure?'

'Absolutely.'

'It's imperative that none of our landing fields are on heather. Am I clear? You must give me your word.'

'May I ask why?'

'You may not. I only need your assurance.'

'Of course, madame, if it gives you pleasure.'

He looked at her curiously. He was right, perhaps she was going mad – wasting operation time on dreams – and the responsibility was getting to her, but it made her feel a little easier.

Thank Christ that meeting was over. By the time they finished it was late evening, and the July sunset was turning the pavements orange on the Champs-Élysées. Eagle pulled her close. The air was sweet without the bustle of civilian traffic, starlings roosted in the elms, and she nestled her head on Eagle's shoulder, tight as new lovers as they strolled the avenue. It was these rare, sweet moments that gave her work the most meaning. Confirmation that all the sacrifices were worth it. Love was always the answer, past, present and future.

At the Arc de Triomphe, they stopped for her to say goodbye to her favourite view in all Paris. She whispered *my country* to the breeze, but Paris replied with a whip of the swastika flags as the waxing moon rose, almost full. Perfect for Operation Renoir, the July Lysander flight tomorrow. One precious, snatched night for her and Eagle awaited.

Everyone had become accustomed to living a life in a moment, to creating a world in the tiniest chink of light, and they both knew every meeting could be their last. They dined at Le Grand Véfour to remind themselves that Paris still belonged to the French, at least in spirit. The place was infested with German officers and, in a delirium of unaccustomed cocktails, and in defiance of fate, Eagle held up his champagne coupe to a drunken table of Nazis. They delightedly raised their glasses in return.

'Die in hell,' she and Eagle whispered through rictus smiles.

The candelabra flickered, the tall white candles belying any idea of rationing. Eagle held her hand across the table.

'I have something for you.'

He handed over a package. Inside was a miniature model of Noah's Ark.

Marie-Madeleine was bemused. 'There are no animals.'

'They're all in hiding, but I'm so proud of you for steering your ark full of agents. I know everyone trusts it will never sink with you at the helm.'

She waved away his kindness. 'I've rather had greatness thrust upon me. I do no more than anyone else.'

'Look inside.'

Marie-Madeleine found the hinge, and opened it to reveal a little family – an eagle, a hedgehog, and a baby hybrid of the two animals. Darling Léon. It was a strange gift, but everything was strange in their new world, and it was imbued with meaning. Her codename was Hedgehog, to represent a seemingly harmless creature that in reality even a lion would hesitate to bite. Léon's was Eagle for his warrior's nature, his bravery, and his hawkish attention to detail. Their child, the smallest figure in the Ark, was a being born of a forbidden union. Marie-Madeleine sent a little prayer to him to grow up strong and kind in a world his parents were prepared to sacrifice everything for.

'When all this is over, we can take a villa in Saint-Tropez by the sea, and I'll float around in silk scarves and a cloud of Chanel no. 5. We'll have an enormous marble terrace overlooking the bay, and I'll stare out to sea with nothing to do but arrange parties and write for frivolous magazines.'

'You'd die of boredom.'

'Not with you,' said Marie-Madeleine.

'I insist on a yacht.'

'And Paris for the season.'

'Oysters.'

'Cigars.'

'Fresh flowers in every room.'

'A wine cellar.'

'Dancing every night.'

'Just you, alive and safe and searingly bright as you always are,' said Eagle.

It was a sweet dream, away from the nightmare. Especially when in reality Marie-Madeleine was already married and they had to accept that their little boy may never know his real parents.

The curfew sent them home to their apartment early, and they were exhausted, but this night wasn't for sleeping. They flung open the French windows in the bedroom and the careless moon offered up her mineral light far away from human darkness and judgement, and made silvery shadows on the bedroom walls for the lovers' delight.

The next morning, Chinchilla arrived at her apartment. She didn't bat an eyelid at the sight of Eagle shaking out a newspaper over eggs and coffee he'd prepared for them. Thank God the army had taught him to cook; Marie-Madeleine didn't have a clue.

'Monsieur et Madame Harrison,' she said with a smile, teasing them. Madame Harrison was the woman the Gestapo had an arrest warrant out for. The French for Marie-Madeleine's codename, *hérrison*, had been misinterpreted, and the Germans had anglicised it. Everyone in their inner circle who knew about the two of them teased them with their 'married' name.

'I hope you don't mind me saying so, Mrs Harrison, but we can't let you go to Britain looking like a tramp. I've bought you a Maggy Rouff suit to help you face the Brits down. All your other clothes are hanging off you, scagged with barbed wire or smudged with mud. You look like you haven't eaten for a year, but at least it makes you a clothes hanger so we can dazzle those Brits with our superior elegance.'

It was true, she was a wraith, and didn't have the time to care about what she was wearing. Nevertheless, Marie-Madeleine was almost ashamed of the long-forgotten thrill she got from opening the beribboned box. She pulled out a couture suit in fine navy wool, with mother-of pearl-buttons, nipped in at the waist, and exquisitely made, with all the hallmarks of her favourite seamstress, Lilou Mistral. Two dresses, a floor-length black silk evening gown edged with diamanté, and a batik-print fitted day dress completed the set. Just another disguise to help get her what she wanted in her ambassadorial role in London, she told herself, as she touched the fine silk to her cheek.

Eagle was already in position on the corner of rue d'Alsace to monitor her safe boarding of the train, his trench coat hunched around him. His eyes glittered a *bon voyage* she was desperate to acknowledge but instead she ignored him, leaving part of her heart behind at the Gare de l'Est.

She kept her head down until the train pulled into Nanteuil-le-Haudouin. Filthy smog from the arms factory killed the moonlight and a westerly was blowing as she disembarked. Please God this awful visibility didn't affect their flight.

A small man with bristled white hair and wire-rimmed glasses waved them over. Doctor Gilbert was on time, engine already running. He sped her and some other agents to the landing spot and reversed the vehicle behind a hay rick.

At 00:59 GMT a familiar hum presaged the sight of the Lysander. The men high-fived and the ground crew flickered landing the code with their torches. Two small bumps and the plane was down, stopping right in front of the trees behind which they were hidden.

Three agents sprang out of the cockpit, pulled out their baggage and ran. Marie-Madeleine wished them Godspeed, and took their place in the cockpit.

They were on their way to England, the July hay moon that had discreetly looked away as she and Eagle explored their tenderest deeps in Paris last night serving as their guide across the water and over the white cliffs of Dover. She was uneasy leaving her beloved France. Her agents needed her, and with Lilou and Eliot in danger, treachery at every step, she felt like her firm hand was the only thing that kept it all going.

However, the trip was a necessary evil. If they could keep Eliot and the documents safe, the promise of the weapon blueprint and its delivery to the British would go a long way towards securing their continued support across the entire network.

The Germans had their V-2s, there were weapons development races everywhere you looked, but Roman Stavinsky's blueprints, containing the most advanced workings of particle beam technology in the world, were her responsibility. If they fell into enemy hands, it could lose them the war. Once Eliot and the Eliot Papers were united, the location unlocked, and the Allied forces in possession of the blueprints, it could win them it, too.

CHAPTER 12

BETRAYALS

Lilou

It was late, and Lilou and Eliot were sitting high up on the escarpment looking down onto Vallon-Doux. If the evenings were warm enough, he loved to watch the lights go down on the village below, even though the sunsets always made him cry. He'd counted them up neatly in his notebook since they'd arrived at the farm, each blazing sinking of the sun another night away from his parents. There was always frustration too, about the numbers he was meant to remember for his papa, that he'd let him down, but he refused to tell Lilou anything more.

This August night, the sultry air diffused the stars on the blotting paper sky, the waning moon mellow and bright, as Eliot snuggled into Lilou and Scout nuzzled him, ears pinned back in solidarity.

'Do you think they're somewhere up there, on their own planet?'

'Who, *ma puce?*' said Lilou.

'Maman and Papa. With a piano and an armchair, so Maman can sing as much as she likes, and Papa can read his books. They must be happy there,' he said hopefully, searching her eyes for affirmation.

'Oh yes, that's very likely,' said Lilou, wishing to God it was as simple as that.

'I don't want her to die.'

Lilou couldn't bring herself to go so far as to reassure him she wasn't already dead.

'She's thinking of you wherever she is,' she said instead.

'You don't understand, you never do! If she doesn't have her medicine she can't breathe. She needs it,' he said, almost in tears.

'They'll have medicine where she is,' said Lilou.

'They won't! It was very *particular*.' He broke away from her and folded his arms. 'Adults never know the right things,' he said to Scout.

She knew by now that addressing Scout and not her was a sign of deep distress. As he sat alone, cross-legged with his arms folded in the dark, she knew she couldn't comfort him with plat-itudes. He was too clever for that.

'What medicine was it?'

'Cigarettes. Not the kind that make you cough. They were made of special dates and helped her breathe again.'

'Datura stramonium?' said a voice she'd missed more than she thought possible. Kristian. It wasn't unlike him to come and go as he pleased nowadays, and he knew this was often their place at sunset, but Lilou looked up guiltily at the waning full moon. She had another mission tomorrow night.

Eliot hugged his legs. 'Yes! That's it! Do you think they have that on Maman and Papa's planet? Can you take some to Maman?'

Lilou and Kristian exchanged glances.

'I might be able to put some in the post to her. What's her name?'

'Rebecca Rachel Stavinsky, 11 rue Ferrachat, Lyon. Is there a rue Ferrachat on Maman and Papa's planet?'

Lilou winced. She'd never told Kristian Eliot's full name. Eliot continued to confide in his friend.

'She has long black hair and big brown eyes and *striking eyebrows* like in her fashion magazines and Papa says she has a waist like a wasp, but wasps sting and she is more like a kind honey bee.'

'I'm sure she is. And very brave, too. I'm sure I have seen that name, Stavinsky, on a list of very important exceptional people.'

Kristian looked at Lilou strangely. She didn't like the idea of a list in this context. Standing there like a sentinel silhouetted by the moon, he looked different, less a friend and more like an officer. Was her latest mission hanging around her like an aura that he could see? These ethereal summer nights could play tricks on you in the half-light. She shook it off.

'Time for bed, my Little Prince,' said Lilou.

'Only if Kristian reads my favourite chapter.'

'The one about the dragon?' he said.

There couldn't be any harm in it, especially as that chapter didn't exist in her key-code version of it. So why did she feel so protective all of a sudden?

Eliot chattered excitedly about the package Kristian would send to his beautiful maman, then Kristian read him to sleep, and he looked so peaceful with Scout curled up on the rug by his side.

She stepped out into the night with Kristian.

'How do the skies look tonight? Suitable for a visit from a German?' he asked. Her hackles rose. She didn't like the suspicion in his voice, and the way he emphasised the *German* was tinged with anger.

'I thought you said no questions asked?'

'I just don't like being lied to, that's all.'

Lilou rounded on him. 'Lied to about what, exactly?'

'About superstitions and full moons. You're taking risks, and Eliot will suffer, and—'

'I don't know what you're talking about.' But she couldn't look him straight in the eye and he knew it.

'Yes, you do.'

'You said no questions asked. I thought you were a friend.'

'I am a friend. Listen, you don't have to lie to me any more. I know that you're running messages for the Resistance. There's an informant in the village – who luckily came to me. I'd never give you away, but have you seen what they do to people who get caught? What you're doing is too dangerous.'

'So is standing aside while good people get rounded up and transported. You say you hate it too. Why don't you help me instead of trying to stop me?'

'I can't do that. I couldn't be directly responsible for the deaths of my countrymen any more than you could.'

He was almost shouting. She put her fingers to her lips so as not to wake Eliot.

'Then we have no choice. We're on different sides. It was ridiculous to allow ourselves to think differently,' said Lilou.

Kristian didn't need to answer; they both knew it was true. He pulled his jacket tighter around him and walked away, and the lonely sky was so vast she could hardly breathe.

Sleep wouldn't come. Out of the window a star fell in a blaze of light, then faded to nothing. She shivered. Luck this bad was as rare as the red flare she'd seen in the shooting star's trail. Lying awake, she picked over all the facts. She was pretty certain Kristian would never knowingly give them away, but he already knew too much for all of their sakes.

She slept fitfully till the horizon began to pale. She couldn't tell the abbé about Kristian, but maybe he'd know who the informant was so that she could be on her guard. If she went now, she could be back before Eliot woke.

The village was still sleeping when she arrived at the church, but the abbé was already getting into his car, wearing a glowering scowl and a thick shaving shadow.

'I was on my way to see you! If those bastards hadn't stolen the night away with their blasted curfews I'd have come last night,' he said after they kissed hello. He looked across the square to the requisitioned town hall. 'We'd better go inside. Even a priest has to hide like a coward nowadays.'

He swept in, cassock swinging as he strode into the church and filled it with his rangy presence. He pulled the door shut and locked it with the oversized key, crossed himself to the altar, then gestured for her to take a pew.

'Sit down. It's not good news. There was a message over the tubes last night. You and the boy need to leave here today.'

So the informant's news about her *had* gone further than Kristian.

'You go first,' said Lilou.

'The vipers' nest at the Hotel des Chasseurs have been somehow informed of your activities. It seems Madame Aveline has turned her hand from flower arranging to informing. Josette, the hotel maid, overheard a conversation between her and that idiot German lad everyone's swooning over – the one who supposedly saved your cat...'

Lilou breathed a sigh of relief. It was via the maid, not Kristian, that the abbé knew. How the hell did Madame Aveline know anything? Lilou kicked herself; she thought she'd got her in the palm of her hand, and Madame Aveline was one of their oldest, if most dreaded, family friends. Thank God the woman had chosen Krisitian to take her information to. But stupid to be complacent. What if he was going to act on the information he was given? No, he'd never have told her what he knew. Lilou raced through all their meetings in her head. Had she badly misjudged Kristian? What would the abbé say if she knew Kristian had even seen some of the stories from Tonio de Saint-Exupéry's code manuscript?

The abbé continued. 'These arseholes have got their tentacles everywhere. They've been watching you like hawks since the visit you had from the Boche last month, but as far as we understand they don't know about Eliot yet.'

The abbé's eyebrow was twitching. She'd seen that expression before, when he came across a juicy bit of confession.

'There's something you're not telling me isn't there?' said Lilou.

'I didn't tell you because the less you know the better, but keeping that confused little boy safe is key to the war effort. His parents were prominent Resistance leaders in Lyon and there's a dangerous secret the boy's helping to hide, though he doesn't know it. That's why you've got him. They need to keep him in France until next July. I can't divulge any more than that.'

Lilou's heart flew to Eliot. What the hell was he mixed up in, and how much was at stake?

'How dangerous is this secret?' she said.

'Classified. But Lilou... it could be world-changing.'

The abbé had a tendency towards drama, but still Lilou was filled with dread. It all made a little more sense now. This must be why Eliot had been spirited away by Marie-Madeleine herself, Alliance's most senior and busiest operative. And the numbers Eliot was always trying to recall, the ones his papa taught him, must have something to do with all of this. What business did anyone have burdening her little Eliot with something so unsafe?

'Do you know where they're holding his parents?' asked Lilou.

'Roman Stavinsky is still being held at Gestapo HQ in

Lyon. Poor soul didn't manage to take his cyanide pill, though God would have forgiven him. They're keeping him just alive enough to torture whatever they can out of him. He's a radar scientist who was developing a weapon of some kind. Please God, they haven't broken him yet. But Eliot's mother is dead. The lack of asthma medication meant she died within a week of being taken. These days choking to death is preferable to what the Nazis are capable of.'

Lilou gasped, sick to her stomach. What fucking nightmare were they all living through? Did they watch Eliot's beautiful mother die, choking on some cold Gestapo floor?

'Jesus Christ, poor Eliot.'

The abbé muttered to the Virgin Mary for his safe-keeping, then gave her the faux-neutral look he used for confession.

'Now, you said you go first. I've told you everything I can. Do you have something to tell me?'

Even the abbé – rebel, warrior, libertarian – wouldn't understand about Kristian. She shook her head.

The abbé looked at her sideways. 'What compelled you to come to me this morning? Not a vision from the angels, surely, though in my line of business I'd like to believe that was the case.'

'Just a feeling...'

'Do you think there's any chance this German lad can be trusted with the burden of information that Madame Aveline landed on him?'

'How should I know? He's a filthy Boche, like the rest of them. I just came to get instructions for my mission tonight.'

'You're relieved of your duties on that score. I've already arranged to take you and the boy to the convent at Sainte Rose-line. No one gets past those nuns – they'll smile and preach peace and love, but get on the wrong side of them and they'll kill you with one pious put-down.'

'I'll be hiding away in a convent?'

'Yes, you will be. Holy orders.'

Frustration rushed through her. 'What about Maman and the farm? I haven't spent a single night away from her or the house since I was born. And what about my bees, and the lavender, and my smallholding?' She could hear a thousand Mistral ancestors turning in their graves in the family cemetery. They had lived through drought, famine, blight, the Revolution and the First World War, and no Mistral had ever deserted their post.

'I'll keep an eye on your maman, like I always have,' said the abbé passionately. It was true, he'd always been fiercely protective of her fragile maman, even when Papa was alive. 'You need to leave today. The farm can look after itself.'

'I have to meet the Lysander flight tonight. You *know* I do. There's no one else who can do it.'

'This is no time for misguided bravery or the famous Mistral pride,' the abbé said gravely. 'If they catch you, and make you talk, we could all die. I won't sleep until you're both safe behind those convent walls. Seriously, Lilou, what you have done so far is more risk than I would ever ask of anyone. You've done your bit. The agents can fend for themselves. They're soldiers, trained to get themselves out of any tricky situation should anything go awry on landing. Our cells here have been blown apart and we need time to regroup.'

No Resistance agent or British soldier was going to fend for themselves on a Mistral's patch. She'd go and meet the Lysander tonight, or die trying.

'Give me till tomorrow morning to sort things out. I can't just leave all of a sudden and let the farm go to rack and ruin. And I can't tell you why, but I know that Kristian won't take this any further. One more night won't make any difference to the situation.'

He looked at her warily. 'No tricks?'

'No tricks, I promise,' she lied.

'I'll be at your place at six a.m. Eliot will have to hide in the boot. It's less than an hour's drive to the Sainte Roseline priory, and if we're stopped you can say you're volunteering there as a nurse.'

The abbé gave her a lift back up the hill and left. Lilou pulled her copy of *The Little Prince* manuscript out of the floor-boards and double-checked the coordinates for tonight, then looked hopelessly around the farm. It was already falling apart. Who'd milk the cow, and cut back the lavender? The kitchen garden was essential to their survival, and— Minuscule concerns compared to what was happening, and nature always survived.

The bees. Apart from Maman, she knew she'd miss them the most. The Sainte Roseline brood had already split and swarmed, but the original queen was still with her. Queens, even miraculous ones like her Queen Roseline, rarely lasted more than two summers, and this was her third. She'd feel adrift without her talisman, her queen of the teardrop swarm who'd tried to warn her of the horror that loomed on that carefree summer's day in the square.

She crossed the yard to say goodbye to the hives. 'You'll be fine without me,' she whispered. 'But what will I do without you to talk to? How will it all this turn out?' she asked. The bees gave her their answer by going about their business like they always did. These fierce goddesses of the sun were right. The world would keep on turning, the sun would rise and set, no matter what happened to her little world, or countless others. It was cruel and comforting at the same time.

When evening came, she read Eliot a chapter of *The Little Prince*, and he eventually drifted off, grew pale and still with sleep, trusting her. The moment of silence, the glut of love and wholesomeness in the peaceful dark, between Eliot falling into a deep sleep and her leaving the room, was an unexpected highlight of her every day.

'I'll be back in an hour,' she whispered to him. Then, to Scout, 'Don't leave his side,' she instructed. He settled next to Eliot proprietorially and she crept out into the night, pausing only to put on her dark clothes and a headscarf, pulling it over her face to become as invisible and silent as an owl.

She'd memorised the coordinates, and had already visualised her route through lonely fields and ancient paths. The moon was bright, and the trees were filigree in her shadow. The mistral blew up, bending the oaks and raising waves in the silvery cornfields. The howling winds were a perfect cover for illicit footsteps, but she prayed the little Lysander would be able to land in such high winds. When she approached the landing field, she stopped short and counted the figures gathered amongst the trees. There were too many people, six at least. She slipped behind an old chestnut with a broad trunk and waited. A rustle too close startled her. She'd know a wild boar at a thousand paces, and this was definitely human.

'Good pastures for the sheep,' a voice said.

'Now that lambing's done,' she replied in the agreed response.

Xavier! Freddie's friend, and the same Resistance operative she'd met the night that Eliot had fallen out of the skies into her arms. She could have cried with relief.

'Who the hell are all those people? It's not a landing crew, it's a bloody rugby team,' hissed Lilou.

'It's the mayor's field, and he insisted on being here for the landing with his entire entourage,' said Xavier. 'He's a good Resistance man now but he's still a pompous fucking idiot.'

'Jesus Christ, it's not a country fair, he's endangering *everyone's* lives,' hissed Lilou.

Over the roar of the mistral, the drone of a plane cut through. They both looked at the little plane's propellers whirling bravely as the aircraft swung in the gusts. The ground crew made the 'L' sign, and flashed the code, but Lilou went cold as a large group gathered at the top end of the makeshift runway. They were sitting ducks if a lone German sniper passed by. Idiots! Hadn't they learned anything from a lifetime of hunting? The Lysander flashed back, and forced its way down through the updraughts as gracelessly as a stag beetle flying at a candle.

The mayor strode forward self-importantly with his entourage. The cockpit slid open and the two agents jumped out with their bags. Lilou's hackles rose as the torch lit the faces of the welcoming committee. Standing next to the mayor was his wife, Madame Aveline.

'*Écoute mon coeur qui pleure!*' Lilou shouted at the top of her voice.

The agents understood, and ducked behind the tail of the aircraft, clutching their briefcases full of precious intelligence and supplies.

Xavier pushed Lilou to the ground. 'Stay low. I'll go that way and shoot to distract them, you go the opposite way and get them out of here. *Courage!*'

He was gone, and she ran silently as she could, holding her breath, skirting the trees.

'*Halt!*' Five Boche emerged from nowhere. In seconds they had the mayor and his gang pinned to the ground pleading for their lives as Madame Aveline watched. Two snipers followed the British agents through their gunsights, but they kept moving, low and fast.

Xavier's gunshot split the night from the other side of the clearing and one of the Boche fell.

'Over there!' yelled someone.

The whole squadron raced in the direction of the shot, leaving the mayoral group kneeling handcuffed on the ground.

In the confusion, Lilou muttered the emergency code word

at the agents, and they joined her in the dip. Their eyes flashed fear as they crouched next to her.

On the other side of the clearing, Xavier made a run for it in the moonlight.

'Don't shoot! We need him alive!' shouted a voice. Kristian's voice.

But Schmidt gave chase, shooting recklessly, until Xavier was felled like a stag, twitching in the dew.

'Now!' said Lilou. The thick maquis slowed them, a bad dream, running but getting nowhere.

The Lysander took off, potshots ricocheting hopelessly off its underbelly rising quickly, soon too high for their bullets.

A splintering crack threw them to the ground, hands over their heads. Lilou forced herself to look. A bullet in the tree. The Germans couldn't have seen the direction they took. A ricochet, or a lucky try.

'This way, keep moving!' commanded Lilou, voice sharp, limbs adrenalin-pumped. The men stayed close, silent, trusting her. She focused on getting them to the ridge, shouts and gunshots fading as they made ground. The gully was deep and blind, but she plunged forward. She landed on solid ground, a searing twist in her ankle snatching the breath from her burning lungs. The stocky one jumped straight after her, landing on his feet as light as a mountain goat. The tall one stopped, silhouetted on the treeless ridge. Target practice.

'Jump!' commanded Lilou. A distant gunshot gave him wings. He lurched forward, landed badly, scrambled to his feet.

Ignoring the hot stab in her ankle, Lilou led them along the gully, through the twisting path of the dried-up stream, screeing on the pebbles, plunging lower and lower down the mountain until they reached a cave that sat behind a waterfall in winter, but which in August was dry.

The men squeezed in with her.

'Fuck me, that was close,' the tall one whispered.

Lilou didn't understand, so they saluted her while her heart pounded. She'd been afraid, but there was something else, like she'd never been alive till she'd had to run for her life. She could have killed with her bare hands. So this was war.

Single, staccato shots rang through the night. Lilou crossed herself and the men exchanged grim glances. They'd be executing the welcoming committee, making their friends watch one by one in sickening fear as they fell pleading for their lives, their families, their loves.

'Who was the brave boy who decoyed for us?' said the tall one. He spoke flawless French. 'Did you know him?'

'Xavier Blanc. My brother's best friend. He was eighteen.'

She'd keep going for every Xavier and Freddie and Eliot and Joseph, their mothers, sisters, grandmothers, and die for them if she had to.

The man took out a notebook from his rucksack and wrote the name. 'Xavier Blanc of... where?'

'Vallon-Doux,' said Lilou. 'Vallon-Doux, Alpes-Maritimes.' Just another name on a list. Xavier, with his shock of black hair and cheeky grin, his blazing spark gone forever. Was his body still where it fell? She'd tell his mother how brave he'd been.

'I'll see he's honoured. And you also. We wouldn't be here without your quick thinking.' He held out his hand. 'Group Captain Peter Vaughan-Fowler, and this is Hugh Verity.'

They shook hands. 'Enchanted,' said Hugh. 'I don't think I've ever been so grateful to be dragged through the thorn bushes by a wild French girl as I am now. I'm sorry about your friend, he was a brave lad.' He held up his briefcase. 'If it's any comfort, us getting through will save many more lives like his.'

At this moment, it wasn't, but she nodded anyway.

'I'll set you on the route, then I have to go,' she said, desperate about the abbé and Eliot.

Peter tapped his watch. 'I'm afraid the protocol is to lay low for at least three hours in the event of a landing attack. By my reckoning, that will bring us to 7.05 a.m. precisely.'

'I have to go before that, I have a little boy back at the farm.'

She jumped up, but he held her gently back.

'Better that his mother arrives late than never.'

It was pointless explaining her relationship to Eliot. What difference did it make?

The men ate their food tablets and studied the silk map for the next leg of the journey. The three of them shared their hopes and dreams. The men listened to stories about Xavier to honour his death, and they were bound together on that brief, cold night by simple shared humanity. But Lilou had to get back. Eliot would wake to find her gone, and she'd promised the abbé they could leave at first light.

Anger and grief weighed heavy on the burgeoning morning, the August landscape tired and ravaged by the harsh sun. Xavier was gone, along with all the colourful village characters she'd known forever who'd given their lives in that miserable clearing.

By the time she reached the farm, the sun was high and hot as a poker, but the old mellow stones of her home were balm. She picked up into a run in the meadow, but stopped short. Doll-face's black Mariah was parked outside the front door.

She ducked into the long grass, skirted behind the wall and rushed to the back of the house to Eliot's hidden room, praying he'd be there. She pushed the door to. His little bed was empty, Scout was gone.

In a frenzy she scanned the yard, and his favourite places, the sun beating down like a reproach. Nothing.

She went to the side of the house and crouched down behind the well. Doll-face was standing at the front door, talking to Maman.

'My daughter is not well, I suspect measles, and it's very infectious.'

Lilou had not seen her so lucid since the day Freddie left.

'How convenient,' said Doll-face suspiciously.

'Illness is never convenient,' replied Maman in her best teacher's voice. 'However, if you're happy to disturb a young woman who's very ill and at the same time risk catching a notoriously infectious disease, I can go and see if she's awake.'

Doll-face didn't hesitate. 'I can wait,' he said.

Lilou was already at the back window, climbing through. She crept up the back stairs, and into her room. It would be no effort to look ill; she was feverish from the horror of the night, lack of sleep, and being sick with worry about Eliot.

She heard Maman come up the stairs, stop for a few beats, and not even bother to open her bedroom door in her pretence. She went back down, and there was a commotion. Heavy footsteps and laboured breathing presaged Doll-face's forced entry, and when he shoved through the door Lilou half-opened her eyes and coughed in his direction.

He covered his mouth with a handkerchief and backed out. A few minutes later, she watched from the window as he inspected the yard, poked the haystack, tried rickety doors to the sheds and barns, set off a bellow of moos in the cowshed. He was meticulous, and Lilou imagined him finding the secret handle to Eliot's hideout and opening it to find the stars and planets decorating his room, the children's toys and his neatly folded pyjamas, if he hadn't already.

He walked off in the direction of the beehives, and it was only then that she heard Scout's wild barking, and Maman's instruction for him to stop, which he obeyed. Shit, was that a sign that he'd found Eliot?

She crept down to the kitchen, unlocked the gun cupboard and pulled out Papa's old rifle. He'd have to come back past the front door to get to his car, and if he had Eliot she'd kill the bastard if she had to.

Her fingers were slick on the trigger as she cocked it ready, not even sure if it'd work after all these years.

The sewing-room casement gave her a good view. Doll-face was walking back with Maman, Scout trotting obediently at her heels, no sign of Eliot anywhere. She slumped back and lowered the gun. Thank God.

Maman's words reached her through the open windows.

'I have been distracted of late, but I can see how you have brought order to the village in these difficult times, and if I can be of any help in return for news of the whereabouts of my son I would be much obliged.'

'Any intelligence or local knowledge is always well received. I don't make bargains with French, especially women, but I suggest you concentrate on curtailing your daughter's wanderings. People talk, and we have to take any allegations seriously. I'm sure you understand.'

'There are plenty of petty gossips in the village if that's what you mean,' replied Maman bitterly.

Beads of sweat had formed at Maman's temples, and she was deathly pale. No one but Lilou could imagine the super-human effort she was making to engage with reality, especially a reality as ugly and incomprehensible as a grown man seeking out a small Jewish boy to torture his father with.

Doll-face saluted her and reversed his monstrous shiny car in a wide turning circle that crushed the mint in the kitchen garden, then disappeared down the hill.

Lilou ran out to fling her arms round Maman, but she was already gone, her eyes blank.

'Where's Eliot, is he safe?'

Maman walked straight past her and continued towards the house without a word, spent. She had already given everything she could, but Lilou couldn't help feeling a stab of anger at her abandonment, leaving Lilou to pick up the pieces. It was a pointless anger though, and Lilou still found a little joy at knowing her maman was in there somewhere, wanting to protect her.

Released from Maman's orders, Scout dashed back to the beehives. Lilou hurried after him and he stopped at the Sainte Roseline hive, refusing to budge. He adopted his guarding stance, glancing from her to the hive and back again.

She carried on past, desperate to find Eliot. Scout gave her a polite single bark, and maintained his position.

'What is it Scout, where's Eliot?'

He continued to look from her to the hive. She found a smoker and pulled out a frame, and there, underneath the structure, was Eliot, curled up with his eyes tight shut.

'It's OK, it's me,' said Lilou, carefully smoking and lifting up the hive so he could crawl out.

She hugged him so tight, buried her head in his shiny mop. 'My brave, brave boy.'

'It's OK, the bees already knew that soldiers have guns for hearts because I told them last time the Germans came, and they turned it to honey. They like boys, especially Jewish ones. Your maman told me that they wouldn't hurt me if I kept very still, and I believed her and she was right and I counted all the stars in the sky to infinity until you came.'

CHAPTER 13

CLOISTERS

ARCS-SUR-ARGENS, AUGUST/SEPTEMBER 1943

Lilou

The roads were teeming with jeeps, and camouflaged artillery trucks choked the lanes. The abbé and Lilou were waved through the roadblocks – a priest and a woman didn't seem to pose too much of a threat to the bored foot soldiers checking papers at the checkpoints. *Milices* on German army surplus motorbikes ploughed through in unruly phalanxes, forcing them to mount the verge on steep drops. Before the war, the abbé would have given them a good talking-to, and their parents would have apologised at church on Sunday. Today they were hated collaborators who abused their petty powers, and Lilou cursed them to the high heavens like her Grandma Mistral had taught her.

She and the abbé had left as early as they could without rousing suspicion but, with every delay and checkpoint, the August heat ramped up, and Lilou was frantic about Eliot, hidden in the dark, airless boot. Only Scout was oblivious, filling the back seat of the abbé's car, hairs shedding, ears flapping, with his nose out of the window, catching scents only he could define. But he also served as a welcome distraction to the Milice boys who'd grown up with Patous and were generally more interested in him than in Lilou and the abbé.

Lilou breathed a sigh of relief when they rounded the bend into Arc-Sur-Argens to ten chimes of the Sainte Roseline Convent bell. Only 10 a.m., and just a few more minutes before Eliot could breathe fresh air.

The abbesse was at the gates to meet them, and she waved them through. The nuns at Lilou's convent school had been dour and prohibitive and had worked hard to cage the carefree, irreverent young girl she used to be. She wished the abbé had found anywhere but a convent for them to hide out.

But this abbesse, an imposing woman with an efficient air, met them at the gates with a respectful smile and waved them through. Lilou could breathe again, and as soon as they were out of sight of the main road, Lilou leapt out and flung open the boot. Eliot was curled up, eyes tight shut.

'You can open your eyes, we're safe now,' said Lilou.

She lifted him out and he clung to her like a monkey, silent, hot and limp. Such absolute responsibility for another being was overwhelming. A child this young was so helpless, and every moment she was away from him she feared for him. It was a fierce burden and a privilege to have won such trust and dependence. She felt that she was caring for someone indescribably precious, something much bigger than was visible to the naked eye.

She carried him through the peaceful cloisters with his eyes still clenched and his head buried in her hair. He wouldn't let go even when the abbesse brought them breakfast in the refectory, although she heard his stomach rumble at the smell of the eggs and fresh bread. When she eventually disentangled his limbs from her and settled him in a chair, he picked at the food in anxious silence. Lilou and Abbé Aloïsi discussed arrangements with Abbesse Honorine and they all did their best to include him, but he was a boy isolated on his imaginary planet, silent and distant.

'He'll talk to me in his own good time,' said Abbesse Honorine to the abbé. 'And we have all the time in the world here.'

After breakfast she showed them their new rooms along the dark corridor, Scout padding alongside. Lilou felt trapped. This quiet place was a far cry from her farm and the freedom of her fields, her missions that filled her belly with determination and fired her senses.

'I'm afraid we don't allow animals into the sleeping quarters,' said the abbesse, shooing Scout, who held back obligingly.

'Tell them I won't sleep without you here,' said Eliot to Scout.

'In that case,' said Abbesse Honorine to Scout, 'tell Maître Stavinsky that a child's sleep is more important than rules, and we will make an exception. You may stay.'

Scout took a tentative pace forward.

'Come on, boy,' said Eliot, smiling for the first time. 'I'll show you our new room, and then you can thank the *imahot* for being kind.'

Scout dashed to join him, and Lilou helped Eliot unpack the clothes she'd made him in the months since he'd arrived. They pinned the stars and planets they'd saved from his hideout at the farm to the walls, and Lilou hoped he'd feel a little more at home. But this was no life for a seven-year-old boy, being pushed from pillar to post. He should be outside, with friends, running after butterflies, falling out of trees, watching the sunset for the sheer joy of it, not to remind him of what he had lost. Please God, it wouldn't be long until his papa got to safety, and his world could widen beyond her and Scout and strange places far away from everything he knew.

The abbé had told her there was radio silence as to the whereabouts of Eliot's papa. No one knew his exact coordinates, or whether he'd been captured and transported.

Sainte Roseline was a world apart. The arcaded cloister whispered around a manicured square of green. Wisteria and jasmine softened the arches and framed the windows of the living quarters, which gave out onto the balcony overlooking the cloisters and square.

To one side was the sacred chapel guarding the glass coffin of Sainte Roseline, whose mummified remains were fully intact and dressed in a nun's habit, and on the other side were the kitchen gardens, both elements that were central to convent life. Beyond, vineyards stretched out across the plain, dotted with crimson poppies and edged with roses. Plane trees shaded avenues for contemplative walks, and a rose garden in honour of the convent's namesake was carefully tended by the nuns. For now, they were safe.

But this was no rarefied retreat. A secret part of the living quarters was given over to nursing wounded Resistance lads, and here the nuns worked tirelessly to bring life back to broken bodies and souls. When she wasn't with Eliot, Lilou helped where she could, fetching water, mopping brows, sewing sheets and clothes, fabricating makeshift bandages and dressings. Sometimes she told stories from the village, or recited the local fairy tales they all knew to dying lads who cried out for their mothers, railing at the injustice of the sacrifice of the golden youth with their desperate, silent lament for the life that was ebbing away from them. These fragile, beautiful boys who shimmered on the edge of death, whose mothers had loved them as fiercely as she loved Eliot, would never see them again, and could not protect them from the evil in the world. Her own maman was tortured by her son being somewhere unknown, powerless to do anything for him. Was this happening to Freddie far away, to Joseph? The earth seemed to resonate with a dark throb, even when the birds sang, and the sun shone.

As the weeks passed, a nip in the August heat hinted at a change of season, the long nights shortened, the trees began to turn, and the grapes fattened and transformed the endless summer to autumn sweetness. Lilou couldn't get her last meeting with Kristian out of her mind. She played it over and over again. Draco's starry eyes had opened in the summer, and closed again in the winter, but he was still there in the sky, reminding her of that first night in the tower with Kristian. Mars was back, redder than ever, and with it a constant stream of injured, broken boys in the field hospital. Her instincts told her that Kristian would never do anything to harm Eliot or give him away, but her head advised caution. He'd notice them missing, that was for sure, and, apart from herself and the abbé, he was the only person in the village who knew of Eliot's existence.

For Eliot, the peace of the convent seemed somehow to seep into his bones, and he began to relax, though he often asked where Kristian was and when he was coming to see him. At least here he could play outside as much as he liked, in the private cloisters behind the great gates. His favourite place was the cloister where the angelica bloomed its great umbrellas of flowers.

That was where Lilou found him one morning at sunrise, crouching right in the middle of the flower bed and staring intently at one of the prettiest blooms.

'I hope the soldiers aren't hurting you,' Eliot whispered to the flower. 'Papa always said you were an angel, so I hope you can hear me. Lilou is nice. We like each other, and she's special now. At first, I didn't like her very much because she didn't understand, and I had to explain everything. She doesn't look after me like you do, and I pretend to like her singing but it's not as good as yours.' He thought for a moment. 'But she is trying very hard, and she's given me Scout, and at night we watch the stars, and we have our own planets.'

He crouched back on his heels, and a morning breeze ruffled his hair. Lilou cleared her throat. He stayed where he was.

'Good morning,' he said, not taking his eyes off the flower.

'Who's your new friend?' said Lilou, hanging back.

'The abbesse told me the flowers are called angelica. This one is mine. She reminds me of Maman, and I am going to look after her. Do you think the abbesse would mind?'

Lilou tried to think. It was autumn, and the flower would die.

'She's beautiful, and of course the abbesse would be glad if you looked after her. That means when she goes to sleep for the winter she'll bring even more blooms next year.'

He nodded, still intently focused. 'There are bugs on her. The Little Prince wouldn't allow that.'

'Do you mind if I come closer to look?'

'All right, but be careful you don't trample on anything.'

Lilou studied the caterpillars. Dark green, with black and orange markings. She knew them well. She'd spent most of her childhood wandering the fields and woods, spent long summer hours watching the lifecycle of everything that grew and blossomed in these parts.

'These will grow up to be swallowtail butterflies. They fly very soft on the breeze, like dancers.'

'But they'll hurt my flower.'

'Why don't we collect them, and you can watch them make a chrysalis and turn into butterflies.'

'Yes! When they're ready to fly we can make a show for the soldiers. They look so sad.'

Eliot loved chatting with the boys who were recovering in the sunny cloisters. He and Scout were a tonic to the soldiers who had left their little brothers and pet dogs behind, and they respectfully stubbed out their Gauloises and curbed their language when this curious little city boy came to draw them pictures and tell them his stories.

Lilou showed him how to make a net cage, and make sure the caterpillars had plenty of the food they liked, and Eliot watched, entranced, as they settled in, and one by one spun little silk buttons to attach themselves to their stalks to pupate and form chrysalises. When the chrysalises turned transparent, Lilou knew, the big moment would arrive. Eliot drew invitations to the soldiers, and a gathering was arranged for two days' time.

When the time came and the caterpillars had metamorphosed into their glorious new selves, the lads gathered, a few who hadn't met Eliot looking slightly cynical and bored, irritated to be rounded up for a small boy's 'show'.

Eliot, set up in the middle of the cloister with his butterfly cage, addressed the soldiers.

'There is a surprise in this net. When I let them go and they fly, you can choose which one is yours and make a wish, but keep it secret or it won't come true.'

The soldiers clapped and Eliot bowed formally, the sun tenderly highlighting his bowl of hair. Lilou gave him a nod, and he opened the lid. A cloud of swallowtail butterflies floated upwards. They were magnificent, with huge wings like great sails, scallop-edged and patterned like the rickrack on May Day dresses. Some found the late-blooming jasmine, or sipped from the last honeysuckle, others skimmed past the soldiers, who fell silent, entranced at the languorous, undulating flight. The sun poured in mellow as honey and the soldiers closed their eyes, mouthing their secret wishes more earnestly than they would have before the war. Lilou guessed that most wishes would be the same; for this horror to end, and to bring back loved ones. She wished it too, but there was another wish she sent off on a wing. *Let me see Kristian again, let him be on our side, on the side of France and Eliot.* An impossible ask, but wasn't that what wishes were for?

Weeks passed and the harvest moon swelled orange, and Lilou looked out for a sign from the abbé or a delivery from the bakery that might contain the code for her next assignment. But as the moon began to wane, nothing came. Eliot needed her, and perhaps that was to be her only contribution to the war from now on. He was rare treasure, but she was itching to be out helping more, guilty at being cloistered away from the action. And, she had to admit, she had come to almost enjoy the sharp edge of fear, the dependence on her sinews and quick wits that her moonlit assignments demanded.

Eliot's spirits waned with the moon as his beloved flower withered. Lilou showed him how to cut it back, ready for an even better show next year, she assured him. But he was sceptical. Why should he believe anything, when the sands were always shifting beneath his feet?

It was here in the garden with Eliot that Abbesse Honorine found Lilou, and she was in a hurry. She beckoned Lilou over.

'There's a Madame Aveline here enquiring after you and wondering about a child. It was obvious she already knew you were here, so I told her you were indeed, training as a novice, but I made no mention of our little astronaut. Here, put these on.' She handed Lilou a white habit and a novice's veil. 'Run, and tell her whatever you need to.'

Then the abbesse took Eliot's hand. 'I have something to show you inside,' she said, and he went, trusting her now.

Lilou had always known this peace wouldn't last. Why the hell couldn't they just be left alone?

Madame Aveline was waiting in the office, perched on the abbesse's chair, sipping coffee that the sisters had brought her. She was wearing a new suit, and the sheer callousness of it winded Lilou like a punch in the stomach. She'd know that fabric anywhere. It was the bolt of fine wool cloth Joseph's maman had ordered specially from Paris, and Madame Aveline had admired it one idle, gossipy day in the shop before all of this. Now it was on her back, nipping her waist in expensive tailoring thanks to Boche black-market money. How could she? It made her sick the way she'd sympathised with Lilou at the ransacked shop, then profited from her friends' hard-earned riches when they were suffering God knew where. But two could play at this two-faced charade. Madame Aveline had no idea who'd led those British agents away from her raid at the mayor's landing last month, so Lilou forced a civil smile, and kissed her on both of her traitor's cheeks.

'Hello. How on earth did you find me here?'

Madame Aveline took off her pillbox hat and gave her a saccharine smile.

'I was worried about you, my dear. I discovered that you'd left your poor mother all alone at the farm. There were rumours, but the abbé told me that it was nonsense about holy orders, and he thought you'd gone to visit relations on the coast. But it's nearly a month now, and in a village rumours become the truth. I thought it worth enquiring myself, and here you are, my dear.' She scrutinised Lilou.

'Yes, here I am,' said Lilou, still standing by the door. 'But I really can't stay. I'm called for Liturgy of the Hours, and in the afternoons we are vowed to silence.'

'Impressively devoted, Lilou. I don't want to intrude, but surely you'd like news of your poor maman? I must say, of all the girls I knew in the village you would be the last I would imagine undertaking such a drastic act, deciding to renounce the world all of a sudden.'

'It's a calling,' she said sarcastically. 'I can't go and fight like the men, so this is the only way I can think of to bring some good back into the world.'

'Goodness me, you sound more like a Resistance fighter than a novice,' said Madame Aveline, sipping coffee. 'Unfortunately, you have a choice to make between the Lord and home. Without you to curb your mother's worst excesses, she is in danger of being incarcerated by the occupying authorities for her own good, and the good of the wider community. As a friend, I thought you should know.'

'No collaborator could ever be a friend of mine,' growled Lilou.

'I'm not sure what you mean,' said Madame Aveline.

'What I mean is, how could you take that cloth from Madame Monteux's shop? How could you fraternise with those Boche murderers and petty criminals?'

'I admire your passion, but you are young, and life is complicated, and even you know that you have to crack a few eggs to make an omelette. Let me be straight with you. This country needs order, and what the Germans are doing is no better or worse than the French government, who've made a royal hash of everything. Indeed, many of us agree with our German neighbours' political views, as long as they are kept moderate and the extreme measures some of them believe in are stopped. Yes, I play a clever game, but I don't take sides. I have always operated on that policy, even when our only troubles on the council were boundary disputes and brawls in the square. The truth is, my position with the German occupiers gives me information others don't have access to. I have reason to believe you are in danger and under suspicion. It's only a matter of time till they find you here. Indeed, it was easy for me to trace your whereabouts. I have been in discussion with the Gestapo, and have given them assurances. They have promised to leave you alone provided you are under my protection, but you need to give up this novice play-acting and come back to the village where you belong.'

'Now *is* the time to take sides. You're either for or against. If you're for, then you're part of a regime of pure, molten malevolence and I will have no part in it, and your protection would be poison to me. Secondly—'

The abbesse bustled in before she could spit more anger at this self-serving, deluded hornet of a woman. Ushering Lilou away, Abbesse Honorine was firm.

'I have already made an exception for your admittance, madame. Visitors are usually forbidden for the first month to give the novice time to adjust, but you persuaded me you were a good friend. It seems the visit has only served to upset her. Lilou, go and join the others for Liturgy of the Hours, and I will finish off with Madame Aveline.'

She left gladly and watched Madame Aveline's car disappear out of sight through the slit window, spitting curses after her. The abbesse found Lilou pacing the cloisters, still cursing in a rage.

'Your passion and pride will be your downfall if you don't control it. Make it your strength instead. Someone in the village thought they saw you arrive with the abbé, and they notice things, especially when a pretty young novice arrives. They speculate about broken love affairs, or overbearing fathers, and no doubt you've been the salacious subject of gossip in all the bars and laundries within a ten-kilometre radius. There aren't many people around here with your fair hair, especially cropped so short, and with that great beast sitting in the back seat you must have really stood out.

Lilou subsided a little. She shouldn't have vented as she did, it was very un-novice-like, but she couldn't just sit there and let Madame Aveline whitewash everything.

'You're right. There were so many checkpoints along the way and the *Milice* are all local boys. Madame Aveline's tentacles stretch a long way, and she's always had spies everywhere. It used to be just for the gossip, but now she has bigger fish to fry. Christ, we should have been more careful... sorry, I mean...'

'Words are immaterial. What's important is that you took the precaution of hiding Eliot for the journey, so no one knows he's here. Now people know *you* are here, that puts us all in danger, including Eliot and all of our brave boys. You have to go back, for everyone's sake. The abbé tells me you're a brilliant guide, and you'll be more use back in the village than here.'

'What about Eliot? He only trusts me, and I can't leave him. He couldn't survive another separation!'

'It's a matter of life and death. Meet me in Sainte Roseline's chapel tonight at midnight and you'll have more information. After that, we will have to make arrangements for your return, and you will play Madame Aveline's game.'

She'd rather be in a forest listening out for snipers than playing any game of Madame's. What the hell did she want with Lilou back in the village?

Thoughts of leaving Eliot drove her mad as she waited in her room for the bells to chime midnight. At the twelfth stroke, she crept out, grateful for the cool night air, and pushed the door open to the chapel.

The glass casket was there as always, Sainte Roseline in her nun's habit the perpetual sleeping beauty, and the abbesse was kneeling, but not in prayer. A cut-out panel from the casket's stone catafalque was on the ground, and the abbesse was working a radio, twisting the controls to find a frequency. It clicked in, and a voice crackled onto the still chapel air.

'The roses are still blooming,' said the abbesse.

'Pray it continues,' replied a clipped, aristocratic voice. It was Marie-Madeleine!

'I have Patou here,' said the abbesse efficiently, waving at Lilou to come closer to the microphone.

'Patou. Congratulations are in order,' said Marie-Madeleine. 'You rescued our two best agents and they made it back to base with crucial intelligence. I have enthusiastic reports of a courageous mountain goat whose knowledge of the terrain saved their lives.'

'Mission accomplished, comrade,' added another voice: Hugh Verity in his perfect French.

'You're a soldier, Patou.' This time it was the group captain, Peter Vaughan-Fowler, who joined in.

'At your service,' she said in her best English, then to Marie-Madeleine, 'And the pup? News of his family?'

'Return to your kennel and leave the pup in the rose garden,' Marie-Madeleine intoned. 'Rabies at large. Duties at the next cycle. Orders from the Shepherd.'

'Ten-second warning,' said the group captain.

Marie-Madeleine exchanged brief instructions in code with the abbesse, then the transmission went dead.

It was final. They wanted her back at Vallon-Doux, and she would be given orders for her next mission from the abbé; so Madame Aveline would get her way. Eliot was to stay here with the nuns.

She spent the whole of the next day with Eliot. They went to all their favourite places, played word-games in the cloisters, checked the long grass for fieldmice and weaved fantastical stories about country cousins and town mice. They asked Scout who he liked the best of the two of them – one blink for Lilou, two for Eliot. They practised handstands in the cloisters, counted the angelica flowers, and her heart broke, and she knew she'd never rest again until she saw him safe on a plane, to a settled life somewhere if his papa survived, where he would never have to be afraid again, or depend on the kindness of strangers.

That night, Lilou went to Eliot's room and read to him.

'I have to go away for a little while,' she said, hating herself for the lie. She might never see him again. 'But the nuns will look after you, they all love you almost as much as I do.'

He thought for a moment. 'It's easier for you to go home than me. You're lucky.'

'But this is your home now, just while we're waiting for the time it's safe for you to be with your family.'

'When will that be?'

'We don't know,' said Lilou.

'Can't I stay with you? We shouldn't have loved each other, and you're sad. If you go, I won't be able to remember our stars and they'll stop shining for us.'

Lilou calculated the night skies to make sure she chose a star that would be visible the whole winter.

'Look out of the window. You see that really bright star? That's ours, and I will be there every single night thinking of you, and it will never stop shining for you.'

That seemed to comfort him.

'Me and Papa have a star, too. A secret one where all the numbers are.'

She prayed fervently that the nuns would guard her fragile, lonely astronaut as fiercely as she did, and pledged to work tirelessly until she could help get him to safety on some Lysander mission on a winter moon.

At the RAF cottage at Tangmere, nestled in the rolling Sussex countryside, Marie-Madeleine cut transmission to the brave young French girl. She was forced to send her Patou back into the wolf's lair but, from what her agents had reported, she had the stomach for it. And she had chosen her codename well. In the mountains, the wolves had no natural predators, and Patous were the only beasts in the area capable of protecting the sheep. She might be going back to collaborators and hostile Germans, but the danger was insignificant in comparison to being with Eliot. Anywhere he was, the full force of the Nazis threatened. Fear was disabling when what you needed was blind courage.

Eagle appeared at the door with a cup of British tea and a ready ear. He'd been waiting all evening for her to finish. She made sure that to her subordinates she appeared impervious to the pressures of her position, but when the responsibility of sending her agents into danger, quite possibly to their death, weighed heavy, he was there, too clever to judge or comment. He just listened.

She took the tea and leaned her head back into him. Everything felt right again, but their time together in England was almost over, and he was flying back to Paris tomorrow.

British intelligence had briefed her that if Eagle returned to France it would mean almost certain death, but Eagle had damned their law of averages.

Ordinarily, she would too. You didn't get to be head of a successful Resistance group, which lived and died on daring and subterfuge, without a certain level of derring-do, but she still couldn't get the dream about the field of pink heather and the Nazi raid out of her head. It was an overwhelming feeling she'd never see him again she couldn't shake. Worse, as Eagle's commanding officer she was forced to send him on his mission, whether she liked it or not. What right did she have to send other agents into dangerous terrain if she wasn't prepared to send her own lover and soulmate? But to be the very person commanding him into the lion's mouth was almost more than she could stand. There was no one else she could trust with this one, and no one else who wasn't already incarcerated who understood the critical nature of it. The Eliot Papers had been safe in her London basement all this time, but they'd found a French astronomer who they hoped could help decipher them, and Eagle's mission was to see them safely into his hands, then keep them safe until the critical date of 30 July 1944.

Their month together in England had been bliss, even though most of it had been work. When they weren't in meetings with the British Special Operations Executive, they were

packing supplies of crystals, collating operating codes, question-
naires and directives, bundling up millions of francs, requisitioning document-forging equipment, Red Cross cards and
anything they could think of to contribute to their colleagues
back home. But in between this, the meetings with ambassadors
in bloated ballrooms, negotiations for supplies and support in
panelled war-rooms, and deals on back stairs in gentlemen's
clubs, they snatched moments. A word or a look could make her
day. A night in the Sussex cottage in his arms was luxury
beyond imagining. And now the transmission was concluded
with the abbesse, tonight was one of those nights.

Eagle held out his hand for her to join him, and she took it,
exhausted with the day's work.

'Even top spymistresses need their beauty sleep every now
and then.'

'You're going tomorrow night. Sleep wasn't exactly what I
had in mind.'

He slipped his hand inside her blouse and her body fired at
his touch. She let him guide her to their room. It was a damp
little hideaway with windows that stuck and bats roosting in the
eaves, but she'd happily live in a cave with this man.

He undressed her slowly and laid her down.

'I want to look at you.'

The night was cloudy, and the room was dark, but she
glowed like a candle in his gaze.

He ran his fingers over her, caressed her hip-bones, each
slender finger, smoothed her temples and felt the softness of her
hair. In different times they would have been society's golden
couple, the fashionable, daring, witty, bored hostess and her
illicit handsome intellectual. Tonight, they were each other's
consolation from the horror far away from home, and they
belonged to no one but themselves.

In the darkness she committed every angle of his face to
memory, the dry fragrance of his skin, his tender touch.

He kissed her, slipped his hand between her thighs, and the night was theirs in dark colours. She fell asleep wrapped in him warm and sweet, until reality seeped through the window with the bloodless sun, and the dreary morning commanded them back to their posts.

The day went too fast, and Marie-Madeleine brushed down the shoulders of Eagle's jacket, which contained the Eliot Papers printed on the finest silk. In Eagle's briefcase were instructions for her agents in the Sainte Roseline area to guard the convent, and Eliot, at all costs. His father still hadn't talked and, if they got to him, what he knew would blow everything apart. The abbesse was one of her most unflappable and reliable agents, but she'd learned to take nothing for granted. She sealed the envelope, put it in Eagle's briefcase and snapped it shut. It sounded so final.

Eagle looked at her. 'Why so glum? I'll see you back in France.'

'I just hate saying goodbye and I don't know what I'll do without you,' she replied with an overwhelming sense of foreboding that she was struggling to hide.

'You don't need me. I'm just the operative, but you're the brains. Listen, you *are* the Ark, the fulcrum. I've had to hold men at gunpoint in order for them to submit to a woman's authority. But when they meet you, they know what the Chief says about you is true. You are the most valuable of us all, with an elephant's memory, the cunning of a fox, the guile of a serpent, the perseverance of a mole, and, when required, a panther's savagery. Let me go with your blessing. Whatever happens, loving you is more than any man can ask in a lifetime.'

There was no more time for goodbyes as they climbed into the jeep along with her agents and an MI6 liaison officer. It was a short drive to the night-flight take-off site, and there was none of the customary bright, brittle banter to bolster spirits. Nobody spoke, and even Marie-Madeleine couldn't muster herself for the obligatory 'once more unto the breach' pep-talk. The feeling of dread would seep into her words, and they didn't need to hear that before such a critical mission.

It was an incongruously beautiful evening, and, as they rounded the corner to the take-off location, Marie-Madeleine froze. The Lysander was waiting for them, the ground crew waving at them from the middle of a swathe of heather, stretching as far as she could see, glorious pink in the setting sun. The whole scene was an exact facsimile of the vivid nightmare she'd had in Paris.

It was all she could do to stop herself from screaming at the driver to turn round. She had to be logical. It was easy to retrofit dreams to situations you were worried about. And anyway, there was no way to stop the mission. Even if she tried, nothing would stop Eagle doing his duty.

All she could do was thrust her hands deep in her pockets as they strode to the aircraft so no one could see them trembling, and fake a bright smile for the departing heroes.

'Lucky you, you'll be drinking proper coffee on the Champs-Élysées while I'll be sipping weak tea in the pouring rain,' she said to agents Eagle and Rodriguez, who had turned to salute her. 'Send my love to my beautiful country, and do us proud.'

'Roger that,' said Agent Rodriguez, climbing into position.

'See you on the terrace in Saint-Tropez,' said Eagle and waved, the last rays rendering his features in vivid colours.

'I'll light a thousand candles,' she returned, smiling through tears she made sure he was too far away to see.

CHAPTER 14

CODE RED

VALLON-DOUX, OCTOBER 1943

Lilou

Once you love a child you are never free and now Lilou felt a profound connection with all mothers. The pietà in the church she'd hardly even noticed before took on new meaning. Mary weeping over her brutalised, beautiful Jesus, the hope of the world, was a universal truth, whether or not you believed in God. And it would never end. Almost two thousand years later, and the world sent its new-minted young men, angular and fresh-hewn from their boyhood, filled with fire and dreaming of greatness, to be shot and tortured in random acts of cruelty in the guise of organised warfare. The stupidity and waste of it made Lilou so angry it almost choked her.

She missed Eliot's warm touch and trust so viscerally she couldn't sleep. Knowing the danger he was in made her live every waking hour in a dread that seeped into everything, and she couldn't rest for a moment without some gut-wrenching scenario appearing in front of her eyes.

Her old, carefree country life, full to the brim every day with the demands of the season, family, friends and love, was out of reach forever.

Maman was even more withdrawn than ever, and muttering incessantly about Freddie, often getting him mixed up with the boy she'd hidden under the beehives, and Lilou worried constantly that somehow she'd give Eliot away, even though he wasn't with her any more.

She missed Kristian, too. She'd never been able to talk to anyone like she did him, and they'd shared Eliot for a little while, the most precious thing that Lilou had ever possessed. She couldn't get the night they'd danced for Eliot out of her head; Eliot's lullaby haunted her. No one in the world apart from her knew that a German soldier was aware of Eliot's existence, and she carried the knowledge around with her like a heavy stone. If they crossed paths in the village, the air was charged with an unfinished melody. What would have happened if they'd met in different circumstances? They wouldn't have met. She mustn't forget that. It was the war that blew him in here on an evil wind.

Lilou steeled herself. Since returning from the convent, she was required to report to Madame Aveline every day to avoid scrutiny and possible arrest by the Gestapo, so she said, and today was no exception.

In the square, Lilou walked past the lads who remained reluctantly in the village, smoking around the statue. *Collaborator*, they whispered, glowering and kicking up the leaves. It was easier to endure knowing that their mates Xavier and Freddie should have been with them, and she was doing this for them all, but she wished to hell she could tell them the truth.

Madame Aveline waved her over and she joined her at the café table. Old Monsieur Latil, the café proprietor, shoved two real coffees down in front of them. Slopping it into the saucer was one of a thousand protests against collaborators made by the villagers every day. It didn't matter; Lilou refused to touch Madame Aveline's black-market spoils. She was used to pretend coffee, made from ground acorns now.

Madame Aveline regarded her frankly. 'You don't trust me, but I know you better than you think,' she said, taking off her expensive hat and soaking up the spilt coffee in the saucers with a napkin for both of them.

Lilou didn't bother answering. Madame Aveline could no more understand Lilou than a snake understood a jay.

'I am working to change things from the inside, and you could help me if you put aside your stubborn Mistral pride.'

'Does changing things from the inside include a new hat?'

'I am in a position of authority and I'm expected to look the part.'

'You're fooling yourself, but you can't fool me. There's still simple right and wrong.'

'Maybe it's more complicated than that. Our families are the oldest in Vallon-Doux. We go back further than anyone can remember. The Mistrals have always been proud and head-strong, and we Avelines are pragmatists. The whole village is falling apart. If we can unite both sides, we have a chance of peace for us all.'

'As long as you're a Mistral, or an Aveline or an Isnard, or any of the old names from around here. Where do you think it's all going to end? They're just using you until they mangle all our boys in their war machine and turn the rest of us into second-class citizens. And what you call the Jewish Question is just a disgusting whitewash.'

'You're so like your mother used to be, always taking on the woes of the world.' Madame Aveline took a sip of her coffee, and surreptitiously checked around her. She needn't have worried. No one was taking any notice of them. The girls from the bakers were gossiping and giggling in the corner, the old men were propping up the bar shouting about how they were going to bring the harvest in with so many gone, and a table of German soldiers were guzzling the only cake in the town. Madame leaned closer across the table.

'I've never told you this before, but when your father was dying he came to me and asked me to watch over you. I made him a promise, which has meant more to me as the years have passed and I was never blessed with children of my own. He at least understood that you couldn't be left to tear around as you pleased, and that your mother wouldn't have the strength to control you. The problem is you let your heart rule your head, and you've never quite grown up.'

'My heart is the only guide I need. Your idea of truth bends with the wind, and the winning side. And if growing up means twisting everything for greed and personal gain, I'd rather not be your kind of adult,' said Lilou. She was missing Eliot's clear-sighted morality more than ever and she didn't care that her own papa had elicited such a promise from this woman. If he had known what would happen and who she would become, he would not have asked.

'I wish I was in a position to be as high-minded as you, but I'm not. My protection may seem stultifying to you, but you should know that I'm making compromises so you don't have to. I just wanted you to know.'

'Are you asking me to thank you?' said Lilou.

'I'm only asking for you to see things from my perspective.'

Madame Aveline concentrated on fixing her hat back in place, but the hurt in her eyes was as genuine as it was surprising. Lilou thought of the whispers of *collaborator* as she passed people in the street despite the fact that she regularly risked her life for the Resistance. Was Madame Aveline trying to tell her she was some kind of double agent, or just trying to gain her confidence so she would pass on valuable information? Then what the hell was she doing at the raid that led to Xavier's death? Everything pointed to her alerting the Germans to the

Lysander landing. She couldn't stay another minute to listen to her twisting the truth.

She stood up to go. 'I'll report to you tomorrow, as agreed,' she said curtly.

Now the most hated part of her day was over with, she crossed back over the square to the bakery. The redhead was there, and handed her the bread she'd prepared for her with instructions inside. They met eyes briefly in recognition and parted with a 'Bonne journée' and a conspiratorial smile, nothing more. There would be no good days until she saw Eliot was safe.

She thrust the bread deep into her shopping bag and took the back road up the hill to avoid prying eyes.

Back at the farm, Scout ran to meet her and her hackles rose immediately. The sheep were back down from the pastures, and Scout never left his post of guarding them unless there was something wrong.

She ruffled his neck. 'Hello, what is it, boy?'

Scout ran to Eliot's old hideout, and paced back and forth. Lilou opened the door with a beating heart, but there was no sign it had ever been a small boy's den, and of course Eliot wasn't in there.

Lilou hugged Scout. 'He's not coming back,' she told him. 'We all miss him. Back to your post, now.' He slinked back to the sheepfold, and Lilou took her package from the bakery into the kitchen, pulled out *The Little Prince* manuscript, and created a code grid to decipher the pickup location for tonight. The code was hidden in Saint-Exupéry's chapter thirteen, the one about the businessman. It was apt; about a man who concerned himself with counting the stars and, in counting them, owning them. Was that what the Nazis thought they could do with human beings, own them and add and subtract them like they were numbers on a ledger? Eliot was right, grown-ups were ridiculous. She concentrated on picking out the letters until the coordinates came into focus. She knew the place, and it wasn't far. At least now that Eliot was being looked after at the convent she could carry out her missions without being terrified of leaving him at night.

The hunter's moon was bright as Lilou set out. The village in curfew was silvered, but no warm lights shone out in the way she used to love. The houses were shuttered and characterless, waiting for better times. She hastened along the chemin de Beliers, then struck out through the woods, taking the old boar's trails she knew so well. Tonight's rendezvous was simple. No landings, but instead a lone agent parachuting to a drop zone nearby, a bag passed over and a radio transmission tomorrow with the abbé.

When she arrived, she helped the agent gather up his parachute, pack it and cover up all traces, then guided him to the route to the safe house. It was easy by the light of the bright moon, and they worked quickly and silently, exchanging hand signals and looks in the dark. He could only be about eighteen, tall, wiry and straight, with ears that stuck out and a crooked grin. He knew how to run through a wood silently like her, no town-boy blundering through, cracking twigs or snagging branches. His feet found the right path instinctively and, she thought proudly, he was a stalwart of the maquis, a tough, wily country lad, the backbone of Provence. They parted at the crossroads, and she sent an old Provençal spell with him to protect him.

Mission accomplished, she made her way back easily, eyes accustomed to the dark, every sinew firing, ears on high alert for humans, she became part of the animal world that came alive at night, super-tuned to danger. She slipped into the house and climbed into bed and tried to close her eyes, but she couldn't sleep from the fizz of adrenalin. The abbe's church bell struck two, then three as she went to the window to stare out at the night sky. The Milky Way was clearly visible, and Auriga joined Taurus and the Pleiades, aligned to a star that shone bright orange. She tried to remember the name that her papa had taught for that one, but it was gone. Kristian would know. She passed the time by naming all the stars she knew, until her body calmed and she drifted off. The only constant in the sky was Eliot's north star, shining like a beacon. *Sweet dreams*, she whispered to him.

The next day was Sunday, and, after helping Madame Aveline with the post-mass gathering where the town eyed each other suspiciously and whispered about collaborators or deviants, she escaped to the sacristy with the documents from last night's mission sewn into the hem of her Sunday dress.

The abbé locked the door, and they pored over the code and gridded it from the code book. The abbé flicked the pages, ran his finger down and across the lines, and called out the letters, which Lilou carefully noted down. The words that emerged screamed her worst fears in stark, staccato sentences.

Eagle captured and held at Gestapo HQ, Avenue Foch, Paris. Whereabouts of the Eliot Papers unknown. Network catastrophically compromised. Sicherheitsdienst SS Counter-intelligence aware of critical date 30 July 1944.

Documents relating to precise location of Eliot Stavinsky in enemy hands. Urgent action to remove to undisclosed location with immediate effect. Knowledge of whereabouts restricted to one person, the abbesse at Sainte Roseline. The child is key to operations and must be hidden and kept alive at all costs.

*Single communication permitted from Vallon-Doux trans-
mitter prior to complete shutdown of all networks. Message to
all agents: cease communication until further notice. Repeat,
cease all communications. Risk level for all agents: Red.*

The abbé shook his head in despair. 'The entire network is
hiding under rocks, and those are the lucky ones. The British
are losing faith in the Resistance movement and withholding
resources. They're worried that with so many security breaches,
those that do get caught will give away all their secrets under
torture.'

'He'll be terrified if they move him again,' said Lilou. 'And
what if something happens to the abbesse and no one else
knows where Eliot is?'

The abbé hugged her. 'At least he'll be safe for now.'

'How do we know? The whole network's compromised. I
want him back with me. I can't just let him disappear,' said
Lilou, frantic.

The abbé threw the documents and Lilou's notes on the
fire.

'Think about it, Lilou, we have to follow orders. The whole
network's on the brink. He holds knowledge his papa entrusted
to him that is critical to the war efforts, and makes him a prime
Nazi target, especially now they might have the Eliot Papers. If
you disappeared again, alarm bells would ring and who knows
what they'd do or who they'd torture to try and find you? If you
tried to hide him on the farm again, who knows who's watching?
The abbesse knows what she's doing and he's one child. One
brave, beautiful boy, but there are so many souls to save.'

*One boy who represents everything that's right and wrong
with the world and means more to me than every star in the
Provençal sky,* thought Lilou. Maybe they'd already moved him,
and Scout somehow sensed his fear, and that's why he was
acting strangely. Sometimes it was worth listening to the old

country signs; but she knew the abbé wouldn't approve of spells and augurs and animal instincts.

'First things first, we have to warn the network. Now's a good time, while the Gestapo are casting a shadow with Madame Aveline and the town council on my church steps,' the abbé said. He unlocked the door to the steeple steps. They crept in and he locked it behind them.

'You know there are only six transmitters still in commission, of the hundreds that belonged to Alliance? All the others have been discovered or shut down for safety reasons and ours is one of the very few left. I still can't believe that young man who rescued your cat didn't see it, or that our local Gestapo thugs haven't detected it. We either have an ally in the German camp, or we've been very lucky.'

'Maybe he did see it and he's just playing a long game.' No, he hadn't ever given her away…

'Spoken like a true Resistance operative,' said the abbé proudly. 'I always thought if you learned to tame your reckless spirit you'd be a force to reckon with.'

They transmitted their warnings, and sent instructions to the abbesse, each letter a betrayal to Eliot and all Lilou had promised him.

The abbé closed down the transmitter. When they came out, the churchgoers were still milling about, including Kristian, Madame Aveline and the other soldiers. Damn them all to hell, standing on the church steps while Hitler played God and preached hate and destruction. She pushed past them and started up the hill to home, sick to the stomach. The abbé told her the boy she'd guided last night had been found and shot on the spot. And poor Eagle – the Gestapo were crowing over the capture of such an important Resistance figure. What lengths would they go to to break Marie-Madeleine's magnificent Eagle? Did he manage to pass on the Eliot Papers before they got to him? If the Nazis had the papers, they had one half of the puzzle Roman Stavinsky had set, and they'd do anything to get to the other half – Eliot.

Each missive they'd sent from the church steeple, in the sparest language possible to save on transmission time, represented an endless story of sacrifice, bravery and suffering. And her own Eliot, at the tender age of seven, could write the book of every child's worst nightmares.

CHAPTER 15

OPERATION LAMB

Marie-Madeleine

Marie-Madeleine had watched from London as the fleets of Allied bombers flew in formation like a giant factory in the sky, the thrum turning to a deafening roar as they headed east towards France. She'd celebrated D-Day with a bottle of vintage Bordeaux, but the taste turned bitter soon enough. The Nazi reprisals were brutal, especially for her Resistance networks in the south of France, for whom support was sparse, with resources focused on the big push north out of Normandy. Whole villages were rounded up and shot or tortured, her networks were on their knees, *maquisards* engaged in vicious fighting with the *Milices* desperate to get their blows in before defeat. That came on the heels of autumn 1943, which was the worst year Marie-Madeleine had ever experienced. After Eagle's capture and incarceration, and lack of security in the south, the British were adamant that she shouldn't return to

France, but how did she have the right to carry on without sharing the fate of her agents?

Codename Stronghold, the grand house in London they'd given her to be closer to the War Office, was incongruously luxurious, so she'd installed herself in the basement with a camp bed to be near her desk and the telephone with a direct line to MI6. As she struck out name after name on her network charts with an aching heart, she commanded herself not to despair. She checked down the list. Patou was still free and alive, still making her night-time missions, fleet as a deer. There was something about her that represented rural France, the delights of Provence, the old ways, the soul of the country and what they were all fighting for. While she was still in operation it gave her a kind of superstitious hope.

That, and intelligence that the Eliot Papers were still in Resistance hands, to be delivered in Operation Popeye, thanks to Eagle's quick thinking before his arrest. The thirtieth of July was fast approaching, and Eliot was still safe, but the closer it got the more danger he was in.

Until, or if, the Eliot Papers materialised, she had to face it: despite her agents' profoundly touching loyalty and their almost crazy desire to carry on, the Gestapo still had the upper hand over Alliance and her Ark of agents. In the dead of night, she visualised her agents on their knees praying for her help, mouths twisted in agony. It was for them, for France, that she would never give up.

She had last seen her baby when he was only three weeks old, almost a year ago, but she slept with the telephone on her pillow ready for any emergency, working through as much intelligence as she could manage on a few hours' sleep a night, constantly petitioning the War Office for help and supplies. Work was the only thing that pushed the horror of it all, including her darling Eagle's incarceration, into the background for a while. The news about him was worse than she could ever have imagined. They didn't want to show it to her, but she'd demanded the full transcript from the Abwehr's meticulously recorded account of Eagle's capture and transportation. Along with this, and her own agents' reports, she'd cobbled together his sickening months since the day he'd climbed aboard the Lysander in that ugly, beautiful field of heather.

The whole ingress into France had been botched, too many people at the landing site, then all the agents travelling together in the same carriage to Paris, totally contrary to basic protocol. It was a stupid risk, and they'd all been immediately neutralised by the Germans. The informant who'd exposed them was still unclear, but there was a snake lurking somewhere within the ranks, and she had people working on that one day and night, but, in the theatre of war, chaos and human error abounded.

Eagle had been separated, bound and spirited away to the *Sicherheitsdienst* SS counterintelligence HQ in Paris. No one had ever been able to imprison her Eagle for long and he'd of course attempted an escape, and almost made it, jumping into a courtyard from two floors up, only to be caught again when trying to bring two less experienced agents with him. In retaliation, they'd smashed his jaw and broken his arms and his legs. The report detailed that the interrogators were so sickened by the bloody sight that they'd left him there on the floor. The next day he'd been transported to fortress Bruchsal, where his convulsing body was thrown into a vault. They classified the prisoner as an expert terrorist and known escapist, and the jailer was instructed to lock him down. The final report she had was that her magnificent Eagle, who'd escaped and defied death time and time again, was chained to an iron bedstead in a windowless Nazi vault.

Today, at last, she was going back to France. The SOE had relented after D-Day, despite the ongoing security risks for the Resistance. Marie-Madeleine knelt while the priest gave her absolution for taking the cyanide hidden in her ring, should the need arise. She'd like to think she could resist blabbing under torture, but no one knew till it came to it.

When he finished, she knelt alone and prayed ardently for Eagle, for her agents, for her children. She begged whoever was up there to give her back the strength she needed to carry on, despite losing her confidant, lover and chief strategist along with so many of her compatriots, the cream of France's bravest, brightest altruists, all turned to dust.

In front of the Virgin Mary, she lit a candle for her two children in Switzerland, then a third for her baby, one year and five weeks and two days, Eagle's son, in the south of France. Lingering as the candles flickered in the cold London air, she watched the flames blur with tears. She wasn't sure she'd ever see her children again, but she was doing this for their future, for every child's future. Leaving the cool safety of the church, she stepped into the waiting car with her suitcase and stared out of the window at the driving rain. The car sped her through the night to meet Tonio de Saint-Exupéry, who was waiting to fly her to the drop zone back in her beloved Provence, to be amongst whoever was left of her network, and try to recover the Eliot Papers before it was too late.

Lilou stared out at the July skies, heavy with the threat of a summer downpour, her wasted lavender fields a purple storm-cloud against the glowering grey. There was no one to help with the harvest this year with Freddie gone, and since D-Day even more men were scattered in maquis camps in the hills, ready to fight. Women land-workers were concentrating only on what could be eaten, or sold on the black market.

So it was just her and the bees this July, and their lazy drift from flower to flower was in stark contrast to Lilou's mood. She hadn't seen Eliot since October, and the critical July date was fast approaching, with no intelligence whatsoever of him, or even whether he was still alive. Whatever secret it was that was attached to Eliot could cost him his life, and she prayed to their star every night to protect him. She'd lain awake so many nights trying to recall his obsession with the numbers his papa had told him to remember, muttering figures that seemed meaningless. She'd given them little thought at the time, thinking it was just part of his love of order, of numbers, of creating a world he could control in all this chaos.

It was useless. Each mission brought more bad news of good men lost in the Nazis' viciousness in retreat, and the parched land looked as exhausted as its people.

She filled her basket as full as she could with lavender, and took the path through the woods to give the flowers to the abbé for his 14 July celebrations next week in defiance of the occupiers. Even her beloved woods were ravaged by war. The Germans were stripping everything for fuel and food. The piles of logs chopped down indiscriminately were heaped up at random, leaving bald patches where worlds of flowers, woodland animals and birds had once lived forever in harmony.

The town square was deserted, and shutters were pulled tight against the heat as Lilou took the passage to the church and into the cemetery for her annual visit to her papa's grave for his birthday. She arranged a few of the best sprigs of lavender in the urn, then sat back on her haunches.

Eliot was on her mind day and night, but there was someone else that she couldn't get out of her head: Kristian. Papa would understand even if no one else would.

'It's almost a year since I spoke to Kristian, but I still think about him every day,' she whispered. 'You would have loved him, he's an astronomer and last night the stars were as bright as a carpet of aconites in the forest. Draco's woken up, too. The orange star, the eye of the dragon. You told me what it was called once, but I've forgotten.'

A tear sprang from a closed-off place inside her as she

remembered nights watching the sky, wrapped in a soft wool blanket, listening to Papa point out references in the constellations. She hastily swiped the tear away. Papa hated to see her cry.

'Happy birthday,' she whispered, running her fingers over the letters of his name on the gravestone.

'The orange star is called Eltanin.'

Lilou jumped up, unnamed emotions flying like startled birds bursting out of a tree. It was Kristian, standing by the cemetery lychgate. She would have to pass him to leave. Her heart drummed.

He smiled as she walked towards him.

'I wanted to talk to you, but I didn't want to disturb you when I saw you talking to a grave. Are you all right?'

'It's Papa, I come here every year.'

'I'm sorry.'

'Don't be. He's been gone a long time, but birthdays are still hard. I can talk to him about anything now, though, and it was him who taught me about the stars.'

'It does sound like we'd get on.' He smiled warmly.

Lilou laughed, flustered. 'That was meant for his ears only.'

'I didn't mean to eavesdrop, but I'm glad I heard it. I thought you hated me.'

'I just hate this war.'

'You didn't have to go away last summer. I would never have said anything to give you or Eliot away. I thought I'd shown you that.'

Lilou had thought about what she'd say if they ever spoke again a million times. Now it was simple.

'You seemed angry, and what I was doing was too dangerous to risk. You changed all of a sudden, and how could I trust a German?'

Kristian hesitated, hung his head.

'The mission you ran, the one that Madame Aveline told me

about, killed my best friend. He wasn't wearing his ID tag, so I identified his body for his maman. He was so badly burnt I only recognised him by his signet.'

'I'm so sorry.' Lilou didn't know what to say. What could she say? That mission had saved lives, and was a major turning point in the war. She wished no one had to die. There were no words.

Kristian shrugged. 'He's one of a million atrocities. But he was mine. He didn't want to be here any more than you or I.'

'If you weren't here, we wouldn't have met.'

'That has been the only good thing. You, and Eliot. How is he?'

'Not here,' said Lilou, wary again.

'Is he all right? I've collected some fossils for him from the mountains. Where is he?'

'I don't know.'

The flecks in his green eyes were autumn leaves. Papa's favourite season. The church bell rang the hour.

'I'm leaving today, that's why I had to find you, to say good-bye. I'm being seconded to an air base on the coast. I won't be coming back, certainly not to Vallon-Doux and maybe not even back to this world if I'm as unlucky as Felix. They're moving me from reconnaissance to fighter jets. So many were lost on D-Day, and I'm fresh meat. Will you say you'll remember me? That will make it easier to go.'

No! She'd wished the Germans away so many times she'd lost count, but not Kristian! Somehow she thought he'd always be there. All he'd ever done was protect her and Eliot and her family and now he was going.

'I'll never forget you. I wish we could have been more than friends,' said Lilou.

Kristian kissed her and the breeze brought them honeysuckle and jasmine to sweeten the summer heat.

Don't let him go, urged Papa from his grave, but he always said the things she wanted to hear. She stepped away from Kristian and shook her head. You never knew who was looking nowadays.

'I know,' he said.

There was so much to say, and nothing more. He was off to war, a fighter pilot on the wrong side, and she was a Resistance agent who would do everything in her power to stop them.

'Goodbye then,' he said. And he was gone.

Inside the church, Lilou handed over the sprays of lavender to the abbé.

'Splendid. But you don't seem much like a girl who's been frolicking in the fields collecting summer cheer. You look like you've seen a ghost. Is it your papa? I saw you going into the cemetery and you always miss him at this time of year.'

'Everyone's missing someone,' said Lilou. 'Come on, I'll help you decorate with the lavender and it'll take my mind off it,' she lied.

Kristian had kept her and Eliot safe, and she was letting him go.

'Before we do that, I have a present for you. Not a very conventional one, but then neither is my favourite Resistance operator.'

He handed her a set of coordinates and a rendezvous time.

'This looks like all the rest. How is it different?'

'Classified information until the rendezvous, but I think you'll like it,' he said enigmatically. 'There is an additional directive to ensure you have Scout with you, but I'm not authorised to provide further information.'

'I don't need a guard dog—'

The abbé cut her short. 'You have your orders, now go in peace.'

'Do you think this war will ever be over?'

'We'll make sure it is. Keep the faith.' Her darling renegade priest raised his fist in solidarity.

Clandestine manoeuvres were always difficult on a full moon and tonight the storm had cleared the way for a glaring thunder moon, throwing everything, including her, into silhouette. Having Scout with her was a comfort, an extra pair of eyes and a nose for danger. She watched him carefully, but he sensed nothing but Lilou's excitement at being out on a mission, and he trotted along beside her in the best of spirits until they reached the clearing. The church in the valley rang out 2 a.m. Exactly on time, she heard the familiar drone of an approaching aircraft and she crouched in a dip, checked the terrain for hidden figures, night vision honed for danger. Not a soul in sight, not even a night owl – she and Scout were the only creatures crazy enough to be out on such a lonely night. She'd been told there'd be no landing crew, so it was just her and the vast windswept plateau.

As it came into view, the plane seemed to descend too steeply, and she was worried it would smash up on landing, but somehow it came down with a few bumps and skidded to a halt on the hard ground.

The cockpit slid back, and she waited for the agent to jump out with a briefcase, but instead a tall, stocky man stood up and waved her over. She hesitated for a moment.

'Over here, mountain girl.'

The pilot jumped down and wrapped his flying scarf tighter round his neck and shoved a novel in his pocket to shake her hand. Lilou was delighted to see it was Tonio de Saint-Exupéry.

Scout sniffed him suspiciously.

'Hello fine beast,' said Tonio, winning the dog over immediately with a scratch behind his ears. 'You're going to be a fine piece of ballast aren't you boy? Glad I took the precaution of a full set of tanks. And how's my Provençal Resistance heroine?'

'Still fighting.' She pointed to the novel in his pocket. 'Is that the documentation?'

He looked down and laughed. 'That? Oh, no, I left early so I could finish the chapter. The altitude and peace up there makes it easier to concentrate. It's not a drop tonight, you're coming with me, and your dog, too.'

'In that?' Lilou definitely preferred her own two feet. She would have happily climbed the steepest crag to see a rare orchid or jumped a ravine for the perfect picnic spot, but not this.

Tonio put his fingers to his lips. 'An aircraft has feelings and you've just hurt them. *That* is the gold standard, with heating, and she flies like a dream. If it makes it any easier, you have no choice. There'll be some very important people waiting for you when we land, and you'll be receiving instructions on a mission that is critical to the entire war effort.'

Lilou looked doubtfully at the plane, all harsh metal and dark shadows. Tonio laughed at her expression.

'I'll sweeten the pill a little. The abbé couldn't tell you before you got here. It's all on a need-to-know-basis from start to finish, but you'll be reunited with Eliot Stavinsky for a night, too. The little fellow has been pining for you and your canine companion, and has hardly said a word since you left him. We couldn't risk detection on the roads or a in a train, and no one else would agree to carry a seventy-kilo Patou, so voilà, your carriage awaits, mademoiselle.'

Tonio bowed, gave her a rascal's smile and unfurled a large sling out of his rucksack.

'This thing has hauled many a Colonel Blimp off the battle-field, so it'll do the trick for this sturdy animal. He'll probably make a damn sight less fuss, too. I'll get in and haul him up, then you jump in the back and hold on tight. Bit of a squeeze but at least he'll keep you warm.'

With Scout and Lilou in the back, Tonio set her up with the headset and showed her how to radio him from the seat behind him if she needed to.

'Comfortable? Sorry, you're going to have to wear this. Orders from the boss, and no one defies her and lives to tell the tale. It's better for everyone that you have no idea where Eliot's located. I'll be your eyes for the journey.'

Lilou had already planned to keep her eyes tight shut, so she was very happy to secure the blindfold and bury her head in Scout's warm fur for take-off. She comforted herself that it didn't really matter about this short journey though, however much she hated the idea of flying. She was about to see Eliot again, and anything was worth it for that.

The engines roared, and the wheels spun, and Lilou tried not to think about the precipice at the end of the plateau as they skidded up to speed, but, sure enough, they soared up and she could breathe again.

She jumped when Tonio's voice crackled direct into her ear.

'OK back there? We're already at five thousand feet. How are you feeling?'

'Fine.'

'That's one of the shakiest "fines" I've ever heard through the tubes. I hear you're a great navigator by the stars?'

'We're shepherds. It's how we've always done it,' shouted Lilou through the mouthpiece.

'It's a beautiful night out there. The moon's a silver dollar, and straight ahead the Seven Sisters are blue as a glacier.'

Lilou imagined the sisters glowing hot ice-blue, with Aldebaran's cold orange glare watching over them.

'So we're going north-west?'

'As good as a co-pilot. How's the beast of Vallon-Doux faring?'

Lilou peeped at him from under her blindfold. 'Sleeping like a baby.'

'At least one of you's relaxed. It's a short hop, not too much longer. We're going to promenade the Milky Way, then hail Ursa Major when we turn. Can you hear them?'

'The engines?'

'The stars. On a night like this the whole sky's ringing like hundreds of carillon bells.'

'I can hear them, it's like heaven.'

'That's the ticket.'

The tubes went silent and Lilou relaxed a little. Scout was sound asleep, the stars were oscillating a thousand tones and they were flying above the madness, greed and tragedy in the pristine night sky. She thought of Kristian in his fighter plane, finger hovering over the trigger, and wondered if he'd remember his star-gazing with Eliot, and hear them ring in the innocent space where Eliot longed to live amongst the planets. Would he still open fire?

The landing was hideous – the plane fell out of the sky like a rock, leaving her stomach in the clouds – but they finally touched down safely and she could breathe again. When the plane came to a halt and Tonio opened the cockpit, Lilou smelled the salt and spray of the sea.

'Where are we?' she asked.

'Classified information, I'm afraid. Let's just say Eliot's planet, or the equivalent of,' said Tonio. 'Come on, let's get the hound on solid ground, then I'll help you out. The blindfold stays until we're inside. Enjoy the trip?'

'I can still hear the bells.'

'That means you're one of us.'

'I'd never make an aviator, I prefer my own two feet planted firmly on the maquis.'

'I mean you still honour the child in you, and go with your heart as well as your head, blindfold or otherwise. It's the surest moral compass you can have.' He helped her unstrap. 'Come on, let's get you inside. There's someone very special waiting for you who wouldn't thank me for keeping you.'

The sea was booming on the shore. They were somewhere wild and remote, and the wind was picking up. Inside, she smelled woodsmoke, and a wall of delicious heat hit her. Tonio took off her blindfold and there was Eliot, giggling like the chiming stars at Scout's overwhelming affection, his great tongue smothering him.

Marie-Madeleine was there too, rather awkwardly holding a baby, oscillating between tears and affection. She'd always been slim, but there was barely anything left of her, and dark circles encircled her fierce brown eyes. Even here, she exuded an air of strength and restless energy, sitting in the corner straight and focused on the task in hand – this time, her baby.

The abbesse was putting candles on the kind of cake that was definitely not possible on a ration-card, and the table was laid with a jug of cream, a bowl of summer fruits and side plates, ready for someone's birthday.

Marie-Madeleine handed the baby to the abbesse, who looked considerably more skilled at handling it, and strode over to embrace her.

'Lilou, welcome to our little birthday feast! It's a joy to see you, Agent Patou. How can you look like a spring day at this hour? Eliot dear, don't let that hound lick you in the face. Come and give Lilou a kiss, she's come a long way to see you.'

'She's not a Patou, you are,' said Eliot to Scout. 'She said that she'd talk to me through the north star, but she didn't, she left me alone.'

Like Marie-Madeleine, the last months had taken their toll on Eliot. He was withdrawn and pale, he'd lost his plump cheeks, and he looked like he hadn't slept properly since she'd left him at the convent. His big dark eyes were wary and afraid.

Lilou fished in her bag and pulled out a star she'd sewn for his wall.

'I kept this with me, and I thought about you every time I looked at the north star. Scout missed you so much – he went to your room on the farm every day after he left you to look for you.'

'Just because people aren't with you, it doesn't mean they can't see or hear you in their hearts,' said Tonio.

'Everyone who's read *The Little Prince* knows that, it's obvious,' said Eliot to Scout, who blinked in agreement.

'That's everyone in this room, and everyone in this room is looking after you in their own way, little man,' said Tonio.

'And Kristian,' said Eliot. 'He's read it too.'

Lilou felt the ground swallowing her up. Thank goodness Eliot had pronounced the name 'Christian', in the French way. All eyes were on her.

'Who's Christian?' said Marie-Madeleine, eyes blazing.

'The man she danced with. He looked at her like Papa looked at Mama. I think he loves her. Scout liked him, didn't you?'

'He's read the manuscript?' said Marie-Madeleine, horrified.

'I'm not sure our agent wants to discuss her dancing partner with us. We must all be allowed our secrets, and my book's published now in America, so there's no reason why lots of people shouldn't have seen it. The versions the Resistance agents have are all different, so someone else seeing it shouldn't compromise our code systems,' said Tonio, coming to the rescue.

Lilou stammered a response. 'Yes... Eliot loved the story so much, so we talked about it, and it was the only way he could get to sleep. He's totally trustworthy.'

'He had a gun, but a kind face.'

'A *maquisard*, a Resistance man, we can trust him,' said Lilou, praying that Eliot wouldn't know the word.

'The manuscript will have to be neutralised. I'll instruct the abbé to issue you with a different key script,' said Marie-Madeleine.

Lilou made a silent pact with herself to make a copy of *The Little Prince* before they made her destroy it. The manuscript was like a trusted friend to her now, it had never failed her, and she'd miss the constant reference to it as her key code; but Marie-Madeleine was right. It was her own stupid fault.

Eliot buried his head in Scout's fur. Lilou was desperate for a hug, to share stories and giggles with Eliot in the few hours they had, but she could tell he was confused and scared by the serious tone the conversation had taken.

'He takes great comfort from that creature,' whispered the abbesse. 'He says he only feels safe when he's there, no matter how much we reassure him. He misses his mama and papa, and now you and Scout, so much.'

Lilou got the abbesse's permission before she offered.

'I can't stay, but what if I leave Scout with you?'

She got the hug she was waiting for, Eliot's warm body folding into her arms. His hair against her cheek was impossibly silky, and everything about him so new-minted, determined and vulnerable at the same time, she didn't know whether to laugh or cry. For Eliot's sake, she laughed, and hugged him tight.

'I'm not sure I can top a large shaggy dog who is the best companion a boy could wish for, but I have something for you, too,' said Tonio. He handed Eliot a messily wrapped package, stuck with duct tape. Eliot opened it carefully, peeling the tape off bit by bit, lips pursed in concentration. Lilou wished for his sake he'd just tear it open like Freddie would have.

He jumped off Lilou's knee and whizzed the red plane through the air. 'Can I fly with you in your plane?' he said.

'Of course you can. I just need to arrange it with the boss, then we can pack ourselves up with a hot chocolate and do a loop-the-loop around the moon.'

'But not tonight. It'll take a little time to arrange, you just have to be patient and be good for the abbesse. Can you do that?' said Marie-Madeleine.

'Will you be taking me home?' asked Eliot.

Tonio looked at the abbesse for help.

'We'll see about that, God willing.' She smiled briskly. 'Now what about the birthday cake? You may be eight years old now, but it's still very late for a young boy to be up. Shall we eat and be merry, and, if I let Scout come with you to your room, do you think you will have sweet dreams tonight?'

'If you all sing me the song I'll be able to sleep for a thousand nights until I can go home.'

'Which song is that?' said the abbesse.

'Lilou knows it.'

Yes, the one that she and Kristian danced to for him.

They ate the cake, and played with Eliot and his plane, Tonio piloting it by dashing around in circles and Eliot providing an enthusiastic engine soundtrack. Even Marie-Madeleine joined in, pointing out the landmarks, and Lilou was the navigator, making sure they kept following the north star. It was a drop of happiness in a deep well of sadness, and they threw themselves into the precious hours with all the dedication they showed to the cause. Tonio did card tricks, Lilou sang an old Provençal song, Marie-Madeleine danced a cha-cha with Eliot, and the abbesse told the fable of the mouse and the lion, and was surprisingly good at the voices.

Outside, another storm was whipping up over the sea and the wind howled like a banshee, but inside the little cottage was temporarily a world of innocence, warmth and fellowship, the world they were all fighting for.

Tonio consulted his watch. 'Time to go, before it gets light, and it's very late for a small boy, even one who can fly,' he said.

Eliot obediently got off Lilou's lap and let the abbesse lead him to bed. Lilou wished he'd scream and cry and make a huge fuss. But he'd already said too many goodbyes for that.

'Will you all sing me the song to get me to sleep?' said Eliot.

'Do you all know "Dream a Little Dream of Me"?' Lilou asked, and they all nodded. Eliot was tucked into a narrow little bed off a room where the abbesse slept. *Just these thin walls, a nun and a dog between Eliot and capture and horror*, thought Lilou darkly. It would be hard to leave him.

It was a motley choir who sang Eliot to sleep. The abbesse had the best voice, Marie-Madeleine was tone-deaf and looked a little uncomfortable singing to a child, Tonio hummed gamely and pulled faces to make Eliot laugh but didn't know the words, and Lilou put her heart and soul into it, remembering Kristian's arm round her waist.

Eliot tried to stay awake, but his eyelids betrayed him, and soon his little body was still as a newborn lamb, his pudgy hand on Scout's head for reassurance.

On his bedside table was a small open notebook, with rows and rows of neat numbers, and in the margins drawings of guns and childish depictions of evil faces.

'He counts the sunsets every day and records them, to show his maman that he thought about her at the end of every day,' said the abbesse, crossing herself for the dead.

'Twenty minutes till take-off,' said Tonio. 'Any longer and we'll be target practice. Orders, *patronne*?'

Lilou kissed her hand and planted it gently on Eliot's forehead. Scout opened one eye by way of goodbye, understanding he had a new and grave responsibility, then the four gathered around the dying embers of the fire.

Marie-Madeleine addressed Lilou and Tonio.

'You two are to be key agents for Operation Lamb, to bring together the boy and key documents, the Eliot Papers. His father got him to commit some coordinates to memory in case anything ever happened to him. The Eliot Papers contain prompts for a geo-location that only the boy can understand. He's used celestial navigation to plot a very particular point on the thirtieth of July. If we can unite Eliot with the documents, we can retrieve valuable blueprints and keep them out of enemy hands.'

'What's at stake here, what are the blueprints for?' asked Tonio.

Marie-Madeline looked into the fire as she spoke. Lilou felt she could barely breathe. 'We have limited time, so full disclosure. There's a Nazi manhunt out for Eliot. His father is a brilliant and, as you know, eccentric, radar scientist. He was using radar technology to develop a weapon and the blueprints in the wrong hands could change the course of the war. The Americans, the British, the Germans and, we believe, the Japanese are all working on the technology – a particle beam something or other, one of many technological races to the bottom, and to mass destruction.'

Lilou hunched forward towards the fire, turned it over in her head, tried to understand. It felt too big to contemplate as the flames raged in the grate, speaking of destruction in their turn. How could she be a part of this, some nightmarish, otherworldly weapon of mass destruction reaching its cold, industrial fingers as far as her fields and pastures?

All the hints she'd got from the abbé, Eliot's desperate attempts to recall the information his papa had entrusted him with, began to make more sense. Nobody spoke, and Marie-Madeleine paused to allow the weight of her words settle before continuing.

'Don't ask me what the hell nightmares it can unleash, and we don't even know if it would be feasible, but by all accounts Roman Stavinsky's calculations are incredibly advanced, and the Nazis are interested. Why on earth he chose the little lad to give the information to, we'll never know, but colleagues suggest he had no choice when he was raided, and the pair had a secret language together, and played games using celestial navigation, using the lad's love of *The Little Prince* and his planets.'

The book, that book, Tonio's beautiful imagination, was the centre of everything.

'It's a tight operation to ensure maximum security and will be run by a small cell of you two, the abbesse and the abbé. The abbesse will have intermittent contact with the abbé, and your job is to get Eliot to where he needs to be on the thirtieth of July, by whatever means. Lilou, you will receive these updates via the abbé, and contact Tonio as you require his services, including his final flight to Switzerland, where he'll be placed with his uncle and aunt and eventually, we hope, his father. You will receive information as necessary via the abbé, on a need-to-know basis.'

'There's a lot riding on that little man's head,' said Tonio gravely.

'I'll protect him with all my heart,' said Lilou.

'I know you will, with all that Provençal wildfire,' said Marie-Madeleine.

Her fierce warrior's eyes exuded pride and courage for her protégée.

Lilou absorbed every last bit of strength she had to give her. Despite her slim frame, her society hostess's demeanour, Marie-Madeleine had strength enough to power an army.

'We all have a creature within us that is not concerned with the physical. That creature gives us wings, joins us with a universal truth, and prepares us to give ourselves, even die, for the greater good,' said Tonio.

Lilou felt it, and joined with Marie-Madeleine, the abbesse and Tonio in a pact that could never be broken. They said their goodbyes and stepped out into the storm.

CHAPTER 16

PANDORA'S BOX

AIX-EN-PROVENCE, JULY 1944

Marie-Madeleine

Marie-Madeleine checked over the Aix-en-Provence apartment. There was a time when she'd have made a shallow inventory of her hosts' class and taste from what she found. Still her old self couldn't help noticing the tasteful parquet floors and silk rugs, the Louis Quinze furniture and the marquetry console. The battered stuffed bear in the children's room was a sudden hammer-blow, but the expensive Alençon lace shielding the empty baby's bassinet was scant protection from evil, and that's what she was here for. Out of respect, she set right the mezuzah on the wall by the door, and focused on an efficient and quick security check.

A fire escape led to a courtyard and exit at the back, and the front door opened to stairs and a shared entrance. The slit of a toilet window was too small even for her emaciated body if she needed to make a quick run for it, but she had just a couple of nights in this place before she moved on, so it was unlikely it would come to that anyway.

In the kitchen, she cut up a fig and made herself eat, washed it down with a black coffee, then sparked up a Gauloise. It was a stupid habit, but she'd started again after Eagle was arrested, and the Brits were generous with supplies on parachute drops.

The doorbell rang three times. She checked her watch: 10 a.m. precisely. Bang on schedule.

'Is this my laundry?' she called through the door.

'Washed and pressed.'

She opened it to Agent Grand Duke. Count des Isnards, her old co-conspirator from her Marseille days, looked the same as ever – the ubiquitous faded jeans, flirtatious eyes primed for mischief, tall and fair with a delinquent's guarded demeanour, as though he was about to get caught for his latest misdeed.

He dumped a large sack on the floor. She checked inside. Huge bundles of documents, critical messages, and a stack of neat banknotes in an elastic band.

'At your service, *patronne*. Plucked off a rock near Saint Raphaël for Operation Popeye in icy rain minutes before the Boche got wind of it. Nearly froze my bollocks off.'

'That would have greatly helped the local female population. You're sure no one saw you?'

'Master of subterfuge.'

'All those affairs have made you an expert.'

'I was young and beautiful. As were you, still are. Seriously, Marie-Madeleine, I'm honoured to do my bit. I always thought you'd do something great, but I must admit it was more along the lines of bagging yourself a stellar husband and making tidal waves in high society.'

'Now it's a matter of staying alive long enough to change the course of history.'

'Speaking of which, you need to leave with me now. My network's buzzing with reports of Operation Guillotine – a lockdown and search of the whole of Aix tomorrow night. They're running around like rabid dogs with all this talk of an Allied landing and they're itching to execute as many *maquis* as they can get their sausage fingers on.'

Marie-Madeleine played through the facts and priorities as she knew them. She shook her head firmly.

'No, you only have your bike with you, and we'd never get this lot transported without rousing suspicion. There are lives at stake in this sack full of documents, and it's a whole twenty-four hours before their clean-up. Pick me up at eight a.m. tomorrow with the car and I'll look forward to seeing Marie-Sol and the old chateau, even in these circumstances.'

'Was the parachute drop gin delivered safely?'

Marie-Madeleine pointed to a crate under the sink. 'Four million francs, nestling amongst Provence's finest charlotte potatoes.'

'Splendid. But what the fuck are you intending to do with all those spuds? They'd feed a maquis camp for a month.'

'Peel them like I'll peel your balls if you don't get out now.'

'Hands off.' He cupped his balls and saluted at the same time.

She couldn't remember the last time she'd laughed.

'Before you go, I need to check for one crucial document,' she said. Please God it was in there as the agent had promised.

She unpacked the sack with trembling hands, and there, at the bottom, was Eagle's jacket. Jackpot! The Eliot Papers were sewn into it, concealed until the critical moment, with just over three weeks to go until 30 July. *Thank the holy lord and all the angels and anyone else who knows me, the network has triumphed on this one, despite everything.*

No time to press Eagle's jacket to her cheek, try to evoke some sense of him from the fine wool, remember how the dark navy matched his intelligent eyes. He'd somehow got this jacket to her over time and through many hands, and she had a job to do.

Grabbing a pair of scissors from the kitchen drawer, she cut the stitches to the lining and the silk documents pooled to the floor. She studied the childlike drawings of a dragon, a house, a star of David and other symbols that presumably only had significance to Eliot and his poor papa. Certainly the most curious documents she'd handled in her time at Alliance.

Marie-Madeleine popped the Eliot Papers into an envelope and gave them to Grand Duke.

'Guard these documents with your life, and deliver them to the abbesse. I've scribbled the coordinates of where she's hiding Eliot Stavinsky on the back. You know the drill – once you've memorised the coordinates, destroy them.'

There was no one she'd trust more with this precious document. Grand Duke touched her gently on the arm. 'You're an inspiration to us all, Marie-Madeleine. You don't have to tell me the strain you're under, we all understand. Any news of Eagle?'

'They haven't executed him yet. Now, get home before curfew and Marie-Sol starts to fret. I'll see you tomorrow first thing.'

Grand Duke left, his lithe, aristocratic figure a reminder of her old, privileged, carefree life, and she was suddenly filled with nostalgia for what might have been. Not for him, but for that spoilt, bored woman she'd been, playing at learning to fly, dabbling in fashion, drawling away on the Paris radio station; anything to defy convention and boredom. For a split second, she longed to run after him and join him and his wife at their chateau for a sparkling evening amongst the servants and chandeliers. But only for a split second. Down to work. She set to getting through the mailbag.

First up, she divided the documents and letters into order of importance, laying out on the study table what she could process today. She took the precaution of hiding the rest around the apartment, in the footstools, behind the mirror, in the leaves of books, and, to save time, a whole stack under a floorboard she prised up, having moved the rug. She made a mental note of the whereabouts of each batch of information she'd secreted, then assessed the current papers in order to begin her message grids.

The minute she sat down, a commotion blew up on the stairs, German voices surging up the stairwell. Her mind tunnelled. She hadn't shot the bolt when Grand Duke had left. Gathering the papers into a hasty pile, she just had time to close the study door and run to the front, where they were already trying the handle. Her slight body against the door was useless.

'German police. Open!' someone shouted as they surged in. Marie-Madeleine counted at least two dozen of them, in grey-green uniform. *Focus.* Each paper she'd left out on the study table was someone dead.

'Where's the man?' they screamed in her face, digging revolvers into her chest. Others with sub-machine guns made a circle around her. She searched the circle for a chink – a flicker of fear, of sympathy.

Fake it. She forced a bewildered look. 'What man? I'm a woman, a woman on her own.'

God, she'd always been a ham actress.

'He definitely came out of this building.' A shiny little boy-scout officer, desperate for his superiors' attention.

Stupid idiot.

'There are other flats here, and no man has crossed my threshold. Why on earth would you imagine he's in the first place you come to?'

'We're wasting time,' said an older officer who seemed to be in charge. Marie-Madeleine clocked his collar for the insignia. Middle-ranking *Oberleutnant.* No real authority.

'Spread out and search every flat now. You stay here and watch her,' he said to the baby-faced soldier.

The kid leaned on the mantelpiece and trained his gun on

Marie-Madeleine. A proper keen little Boy Scout; she'd have to watch out for his hair trigger, but he couldn't look her in the eye. Marie-Madeleine stood in his gunsights, mentally scanning through the document hiding places, including the papers still out on the table in the study. They were a priority. Doors banged, tenants shouted and screamed. The men were whipping themselves up into a pretty frenzy as they rampaged through the building. Boys will be boys.

'Who are you looking for?' she said, careful to add a tone of respect. He liked that.

'A man who's causing us a lot of trouble, a *terrorist*.' He emphasised the word portentously.

'What does he look like?' she asked in a flat voice.

'Tall and fair. The Gestapo call him The Grand Duke. He came into the building about forty-five minutes ago.'

Marie-Madeleine's stomach flipped. They were on to them. Grand Duke was exceptional, a diamond in a jewelled crown of exceptional people. If they lost him it would be tragic, but, more than that, he was carrying location information about Eliot Stavinsky.

'Thank God you're here. To think that a terrorist was in this building!' She sneezed. 'I need a tissue, do you mind? They're just in there.'

He waved his gun by way of permission. In the study she shoved the papers under the divan, and came back out blowing her nose.

'Thank you.'

'It's a cold winter,' he commiserated.

At that moment, the Gestapo chiefs marched back in.

'This woman is lying. We know the couple upstairs, and they say the man was here, in this apartment.'

'They would say that, wouldn't they?' said Marie-Madeleine coolly.

'Then why did you push against the door when we asked you to open it?' asked the Oberleutnant.

'You lot gave me a complete fright! I was terrified it would be maquis terrorists. As soon as I heard you shout German police, I was so relieved.'

He retracted his claws a little, but set his men about searching the apartment.

'Quite right. What are you doing here by yourself?'

Being a woman is the best disguise I have. Keep it plausible, but don't over-explain.

'I hate this war! I came here to get away from the bombing in Toulon, the raids were driving me mad! I thought Aix would give me some peace and quiet, and now all this talk of Maquis, then you bursting in! If you'd just told me you were Gestapo straight away, I'd have been glad of your protection. I've heard how courteous and polite you are compared to those dirty mountain communists.'

Her insides were melting, and his men were still blundering around the apartment chipping the good furniture. The book-case and the footstools remained untouched. She had to keep it relaxed.

'Is there something particular you're hoping to find?'

This man was more stupid than she thought, full of his own importance; he couldn't resist babbling. He gave a terrifyingly accurate description of Grand Duke, his importance within the network. Apparently they were on a mission to annihilate the whole of an organisation called Alliance who were running messages, destroying infrastructure, infiltrating everything. There were also rumours of plans for a weapon that could cause untold damage that 'some Jew' was developing, and Alliance were protecting. Her blood slowed. So it was indeed Alliance, the whole network, and the Eliot Papers they were on to. And they were so painfully close. If he knew who was standing in front of him, she was dead, slowly and painfully, as were many others.

'I do hope you can hunt them down, I won't feel safe until you find them. Is there anything at all I can do to help you?'

'Nothing suspicious, Chief.'

The ferrets were more careless than she'd hoped, thank the holy lord. The Oberleutnant lowered his revolver and handed her a card.

'Here's the address of the office. If you see anyone of his description, or he returns to this building, you must notify us immediately.'

Boy-scout pointed to the Gauloises on the console table.

'Cigarettes are rationed.'

Shit. It didn't look good – it was a year's supply.

'A terrible habit, and I must admit I did make some swaps on the black market. Some people would rather have butter. Are you going to arrest me? Or can I offer you one?'

They were made in England as a prop for British SOE Agents, and Marie-Madeleine put her finger over the anomalous words and betted that they wouldn't notice anyway. They seemed to be in no hurry, and several of them took her up on her offer.

'All those guns are making me nervous. Do you mind?'

Sheer force of will stopped her hand from shaking as she lit up. She took a deep drag and ran every possible escape scenario through her mind. The courtyard was a possibility... a dash out of the front door was a stupid risk. She forced a smile.

The Oberleutnant gave a few brief orders, and the men pocketed their weapons, bored with such small fry as her, and began to muster.

She concentrated on smoking, and betraying nothing to arouse their suspicion, but inside she was beside herself with her success. Just a few more minutes and they'd be gone. Bells rang in heaven, joy surged, and she was so close to getting away with it, it was harder to contain than the fear.

The Oberleutnant gave her a polite bow and repeated his instructions to inform him should the man return.

But Boy-scout was still in the study sniffing about. He crouched on all fours and his arm shot under the divan. The nosy little shit hit the jackpot. Her legs buckled. It was all she could do to stay standing. Boy-scout studied the papers, and thrust them triumphantly under his boss's nose. With that small gesture, he was up for promotion, and she was dead.

Pandora's box opened and, like in a nightmare, the Furies were loosed on the apartment. They found everything, pulled up the loose floorboard, tore open the footstools, shook out the books. Reports fluttered out like flights of butterflies. Each one a life. Thank God Grand Duke had taken the Eliot Papers. If it wasn't so fucking gutting and terrifying she might have laughed. Their eyes were literally goggling.

'*Ach so! Geheim... Sehr geheim!* Secret... top secret!'

They helped themselves to the good cognac in the cocktail cabinet and swilled it down like peasants. Boy-scout handcuffed her. High on looted booze, he fondled her breasts, and she could have bitten him for the disgrace. The Oberleutnant finally showed some discipline over his troops and called him off, but he hurled abuse at her, apoplectic at being duped.

Positive. Losing your cool is a sign of weakness. The scene blurred, then sharpened, and time slowed. It was always going to be at some point, and it was now. Anything else would have been unfair to all the brilliant people who had faced this before her.

The Oberleutnant shook her like a rag doll.

'Who the hell are you?'

Marie-Madeleine drew herself up to full society-goddess stature.

'You're far too unimportant for me to tell you.'

He dug his revolver into her chest. 'You're British.'

'No, French.' *Give them something, but no names. Keep to the bare facts, speak like a soldier, stall for time. There's always hope.*

'When did you get here?'

'Two days ago. I was parachuted in the dark. I am not familiar enough with the territory to give you exact coordinates.'

'Who is the man who visited you?'

'I've never seen him before. We're not given names.'

'The purpose of his visit?'

Marie-Madeleine was firing on all cylinders. She'd read enough directives to make up a million stories on the spot.

'To instruct me about a rendezvous tomorrow in the Place du Marché. I was to meet someone, who'd take me to meet someone else. That's all I know.'

'Where?'

'I was just carrying out orders, on a need-to-know basis. We never know more than our part.'

'Who were you going to meet?'

'A network agent.'

'How will you recognise him?'

Marie-Madeleine was already ahead.

'*He* will recognise *me*. I have a very particular Hermès scarf.'

'What's your name?'

Boy-scout was on a roll; he'd found her identity card. He waved it in the air.

'Germaine Pezet.'

Marie-Madeleine laughed, and that shut him up. 'It's obviously a false name.' She let herself falter and it had the desired effect – they didn't believe her.

'We're wasting valuable time with Madame Germaine Pezet. Lock her down, we'll deal with her later.'

Marie-Madeleine braced herself for a lynching. Two

drunken teenagers in uniform pointed their guns, itching for a kill, and the Oberleutnant had a struggle to stop them. What a loser. There'd be no drinking on the job in her ranks. She stared them both down, fierce as a woman who had nothing left to lose.

But the Oberleutnant wasn't stupid enough not to recognise he had a prize. She needed to convince him that she was too valuable to damage quite yet.

He admonished his trigger-happy halfwits and dragged her into the study. Boy-scout won the prize of guarding the door.

'I'm impressed. You didn't betray the slightest bit of emotion apart from perhaps a trembling of the fingertips. Why are you not afraid?' he said.

'I've done nothing to reproach myself for.'

'Tell me who you are.'

Marie-Madeleine let all the contempt she felt for this man show. She held his gaze until his eyes flickered momentarily away.

'I'm not authorised to negotiate with such a low-ranking officer. I'll tell your commanding officer and no one else.'

'You're lucky, the general is arriving tomorrow morning, and I will arrange for him to see you.'

I bet he will. You've got a big fish gasping for air in your net, and you know it.'

'Pack your bag, you're coming with us,' said the Oberleutnant.

Marie-Madeleine took the precaution of turning the gem of her cyanide ring to the inside of her palm, so it looked like a simple band. Then she threw a few things into her bag, including her Hermès scarf and Schiaparelli perfume. If she was going down, she was going down in style.

They paraded her handcuffed through Aix in the car with the internal light switched on for all to see. Agents she recognised looked away, old ladies crossed themselves as she passed. She was dead meat. At the army camp they drove her through the barbed-wire gate, deep into an army complex, and led her down the grimy steps to the cells.

They filed her past a bare room with a narrow table. A man was tied to it, covered in excrement and blood, screaming for his mother as a soldier approached him with a poker. His face was handsome and young, with dark curls like her son's. Marie-Madeleine swallowed her bile. *Don't show fear.*

They threw her into a stinking cell with a single cot and a soiled bucket, and locked the door. She vomited in the corner for the young lad on the torture table, for Eliot, for Operation Lamb. They hadn't taken her ring, and she reassured herself the cyanide pill was still in there. If she talked, death and destruction was inevitable.

CHAPTER 17

THE MASON'S BAR

MIOLLIS BARRACKS JAIL, AIX-EN-PROVENCE,
JULY 1944

Marie-Madeleine

The heat was unbearable; she was slick with sweat. She sat on
the cot and contemplated the humiliations and torture to come.
They'd walked her past that poor boy's cell on purpose, but she
already knew. She'd read too many gory reports she wished at
this point she hadn't. Hot pins under the fingernails, breasts
mutilated and burned, broken bones and teeth, hanging upside
down by the ankles while soldiers did what they wanted with
you, then they cut you down, and kept you just alive enough to
do it all again.

Marie-Madeleine forced herself to stand up and pace, keep
moving, and run through the scenarios.

No use thinking about any of it until it happened. People
could divorce their minds from their bodies in extremis,
couldn't they? She'd only know if it was possible for her if – no,
face it – *when* it came.

Keep moving. Shit, she was so scared she could barely walk. Don't let the tears come, *fucking no!*

A turquoise bay, diffused sun in the glassy water swirling over white stones dotted with waving urchins. Her newborn daughter's eyes opening, an electric spark of love like lightning. Her son at the top of the cedar tree in their garden at Marseille, the pride at his reckless nerve, the wrench of fear for his safety. The Shanghai colours of her childhood, her mother's embrace, sparkling condensation on a coupe of champagne on a balcony by a sparkling bay. Eagle's intelligent smile, their last night at Tangmere so sweet it hurt, his eyes reflected in their newborn son's. Facing death, she'd never felt so achingly alive.

The church bell tolled the hours, her clarion bell, and the hours slipped away. Six, the angelus, seven, the witching hour, eight... would nine be the time they came for her? Outside, in an impossibly sweet world, people were cooking supper, pulling shutters closed against the heat and the unknown, children tucked up and stories read a hundred miles from this nightmare. No one came. The waiting was terrible. God, she wanted to live. Grief, what might have been, thoughts of her beautiful children exhausted her until she was hollow as a reed. She lay down on the cot and closed her eyes.

A key rattled in the door and she sat bolt upright.

The Oberleutnant stood next to a man with a metal box. He was thin and wiry, with a feral air and a stained shirt. It was the same soldier she'd seen at the torture table earlier.

He lit a cigarette.

'Take your blouse off.'

She didn't move.

'You'll either take it off yourself or, when I've finished, beg me to do it for you,' said the man in a thick southern-French accent. *Traitor.*

The Oberleutnant looked apologetic, but the torturer was alight.

She unbuttoned it. What the fuck was she thinking, Schia-parelli perfume? She wanted more than anything to void her insides right there and then.

'And that.' The man pointed to her bra with his cigarette, making a smouldering red tip with a long drag.

She did so. The Oberleutnant looked away. 'Get on with it,' he said.

'Just a little taster to begin with.' The man pressed his cigarette into her nipple and kept it there. 'Like that?'

Damn it, she couldn't help but scream. Her burning flash stank and all the world was pain. 'I think you're enjoying it more than me,' she managed to spit out through her teeth.

He slapped her hard over the jaw and she screamed again.

'Enough!' said the Oberleutnant. The man left the burning ash where it was, and lit the cigarette again, relishing the smoke.

'Bring the photographs,' said the Oberleutnant, still averting his eyes. The bastard didn't have the stomach for this any more than she did.

The man opened the metal box, pulled out an envelope and handed it to the Oberleutnant.

He opened it and pulled out some photos, wincing, and flicked the top one under her nose. It was Eagle, eyes so swollen they wouldn't open, jaw at a strange angle, dislocated. She looked away. Fucking bastards.

'He's still alive, Marie-Madeleine Fourcade. The general doesn't have much time tomorrow, so we're giving you something to reflect on tonight to speed up what will be a tedious and messy process for us all if you don't cooperate.'

'What do you want to know?'

'Names. Locations. The Eliot Papers.' He waited for a reaction. She gave him none, despite the shock that they actually had the words to describe the documents. 'We'll keep you alive long enough to check, so no funny business. And if you don't care about yourself, your boyfriend here will feel your pain for you.'

He peeled off another picture. They'd mutilated his genitals and his entire body was a bruise. Rusty shackles pinned him to a filthy bed and sores spilled out from the rust.

'Still intact, but only just,' said the traitor. 'We have a very good communications system, so his punishment will be instantaneous.'

She snapped her eyes shut.

'Open them.' He checked his watch. 'We will remain here in silence for five minutes. If you take your eyes off the pictures for one second, something similar will befall you. We'll start with your nails.'

Marie-Madeleine forced herself somewhere else. Flesh was immaterial now, near the end that came to everyone. She still had her mind, and so did Eagle, and that was their last weapon, their own to keep as best they could.

And these people couldn't make wrong right. She let the pictures blur, watched out of the corner of her eye as the Ober-leutnant fidgeted uncomfortably, smelled the unhealthy sweat of the torturer as he eyed her naked breasts, and pulled on the hot rage that was so close to disabling fear. If she wasn't so weak after years of stress and malnutrition, she'd tear them both to fucking pieces for what they'd done.

'It's just a war,' said the Oberleutnant. 'Someone has to win, and there's no point in getting yourself hurt, because if you don't tell us we have enough information from our search yesterday to find someone who will.'

'No one else can tell you what I can. No one knows any more than their single missions,' she said straight away.

If anyone was going down, it was her. It was her fault for not going with Grand Duke when she had the chance, and now she had to take the consequences.

The two of them left. She put her blouse back on and the

light fabric was excruciating on the burn, but she felt safer with it on. A blood and pus stain seeped across the silk and she hugged herself against the terror. Don't crumble, keep your head. You're still here, only a bit hurt. They needed her as much as she needed them.

A moon shadow crept through the gap in the window. She looked closer. The glass was long gone, and a thick board was in its place, nailed to the frame, with a small opening, she presumed in order to let in air for the prisoner. Behind it there was a small gap, then bars. Without tools, there was no way she could remove the board, and even if she could she'd never squeeze through the bars.

What if she did talk? No one knew until it came to it, and no one would blame her. The cyanide pill would be better for everyone.

Not too hasty. She sat down to think. Eagle, her darling, indestructible man, how could they? At her leisure now, she ran the images through her mind, just as they wanted. She gathered what strength she had left, and gave it to him, sent it out across the ether to salve his wounds and steel his resolve.

Bonne nuit, she whispered to the full moon. They always said goodnight to each other whether they were together or not. This would be the last time.

She hinged open her ring. Another piece of incompetence on their part not to strip her of everything, but another advantage of being a woman. The pill was such an inoffensive little ampoule, filled with powder, only the size of a pea but enough to make her heart stop almost immediately. Had she really explored all the options? They might have found their queen, but does a queen give up that easily?

Noises seeped into her cell from the guardroom. Through a crack in the door she spied soldiers coming on and off duty, flopping down on narrow beds, swigging beer and swapping stories.

She hammered on the cell door, and an irritated soldier

came running, riled at having to leave the party. She made him understand she needed the lavatory and he followed her with a gun to the courtyard. Marie-Madeleine made a quick assessment. No bloody chance. The place was in the epicentre of the barracks and she'd never make it. She sat on the toilet trembling – *Breathe* – and let the soldier lead her back to the cell.

Think, think. She needed to sleep, she couldn't sleep. Action. All that was left now was to salvage what she could for Alliance. She hadn't got this far only to let it all collapse at the final hurdle, which she knew would always come. Knowing that compatriots had gone before was a comfort.

Would living kill more people than death? And what about Eliot? They were so close to the date. She'd always imagined she'd never talk, but now she wasn't sure. God knew what they'd do to the queen of Alliance to drain her of everything she knew. And no one knew more than her. What if they found her children?

Then it struck her like lightning. Grand Duke would arrive at the apartment tomorrow morning and walk straight into their trap. He had the Eliot Papers. Even if he didn't talk, they'd find them, then they'd find the blueprints and God knew where that would end.

If she could escape, she could warn Grand Duke and something could be salvaged.

But there was no escape. The pill. If she died at least some people would be saved, and she wouldn't have talked.

She flicked open her ring again. What was it about the human body that will live at all costs? Her hand wouldn't move to take it out. A last act of mind over matter, a pill on the tongue, and... the rest is silence. Easy.

An owl called. One last kiss to the indifferent July moon, to Eagle and her children. She went to the window: and there was a face. A beautiful, ethereal face full of warmth and determination, the soul of Provence. Hallucinating, she squinted through the gap.

'Lilou?' she whispered.

'*C'est moi.*'

'God, it's good to see your face. I can die knowing you're there with me. One last mission for you. You have to warn Grand Duke, Chateau de Vauvenarges. Tell him to clear out immediately.'

'You can tell him yourself.'

'No Lilou. I'm taking the pill, there's no way out and I can't trust myself.'

She hated herself for the shake in her voice, she had thought she'd be bigger than this.

Lilou pointed to the second bar in on the window.

'The bar of freedom.'

'What?'

She pointed to a gap, which on closer inspection was a little wider than the others.

'It's the bar of freedom, a maquis secret. The masons round here always push the bars wider while the concrete's still wet after the final inspection. A country insurance policy.'

Lilou's wild eyes flashed in the Provence night like a deer in the forest. She slipped a phial through the gap in the board.

'You'll have to use this, and go naked so you can slip through. You'll arrive straight out onto the street. Pick your moment. I'll stay near, and owl-call so you know I'm there. It's not your time to die,' she said with all the authority of someone who'd spent their life watching the sky for the messages it had to give.

And she was gone, a night-phantom. Marie-Madeleine was in such a heightened state that she thought for a moment she had been a mirage. But the oil in her hand was real.

It would be easier to just take the pill and lie down. If she was caught escaping— don't think about it. You have to try, Marie-Madeleine. You signed up to this the day you took the baton from Navarre to head up Alliance, the day you faced down all those big beasts who formed the senior committee. Death or glory. Quite possibly both, but she was going down in a blaze.

She dragged the bed over to the window, turned the bucket upside down and stood on it to get a better view.

Lilou was right. Her father had told her that in Shanghai the burglars did the deed naked, having greased themselves in order to slip through narrow gaps. Timing was crucial, as was human error. Eagle had made many unfeasible escapes, and he had told her that there was always some idiot, some chink in the armour, you just had to work out what or who it was and be ready to act.

She'd heard that drowning was easy, once you'd given up hope, that it was sweet and peaceful, and that was how she felt now, with nothing to lose. She was almost certainly going to die, but fear would give her frantic strength, imminent death a clear head.

The soldiers were playing cards now behind the door. They'd had a lot to drink. She looked at her watch: 2 a.m. From what she knew of the workings of barracks, the morning shift would clock on early, around 5 a.m. It was the wee hours of the morning, quiet. They were already prone on their beds, and these boys would be only too glad to get some kip in.

She waited. The hands of her watch were on a deadly go-slow and every second threatened to weaken her resolve. *Keep your nerve*. The sounds from the guard room quietened down, the night was still as a grave.

3 a.m. Those boys could snore for Germany. *Now*. She rapped on the cell door, intending to ask for the lavatory again if anyone came. No one heard her. She slinked off her clothes,

smothered herself in the olive oil, the salve soothing on her burned breast, and crept up onto the upturned potty on the cot. The night air was sweeter than she could ever have imagined.

She squeezed between the board and the bars and studied the mason's gap, the bar of freedom. Thank God she'd lived on Gauloises and black coffee for as long as she could remember. Her head would be the worst, and getting purchase for the thrust out was almost impossible. She shimmied herself into position, the rough board tearing her back, and tested her head on the bars. The iron was uncompromising. Was it narrower than the width of her head? It would take a superhuman push but, if she could bear the pain, the rest of her body would follow. Wrenching her body into as good a position as she could, her hair and skin slick with olive oil and the sweat of terror, she closed her eyes, and pushed with all her might. Her head was through! A headlight swept metres away. She was pinned like an insect. She twisted her head back through, felt an ear tear, blood pouring. The pain was excruciating. Claustrophobia stole her breath till she was gasping, and her heart thumped like a funeral drum.

A German voice hailed the driver. It was a sentry, posted a few metres to the right. She hadn't seen him, fuck! He shouted to the convoy and gave them directions. It had missed its way. Thank God, it turned round and headed back the way it had come. From the papers she'd studied yesterday, a lifetime ago, she ascertained it was a unit they knew were being sent to the Normandy front. Marie-Madeleine had already warned the maquis, and they'd laid their booby traps. This convoy would never make it to the front in the north. The thought gave her the strength she needed.

She thrust her head back through the bars, skinning her nose and forehead. Warm blood trickled into her eyes. She blinked furiously, her arms still trapped. She'd have to be quick.

She pulsed forward, inching till her shoulders and arms were through. Her burnt breast scraped painfully on the bars, but with her arms free it was easier to pull herself forward. Her displaced hips were agony; they could slip right out of the joints as she wriggled forward. She was half in and half out, bent at an excruciatingly twisted angle. She closed her eyes and inched forward and, when it got to her legs, she was out like a baby flying from a womb.

Beached on the pavement for a moment, she gasped the air, stayed flat on her stomach and searched like a bug for a dark space to scuttle into. An owl called to her left and she scurried on all fours towards the sound. In the alleyway, there was Lilou, poised and quivering, like a cat ready to pounce.

'You did it! Just hold my hand and trust me.'

Lilou's warm fingers folded around Marie-Madeleine's icy, trembling paw and led her through the dark.

Sweet, sweet freedom, despite the ground spiking her feet and the air freezing the sweat and blood to a noxious crust. They came to a cemetery and ran through neat rows of looming crypts and tombs. Marie-Madeleine silently saluted the dead who'd faced what she wasn't ready to. When the time came, she wouldn't be afraid.

Lilou pulled her deep into the cemetery, gestured for her to wait, unlocked the door of a mausoleum and pulled her in, slamming the door behind them. Inside were two tombs covered in dusty pall-cloths, the memorial ephemera of country lives lived, and fresh flowers. Safe. She sat on the cold floor and shook violently.

'Catch your breath,' said Lilou, gently helping her to her feet. 'Just stand there a second.'

Lilou shook the dust out of the pall-cloths covering the tombs, and with a few deft folds she draped one round Marie-Madeleine, knotting it at her shoulders. A worn bridle made her belt, and the second cloth a shawl to cover her arms.

'That's the best outfit you've ever made for me,' said Marie-Madeleine.

'It's your colour,' she said, hugging her. 'My aunt on Papa's side, it's her mausoleum. She would have been honoured to help.'

Marie-Madeleine's teeth were still chattering like crazy. Lilou squeezed tighter.

'Ai! That hurts!'

Lilou jumped backwards. 'Sorry. You just looked like you needed it. We hug our newborn lambs to keep them alive when they've lost their mamans.'

Lilou smelled like herbs and wool and her bony arms were balm, but outside the sky was beginning to turn.

'I could curl up in your skinny arms and sleep like a baby with you here to protect me, my angel girl. But we can't stop here, they'll be checking my cell at first light and then they'll lock the whole city down. We have to get to Grand Duke before he leaves at seven thirty a.m., or the Eliot project is lost. How far is it from here, how much time have I got?'

Lilou peeped outside to study the sky. 'Five forty-five a.m.' As she said the words, the church bells rang out the quarter-hour. 'They'll have dogs, and they're well trained. I've seen them scent a cache of explosives at a hundred metres. They'll have your clothes from the cell, and fear is the highest smell there is for trackers. We'll have to find a stream for you to wash in. Do you know the way to his house?'

'It's a chateau and farm, on the road to Vauvenarges. The only way I know is across the bridge, and they'll be all over that like demons.'

Lilou whispered some kind of oath to her aunt's tomb in Provençal dialect.

'The Mistrals have lived here for generations, and the knowledge they've passed down will help us. I know all the signs to find a river. It can't be far from here.'

. . .

The world was waking up, cars and trucks mustering on the roads outside. She might have made a miraculous escape this far, but most agents were caught on the run. The elation of freedom made them careless, and the advantage of surprise that helped spring them free was quickly overcome by their pursuers once the alarm was raised. She was not going back to that hell-hole. It was her and Lilou against the pack.

'Wait here,' said Lilou. She stood outside and listened, watched for the direction of the water birds, tuned in to the land.

The dawn chorus bubbled up in the gold of a Provençal dawn. Another sweet day alive. For Lilou the dawn was full of information.

'OK,' said Lilou. 'I think I know where it is. Follow me. There'll be stones and jumps and your feet are already cut, but a fox can evade the hounds if it keeps its nerve.'

'I've danced three nights running with feet worse than this,' said Marie-Madeleine. 'Lead the way.'

Marie-Madeleine's finishing school education was nothing on what Agent Patou knew. She found a tributary to the river as instinctively as a kingfisher. It was shallow and rocky, and Marie-Madeleine plunged into the freezing water. She must stink of fear, and she was covered in blood and bruises, but Lilou gently helped her wrap the makeshift dress back around her while her teeth chattered.

'Keep going. We'll follow this creek and come to the river. Fear gives you speed. Use it,' said Lilou.

They scrambled through the undergrowth, Lilou slashing what she could with a knife, until they came to the river, right underneath the bridge. Shit, shit, shit, they were crawling all over it, just above their heads, dogs, trucks, soldiers everywhere.

She and Lilou ducked behind a boulder, stayed close to the shadows.

Downriver, women were filing into a stubbly field.

'Come on, you'll pass, even without shoes,' whispered Lilou.

The women were gleaning, picking through a few old cauliflower stumps that the farmer had rejected last harvest. The two joined them, doubly invisible as women *and* poor. It was the only good that had come out of this war; the likes of Marie-Madeleine had learned that snobbery was just ignorance. The women looked up at the soldiers on the bridge, and at Marie-Madeleine's bruised face and cut feet, and silently turned back to their work, surrounding her and Lilou, moving them away from the bridge towards the river.

'Where do we cross?' asked Lilou. She gave them Grand Duke's name, Helen des Isnards, and they knew the place exactly. One of the women gave Marie-Madeleine a pannier dotted with a few meagre pickings she'd collected.

'Here, take these. They're used to seeing us here and no one'll stop you dressed like that carrying the gleanings. You can cross about a hundred metres from here, there are stepping-stones.' She looked Marie-Madeleine up and down. 'Watch your step, mind, it's slippery this time of year. My son's up in those hills somewhere, good luck to you both.'

'Thank you, courage to you all and vive La France,' said Marie-Madeleine.

The river was high, but the stepping-stones were still visible, and Marie-Madeleine barely felt the cold. Lilou helped steady her, arms as strong and slim as hazel.

They scrambled up the banks and, at the top, the road to Vauvenarges greeted them like an old friend. They skirted along it, a barefoot woman carrying a gleaning basket in a makeshift dress, and a willowy country girl with a confident gait and a blond crop. Nothing to see here. The church at the crossroads was the church of Sainte Marie-Madeleine. Finally a landmark she remembered very well.

'It's this way, but it must be ten years since I visited and everything looks so different with all the landscape ravaged and the signs changed. Damn it all to hell, I wish I had your instincts. We're so close but my chauffeur always drove, and I never took much notice of directions. What time is it now?'

Lilou glanced up at the sun.

'It must be nearly seven fifteen.'

'We have to get to them in the next ten minutes, and it could be any one of these farms.'

On the plain below, olive groves, cypress trees and dry-stone walls dotted the landscape, to Marie-Madeleine an indistinguishable jumble. She searched it desperately for a familiar sign.

'They're rich?' asked Lilou.

'Very,' said Marie-Madeleine, slightly ashamed.

A motorcade rumbled in the distance, dogs barked. They were on the road advancing towards them. They'd tear her limb from limb if they found her.

'We've got to keep moving,' said Marie-Madeleine.

Lilou ignored her, standing still and imperturbable as a falcon focusing on its prey.

'It's that one, two fields away,' she said. 'It's the only one with straight hedges.'

They dropped down, made their way through an olive grove, along a stony path, and, as the motorcade stopped at the crossroads, they ducked through thick undergrowth.

The front door to Grand Duke's house was unlocked. *Careless*, thought Marie-Madeleine as she and Lilou stumbled into the grand entrance hall. The count and his wife rushed down at the noise, stark naked and beautiful.

'Thank God you're still here. I've just saved your lives, and hundreds of others. We have to leave straight away. Where are the Eliot Papers?'

The count looked stricken.

'I left them at the apartment, I thought they'd be safer there till I could pick you up in the car. I was due to leave in five minutes.'

Marie-Madeleine collapsed, and everything went black.

CHAPTER 18

THE BROKEN VIRGIN MARY

AIX-EN-PROVENCE, JULY 1944

Lilou

It was too dangerous to stay together. Lilou had waved goodbye to a deathly pale Marie-Madeleine, who was in shock as Grand Duke hastily packed up the car, bundled in his pregnant wife and two-year-old little girl and whisked them all off up into the hills to hide out with the maquis. Lilou had been appalled to see Marie-Madeleine's naked body, painfully skinny, bruised and burnt from torture, childbirth, grief and the huge burden of responsibility she carried. But she was unstoppable. Effective, uncompromising and focused as an arrow. Lilou knew jail would never contain her; all she had needed was the chink of hope Lilou gave her through the prison window. The bar of freedom was a lie, but it worked.

Grand Duke dispatched a farmhand to rush Lilou to the train station at Aix. If they hurried, she'd make the eight thirty train, and there was a small chance she could get to the abbé in time to transmit a message to warn the abbesse and Eliot.

The train was packed with German soldiers on the move, checking papers, roughing up anyone who dared to defy them. The bubbling, impotent resentment was everywhere, a tinderbox of French petty rebellions and German reprisals. Everyone kept themselves to themselves, unheard of before the war, when the carriage would have been alive with people passing round packed lunches, news and gossip. But now, suspicion reigned. Was the old lady knitting in the next carriage an informer? The young lad with the darting eyes, was he running messages, terrified the office worker in the fedora was a German about to arrest him?

Lilou rolled her sleeves over her scratched arms, folded her hands in her lap to cover her torn dungarees, and kept her eyes down. Surely they'd hear the voices screaming in her head? What if the Germans already had Eliot? What would they do to him? Would they tell him his mother was dead, torture his papa in front of him – or worse, the other way round? Axles turned, pistons hissed, wheels clicked in a rhythmic nightmare, *he's dead, he's dead, he's dead,* until she wanted to scream out loud for it to stop.

At Vallon-Doux the town was going about its business, but there was change in the air. After D-Day, the tide was turning. The three girls from the boulangerie were walking through the square, arm in arm, giggling as they always did, but the first wore a blue dress, the second a white and the third, her redhead ally, wore a red dress – the French flag. The redhead gave Lilou the faintest acknowledgement with a flick of the eyes as they passed.

Lilou rushed past them. If Eliot and the abbesse were exposed now, just as the tide was turning, it would be a disaster.

The abbé's church bell struck three. Almost twenty-four hours since the Eliot Papers had fallen into German hands. Lilou stepped into the church, threw a silent prayer at the Virgin Mary to protect her little child and called out for the abbé. He was nowhere to be found. The door to the steeple was unlocked. Uncharacteristically careless. She took the winding stairs two at a time. The radio case was open, the microphone still crackling. What the hell was he playing at? She hastily shut it down and ran downstairs into the crypt and squinted through the gloom. A cough gave him away.

'Father Aloïsi?'

She found him slumped on the floor in a far corner with his head in his hands, a smashed statue of the Virgin Mary at his feet.

He looked up in a daze. 'I'm sorry,' he said.

'Eliot?!' She already knew somehow.

'Those bastards swooped in the minute they got their hands on those documents. The abbesse was transmitting to me when they stormed the place. She wouldn't have had time to hide the radio set. A maid escaped and got word to us. The abbesse is arrested, they dragged Eliot screaming from Scout. He attacked, and they shot him right in front of the boy. The last she saw of him was a soldier dragging Eliot off sobbing so hard he couldn't breathe.'

CHAPTER 19

THE CAT-BOTHERER

VALLON-DOUX, JULY 1944

Lilou

Lilou plunged into the swimming hole at Montferrat to wash away the horror and try to think straight. The place was always deserted, and the water was just the same implausibly translucent jade as it ever was. She used to think it was like a fairy pool, scintillating and glassy, dewdrops trickling into the water and ruffling the surface from the gentle waterfall that fed it. Now new frames of reference skewed everything: the water glowed the mineral of Tonio's phosphorescent instrument dials, the rocks glowered, trees creaked and the world was toxic.

She ducked and surfaced, heaved in a breath. It used to make her feel newborn, but now the freezing mountain water intensified her ache for Eliot, made her skin raw. Lilou longed for him, his trusting head on her chest, growing heavy with sleep, his hot hand on Scout's warm coat for reassurance, wary brown eyes trying to make sense of everything, his contempt of the adults who were incapable of understanding the glaringly obvious. Was he cold? Had they let him keep his satchel with his *Little Prince* manuscript and notebook with all his numbers, the star she'd sewn? Was he still wearing his pyjamas, had they forgotten the clothes she'd made for him? *Please, Eliot, don't be rude or difficult with them, they'll hurt you. Just wait for me on your planet, little astronaut, block it all out like you've always tried to.*

The last time she was here, she was with Freddie, not much more than a year ago, and they still had absolutely no idea of the atrocities that were to visit their little part of the world. Scout was Freddie's dog. They'd both trained him from a puppy the way Papa had taught them, and he was the noblest soul she'd ever known. He'd guarded Eliot with his life; which was more than she'd done and, if there was one certainty in life, it was that a Mistral protects their own.

She dried off and put her dungarees back on, then took *The Little Prince* manuscript out of her rucksack. Was there a clue in here, hidden in the text, in the charming line drawings of stars and planets, flawed archetypes and universal wisdom?

Why did Eliot's copy have an extra dragon chapter? Was there some sort of code in it, or had his papa just indulged him using a character he loved? She stared at it till her eyes watered, but, if there were any secrets, the pages refused to yield them.

She trudged home. The oak woods were a tinderbox and the bleak sun sucked everything dry. She still hadn't slept after her night with Marie-Madeleine, so the abbé had persuaded her to go home and get some sleep so she'd be ready to act on any new intelligence. She wouldn't leave until he'd sworn to her that he'd man the radio in the steeple for any news, and come and get her immediately he heard anything. He'd agreed, but he was just being kind. Eliot could be anywhere, transported even. She was dizzy with grief and exhaustion when she got back to the farm, but she couldn't bear to sleep, not when Eliot was somewhere out there. Everything was a reminder. At the end of the track there were no bright eyes and wagging tail to greet her with unalloyed joy, in the fields the lavender was dried and greying with no one to harvest it, and Maman's shadow retreated from the window as she approached, to fade away and shut itself in a dark room until her stolen son returned.

She couldn't bear to go into the house, so she went to the beehives, and sat on the old chair that Papa had made to watch them come and go. They were nearly all home now, with the light fading. Another sunset, another night for Eliot away from his parents, another night for Lilou away from Eliot.

Inside the hive they'd be working away, transforming the fat of the land into sustenance, like country people always have. A few stragglers meandered in, the sun turned the mountains orange and everything that had ever meant anything to her was lost. She stayed there until it was dark and the dew chilled her bones. She looked down the track for the abbé's Renault straining over the potholes with news, but nothing. Just silence, the owls mournful and sinister, the boars snuffling in the trees.

It was gone midnight by the time her mind relinquished control to her body for a fitful sleep, only to be woken by the abbé outside the window singing a tuneless and respectful 'Morning Has Broken'.

Lilou leapt out of bed and ran to the door. He was standing there, a big bear with a pistol shoved carelessly in his belt.

'Have you heard anything?'

'It seems your cat-botherer has come up trumps.'

'Kristian?'

The abbé looked surprised. His name had come a little too easily to her lips. 'Until now I've known him as Air Commodore Meyer. He contacted me on the radio last night. He couldn't say much, but he says he knows where Eliot is, and for you to meet him in Nice on the Promenade des Anglais this morning. I'll drive you there and keep a safe distance.' He tapped his pistol. 'I'll keep this on me in case he tries anything. He's given us a

specific location, the Hotel Negresco, which will be crawling
with German soldiers, so you'll need to wear something that
looks more like you're a collaborator meeting her boyfriend, and
less like a wild girl who's about to sneak through the undergrowth to annihilate them all.'

Lilou hugged the abbé and kissed him on both cheeks. 'So
there's still time, Eliot's still in the south?'

He pushed her away. 'On with you. We don't know, it might
be a red herring, but it's all we've got. The commodore seemed
earnest enough, but you can't trust the Krauts as far as you
could throw them.'

I sort of know I can trust this one, thought Lilou as she
rushed to her sewing room. She knew just the thing to wear. A
red dress, plunging neckline, ruched bustier, fitted waist and
pleats. Marie-Madeleine had commissioned it a lifetime ago,
but had no use for it now. There was a matching pillbox hat that
would look the part. Shoes would be trickier, she'd have to wear
her espadrilles, but very few people had matching outfits *and*
shoes in these times.

Lilou looked at herself in the mirror. Not bad. The pillbox
hat actually went with her short crop, and she was tall, so the
flat espadrilles didn't look too awful. She'd pass.

The abbé's Renault was in a bad way, there were roadblocks
everywhere, and progress was so slow. They passed the journey
in tense silence until the sun was high, and the Notre-Dame de
Nice struck twelve as they drove into town.

The abbé dropped Lilou a few hundred metres away, and
Lilou hurried to the hotel, saddened by the once-grand boulevard. Most of the elegant old buildings were boarded up, and
the beach was littered with barbed wire, artillery, sandbags and
rusting metal. German soldiers promenaded with girls on their
arms, or in groups, laughing and mucking about. They could
have been Freddie and his friends, but Lilou knew the reprisals
here had been terrible since D-Day, and they'd hanged Resis-

tance fighters from the streetlamps in the arcades as an example. What happened to men in war?

Kristian had already spotted her when she saw him sitting at a table outside the grand hotel.

'You look beautiful,' he said, pulling her close and kissing her lightly. 'My apologies, everyone's watching and it's safer this way,' he whispered into her mouth. When he stopped, she felt like she'd surfaced from a mountain pool. They held each other's gaze, his eyes a forest in autumn, and he gestured for her to sit, then took a seat opposite her. He held her hand across the table, leaning in close enough to whisper sweet nothings. She wondered guiltily if the abbé could tell she meant it from his vantage point.

'Do you know where Eliot is?'

'They're holding him in my barracks in Nice. I'm part of the deciphering team. They needed an astronomer to help interpret the documents.'

The relief warmed her bones. He was alive, and, miracle, he had an ally at his side in Kristian. 'Thank God. How is he?'

'Silent, scared. Apart from when he saw me. He told me off for being in the fucking German forces. He was so angry. I managed to get to him before he could say he knew me, but he doesn't trust me. Who can blame him?'

Lilou laughed and cried at the same time. 'Is he hurt?'

'Apparently he went crazy when they shot Scout, and it took two men to restrain him. He's got bruises around his wrists, and a cut on his forehead where he banged it in the struggle, but apart from that he's unharmed. They're trying to gain his confidence to get information, so, thank God, so far he's all right, at least physically, and I've been guarding him with all my might—'

He broke off as the waiter put two cocktails on the table.

'Can we get him out of there?'

They chinked their glasses and leaned in. There were

German officers everywhere, bantering at the bar, playing drinking games at the table, eyeing her up like she was fair game.

'Keep looking at me,' said Kristian. 'I've got a plan. Not a very good one, but we have to try. God knows what they'll do to him once they've got what they want. Take a couple of sips and we'll promenade.'

They linked arms, the sea indifferent to the barbed wire and sandbags, clear and deep, the ripples sparkling shards.

'I know from past experience how long their patience lasts in a soft interrogation, so it has to be today. It's risky, but I'll be there with you the whole time. I've told them I've deduced that your farm is the geo-location they're looking for. They're travelling there with Eliot now. That's why I asked the abbé to get you out of there, so we can prepare.'

Lilou's mind raced. The Germans trampling all over her home again in their jackboots. Maman would be out pounding the roads at least.

'We have to get back there now!' she said.

'That's the plan. They're banking on surprising you, and I'm banking on Eliot running to you when he sees you, so that will confirm my theory to them, that he's familiar with the place, and that the Resistance placed him with you because of the location. As the sun goes down, I'll persuade them that they need to let me accompany you to the escarpment, the site of the geo-location, and for you to coax the final coordinates from Eliot. Once we're out of sight, you can escape into the hills and I'll tell the Kapitän that there was an ambush. I won't ask where the maquis are located, but I'm sure you know. All I ask is that you somehow inform the abbé that you are both safe. I'll maintain radio contact with him until I know that you and Eliot have escaped, and then I'll disappear forever.'

'Don't you dare. After all this is over you have to find me.'

'I'm not sure how many of us are going to survive this shitshow. It looks like we're on the losing side now and they're chucking us up in the sky like metal filings. Some of us will come back, some won't.'

'I don't even know how old you are.'

'Twenty-two.'

'And you're being asked to accept death for a cause you don't believe in?'

Kristian kicked a pebble down the promenade. 'Correct. Somehow we're all in this together, the good, the bad, and the ugly. Born in the wrong time and the wrong place. Someone else's war. Mine to fight. If we save Eliot, I'll have made one small difference, put one wrong right, and I'll die knowing that.'

'Don't talk like that. There's always hope.'

Kristian stopped. 'And there's always you. If there's another world, I hope you're in it.'

Lilou put Kristian's arm round her, leaned her head on his shoulder, and the sea dispersed the sun's rays and threw them back in constellations.

When Lilou returned to the abbé's car, he looked at her quizzically.

'I always wondered who would capture my wild Lilou Mistral's heart. It's a shame he's a Kraut, but I'm trusting he has other qualities.'

'I was just playing a part,' said Lilou. She wasn't about to admit to anyone, least of all the abbé, how she'd felt like melted snow in Kristian's arms, how the world had iced over again when he'd said goodbye.

Kristian followed them back in his army car, staying as tight behind them as he could. Lilou explained the plan to the abbé, every now and then checking in the rear-view mirror. Whenever she looked, he was always there, ready to catch her eye.

By the time they got back to Vallon-Doux, it was already dusk. Kristian veered off to check into the Hotel des Chasseurs and give them time to go ahead, and, when they reached the farm track, sure enough there was the German truck, as Kristian had planned.

As they approached, Doll-face emerged, flanked by Schmidt and another soldier, and in front of them was Eliot, standing very still, trying not to cry, dressed in trousers that were too short for him and a jacket that drowned him. Surplus from a child who hadn't made it? She shuddered.

Doll-face pushed him forward. 'Do you know this woman?'

Eliot hesitated, unsure. Lilou crouched to his height and threw her arms wide. 'It's all right,' she said, smiling through tears, overwhelmed that *he* was trying to save *her*.

He ran, buried her head in her chest, and she lifted him up and hugged with all her might.

'It's all right, I'm here, don't cry.'

'They killed Scout,' he sobbed.

She set him on his feet and brushed him down, wiped away his tears with her skirt.

'I know, I heard,' she whispered. 'He died doing his job, protecting you, and that would make him happy now he's in heaven.'

'Heaven is stupid,' said Eliot.

'There are good people, too,' said Lilou, thinking of Kristian.

'So the mad dog was yours,' said Doll-face. 'You led us a pretty dance, didn't you, looking all coy and innocent and fresh when you were hiding this little piece of filth all along.'

Eliot's hand started to tremble in hers.

'With good reason, it seems,' said Lilou. 'The poor child is terrified. If you've hurt him, I'll—'

'His kind have fewer sensibilities.'

'Just tell me what you're doing here, and what you want with Eliot,' said Lilou, also shaking, but with pure hate for him, his ignorance and his power over them.

Just then, a black car crawled up the drive. Kristian.

'Ah, just the man,' said Doll-face, lighting up. 'Our Aryan astronomer.'

Kristian clearly had his complete trust, admiration even.

'He'll take it from here. All you need to do is keep the brat calm, and follow instructions. We'll do the rest.'

Kristian saluted Doll-face with a Heil Hitler. Doll-face slapped him on the back. 'Bullseye, my friend. You were right, the girl was obviously hiding him at some point, and the boy knows her. Good work.'

Doll-face crouched down to Eliot. 'Now, you do what the nice man says and nobody will get hurt. Your friend here will hold your hand, and you just need to remember what your papa told you and we can all go home.'

Doll-face stretched his mouth over his teeth in his version of a smile. This overfed drunk trying to be nice was more chilling than him spewing racial hatred. But he believed Kristian's story and that was all that mattered now.

'Do you have the symbols?' said Doll-face.

'Yes, sir,' said Kristian.

He reached inside his jacket, and showed them two silk squares printed with pictures. Lilou recognised them immediately; the same drawings that were in Eliot's extra dragon chapter in his *Little Prince* manuscript, but all out of order. It was an effort not to look surprised. What did they mean?

'Now,' said Kristian. 'You say you don't remember, but do you think Lilou could help you? If you whisper to her, she can keep your secret safe.'

Eliot looked sceptical, and stayed silent. A blush of anger travelled up Doll-face's neck.

'You will speak when spoken to.'

'Yes, sir,' said Eliot in a very small voice.

Kristian put his arm round Eliot's shoulder. 'I'm going to take you up there.' He pointed to the escarpment. 'There's a constellation your papa told you about, isn't there? If it's just me and your friend Lilou, would you be less afraid? Shall we go and look and see if you can remember?'

Eliot nodded. Good boy, clever kid.

Doll-face flicked a nod at Kristian to release them. They started walking, Lilou and Eliot in front, Kristian pacing behind. They walked through the courtyard, past the hives, along the stony path alongside the dying lavender and up onto the escarpment, the sky a pincushion of stars. None of them dared to speak, and the ten-minute walk was the longest of Lilou's life, heart pounding in her ears, Eliot's hand cold in hers, stumbling on the rocks in the dark in shoes that weren't his.

At the rock they used to sit on to watch the sunset, they stopped. Below them, a gully. Lilou ran through the route in her head, the way down on the edge of the gully screened by oaks, double back under the rock, then onto the secret byways she'd known all her life.

'This is it,' said Kristian. 'Goodbye.'

Lilou turned to face him, but Doll-face and Schmidt had followed them, close enough to shoot. In the moonlight, a lumbering figure appeared behind them, straining to run, brandishing a pistol. The abbé! A shot rang out and Doll-face fell. The abbé ducked as Schmidt pulled his gun and missed. The abbé sidestepped into a dark thicket, disappeared from view. Lilou knew the way he would take; beyond there was a road where his car would be. Please God he made it!

'Run!' hissed Kristian to Lilou. Then to Schmidt, 'Pursue the gunman, I'll bring down the woman and child!'

Lilou was already running, with Eliot on her back, limbs fizzing, not even feeling his weight. Kristian followed them so far and fired a shot in the air. She looked back, and he urged her on.

Another shot in the distance, a different register from the abbé's old pistol. *Not him,* please let it be Schmidt, not the abbé.

Eliot clung to her so hard it hurt, and she was so afraid that they'd be stopped in their tracks when they'd got this far that she couldn't think straight. But her feet knew the way. The old paths she'd walked all her life seemed to will her forward, all obstacles removed in her honour, the land of her forefathers urging her into its secret places, away from occupiers and inter-lopers. Or perhaps the animal instinct to survive was a kind of magic. It didn't matter. She took a zigzag route, and reached the cave that only she and Freddie knew about, and set Eliot down. She hugged him tight, felt his heart pulsing fast and furious.

'Kristian had the maps, does that mean Papa is dead? And what about Maman?' said Eliot.

'We don't know,' whispered Lilou.

Eliot let out such a cry of anguish she had to clamp her hand over his mouth. She rocked him until he stopped shaking. The cave was dark, and as silent as a country place could be with all the nocturnal comings and goings and she held him close, their own refuge from the world.

'Hush. We're safe now. You're never going to see those soldiers again and we'll do our best to find your papa.'

Was now the time to tell him about his mama? Of course not, but he'd have to find out at some point. Kristian was right though, the Germans were losing. She'd heard talk of it in the village square, seen it in the way the Milice began to melt back to their families, say that they'd had no choice but to cooperate with the Germans, that they'd hated them all along. Maybe somehow Eliot and his papa would be reunited again.

Lilou made them a nook to sleep in as best she could, a nest made from grass in the back of the cave. He snuggled into her like a lamb, and they looked out. The moon was new, and there was an explosion of stars.

'That's it!' said Eliot.

'What?'

'Draco, the orange eye. I remember now, from the symbols that Kristian showed me, I remember everything.'

She had Eliot safe, but the blueprints were still there to be discovered. From what Marie-Madeleine had told her, they contained information that could give the Germans the upper hand again. If Kristian had held on to the silk maps, and managed to convince them that there was a raid, maybe there was some way of contacting him, and finding the location, with Eliot's help.

'Your papa knew you were the best person for the job,' said Lilou, kissing his cold forehead. 'He would be very proud of you, wherever he is. Now get some sleep, and tomorrow we'll find somewhere safe to go, and you'll have a whole camp of Resistance boys to protect you.'

'It's the thirtieth of July 1944. That's the date. And I think I can remember the rest, if I can see the symbols again.'

'Sleep, my little astronaut. We'll think about the rest tomorrow.'

They had to keep moving. In the distance the church bell rang 3 a.m. Lilou reluctantly woke Eliot and his eyes snapped open immediately, alert for danger.

'Can you walk a bit more? We have to get as far away as possible to make sure we're really safe.'

'I'd walk 382,000 kilometres to the moon to get away from that arsehole,' said Eliot.

He could still make her smile, even in a dark cave with the Gestapo on their heels. They walked up through the oak forest, keeping away from the trails, knee-deep in dried leaves and forest debris, the boars affronted at their intrusion but not another soul around. They emerged above the treeline scratched and weary, and reached the high pastures where the Patou guarded their sheep, and the air was cooler. The sun laid out a dawn for them that bathed the fields in gold and reminded them that there is always a new day.

They kept walking higher and higher until the fields turned to rocks and the air was cool as a mountain stream. Eliot took off his shoes to tip out the stones. His feet were raw with blisters – whoever's shoes they'd given him were too small – so Lilou carried him on her back. Progress was slow in the rocky terrain. The sun reached its zenith and burned them, searingly hot even at this altitude, but they pressed on until they came to the place. As they approached, the shadow of a man shouldering a rifle disappeared behind a boulder to observe them.

'It's late for lambing,' she whispered.

The man showed himself, rifle cocked.

'I'm Lilou Mistral, and this is Eliot Stavinsky. He's eight years old and he doesn't need to see any more rifles pointed at him. What we need is shelter.'

The man kept the gun trained on them. 'We have snipers everywhere, so don't move. Wait there,' he said, and disappeared.

They huddled together, exhausted and thirsty in the hot sun. She didn't blame them for checking them out before they allowed strangers into their camp. She knew what was up there, just a few metres higher. A kind of natural fortress surrounded by high rocks, with a grassy plateau protected by sheer drops, and a life-sustaining stream that trickled down the mountain even in summer.

Lilou wasn't sure if she'd waited five minutes or an hour by the time a slim woman in camouflage and a belt full of bullets appeared, beaming from ear to ear.

Marie-Madeleine! She scooped them both into her skinny arms and smothered them in kisses.

'My brave little soldier and my spirit of Provence, you're a sight for sore eyes! How on earth did you know where to find us, and how did you spring this little one from the bowels of Nazi hell? Come to my summer abode and tell me every single detail. I thought everything was lost! But here you are, a vision with fire in her eyes and a brave boy who looks far too serious for an eight-year-old! I can't imagine what you've been through.'

She waved over a maquis boy, who scrambled to obey the *patronne*. Marie-Madeleine had a way of making you want to serve her while thanking her for the privilege.

'Carry this poor mite up to the camp, and we'll follow. Go to the stores and cook them up whatever feast you can muster. I want a blow-by-blow account, not a single detail spared.'

Lilou bathed Eliot's feet in the stream, and one of the lads brought them British bully beef and hardtack from the latest parachute drop, washed down with cold mountain water. At this point it was the most delicious food she'd ever eaten, never mind it was British muck. Safe in the midst of the Resistance camp, Eliot carefully assessed the scene from her lap.

One of the lads offered Eliot his camp bed and promised to guard him while he slept. Lilou tucked him in.

'Does Kristian love you?' said Eliot.

'Don't be silly.'

'He does,' he said firmly. 'His eyes go all hot when he's near you and when you speak to him he looks like he's lost something.'

'Time to go to sleep,' said Lilou.

'I'm glad this place is closer to the sky,' said Eliot, curling up and hugging his pillow.

'Why's that?'

'The Little Prince's planet is nearer, and even though it's lonely there's no war there, and maybe they like Jewish people,' he said.

'They love them here, too. They're fighting for them,' said Lilou.

He allowed his eyelids to close at that. Lilou crept out of the tent. Marie-Madeleine was waiting outside, a quizzical look on her face.

'Who is this famous Kristian? That's the second time I've heard his name.'

The two sat by the stream, and Lilou told her everything. It was such a relief to talk about him, to admit how she felt. She knew Eliot was right. Love was a big word, but she felt it, too.

'So you're asking us to contact a German Luftwaffe pilot and get him to help us recover the blueprints for a weapon that in the wrong hands could alter the course of the war? A little far-fetched, even for a girl who believes in augurs and country lore.'

'He's proved himself so many times over. Don't you want to recover the blueprints? In our hands, we'll use them for good.'

Marie-Madeleine regarded her gravely. 'With Operation Dragoon on the horizon, we can't risk Roman Stavinsky's calculations getting into the wrong hands. Even though we have Eliot, who knows what other poor agents are being tortured for intelligence, including Eliot's father, who still hasn't talked.'

'He's alive?' Lilou sent out a prayer for him to stay strong for Eliot.

Marie-Madeleine explained about Operation Dragoon, the D-Day-style operation planned for August to aid the liberation of France from the southern front. US Allies had mustered troops to swell the ranks of the French Liberation Army, take the ports and push forward to join with the northern fronts. The attack was planned by land, sea and air. Lilou concealed a stab of fear for Kristian. He'd be on the front line, but she could never tell him about it.

'What about Eagle?'

'Still incarcerated.' Marie-Madeleine chucked a stone into the stream so hard it smashed in two. 'Nothing I can do about it. I'm only dealing with what I can control. I can send one of the boys to find a way of making contact with your German pilot. We do have some double agents who may be able to get a message to him.' She checked her Cartier watch. 'Twentieth of July, 1600 hours. That gives us ten days until the crucial date. Good work, Agent Patou.'

Marie-Madeleine strode off. She was still bruised and

scarred from her escape and torture, and she'd only been living in this camp for a few days, but she already looked like one of them in the British-supplied army fatigues, the belt cinched tight on her tiny waist.

In fact, not so much one of them, but a general in command. Her orders were taken reverently, and immediately executed. As she walked through the camp, the tough country *maquisards* stood to attention, or brought her intelligence, which was quickly dealt with. Outside her tent, where she'd set up a temporary desk and chair, queues formed and orders were dispatched, lads taking off at a run with whatever task she'd assigned to them. Even the old hunters who hadn't submitted to a woman since they'd outgrown their mothers were grudgingly admiring of her, and mustered their units at a one-word order from her.

Marie-Madeleine had a forcefield of energy Lilou had seen the day she'd recruited her two years ago, and in this country fortress she was the queen bee around whom the whole camp centred.

It was too dangerous for fires, and the camp went to bed with the sun, the nightwatchmen watching the stars and listening out for enemy attacks like the shepherds they used to be. Eliot was still sound asleep when Lilou crawled into the cot next to his. Safe, for tonight, but it wasn't over yet.

CHAPTER 20

ELLIPSIS

BARGÈME, VAR, JULY 1944

Lilou

When Lilou woke, the sun was already high in the sky, and she heard Eliot's husky laugh blending with the birdsong outside. She sank back down into the pillow. It was wonderful to hear him happy again, and unusual for him to trust so quickly.

On the grass outside, Eliot was playing pick-up-sticks with Luc. Lilou recognised him as a Resistance soldier she'd helped the nuns patch back together at the Sainte Roseline convent, one of the lads who'd been delighted by Eliot's butterflies in the cloisters.

Eliot flung himself into her arms as she stood at the tent opening, blinking, then insisted she joined in the game. Swifts darted, the stream played with the sunlight over the rocks and the whole camp was delighted to have a rescued boy in their midst, especially one who'd been snatched from such danger. She knew they'd all guard him with their lives. Like Scout had done.

Marie-Madeleine thrust an acorn coffee into her hand and asked for a swift word.

'I've got good news and bad news. Which do you want first?'

'You choose,' said Lilou.

'The abbé was badly injured during your escape, and was unable to make a getaway. They found the radio in the steeple, too, and smashed it to bits. I'm afraid there are severe punishments for radio operators, especially people they've trusted all this time. The word on the network is that he's already transported. I'm sorry.'

Her rebel priest? Always there for everyone with a foul-mouthed word of wisdom or a well-placed bear hug? He was part of this place, as much as the oak forests and the boars and wolves, impossible that he'd be in a prison camp, in hell.

'How many more can they take?' Lilou said.

'They've already taken the cream of a generation, but each and every one of them has made a difference, reminds us that there is love and hope in the world. The abbé will go knowing that he saved Eliot's and your lives, that his sacrifice was worth it. He's a tough old boot. so don't give up hope. If anyone can survive that nightmare, he can.' She re-pinned her chignon. 'Now, we still have work to do.'

'I just can't believe he won't be there any more.'

'It doesn't pay to dwell,' Marie-Madeleine cut in. 'We'll repay his sacrifice by winning the war. Now, to the good news.'

'Yes, *patronne.*' Lilou spirited the abbé into a little part of her heart to grieve later.

Yesterday's rapturous welcome for the conquering farm girl and the little Jewish boy had disappeared. Lilou understood. Marie-Madeleine was responsible for so many lives, she couldn't allow herself the luxury of grief. That was for firesides, carefree café tables, and anecdotes about the men who used to occupy the empty chairs in the village bar, at some nebulous time in the future when the world stopped burning.

'The same agent who brought intelligence of the abbé has made contact with your Luftwaffe pilot, and he's willing to cooperate. He still has the Eliot Papers.'

Thank God, Kristian, you've still got them, there's still a chance. 'What's the plan?' asked Lilou.

'Do you have somewhere you can hide out for nine days? Much as the lads love having a Provençal pixie in their midst, you're another mouth to feed, and a potential risk. We'll keep Eliot here with us, and you can liaise with the German as you see fit. We'll deliver Eliot to you on the thirtieth of July and the three of you can retrieve the documents as his papa instructed.'

'I'm not letting Eliot out of my sight for another second,' said Lilou fiercely.

Marie-Madeleine's eyes blazed. 'You will do exactly as I tell you. I will NOT tolerate insubordination. Especially not at this vital juncture. Those are your orders.'

'But why wait?' she dared to ask.

'The coordinates relate to a certain celestial alignment, which happens on a specific time and date. It's the longitude method, the way that sailors and navigators have pinpointed their whereabouts for centuries. It has to be that exact date and time for the geo-location coordinates that Roman Stavinsky has left us to work.'

Lilou was lost. How could she leave him again?

Marie-Madeleine subsided. 'You must see that we can't have you here while you're liaising with a German officer, however much you have him under your spell. And Eliot is safe here with us. It's only nine days. Our agent in Paris informs us that Eliot's father is likely to be transported, and with the Gestapo on the back foot we are planning an ambush before they can get him on the train. There's every chance that Tonio can fly Eliot to Switzerland to be reunited with his papa on the thirty-first of July, once we have the blueprints in our possession.'

It was a triumph of hope over experience, and they both knew it. If they managed to save Roman Stavinsky, he'd be one of the very few lucky ones, but Marie-Madeleine and her team had already achieved some unlikely rescues. If his father didn't make it, Lilou decided, she'd take Eliot herself and walk over the Alps to freedom.

'I have my refuge in Bargème, close to where you dropped Eliot for the first time. It's just down the mountain from here, so I'll be near enough to liaise when the need arises,' said Lilou.

'Give me the exact coordinates. I know the village, it's a friendly one, and most of the lads in this camp are from around these parts. We'll ask them to put the word around not to trespass onto the surrounding area, and to let the German officer pass un-hampered, as long as he travels alone. We'll give him a series of safe-words he can use each day, until the thirtieth of July, no longer. After that, you're to cut all ties and you will be taken to an undisclosed location for your own safety. Arrangements will be made to transport Eliot away from France with Tonio de Saint-Exupéry. We can't have responsibility for a child with Operation Dragoon on the horizon, and he's seen enough for a lifetime already.'

'What about your children?' said Lilou.

'They're being well cared for,' Marie-Madeleine said tersely.

'Thank you for everything, all you've sacrificed.'

Marie-Madeleine brushed it off with a wave of her hand. 'I don't expect thanks, just unquestioning loyalty, please. And Patou...'

'Yes?'

'You're sure you can trust this man?'

'With all my heart.'

. . .

Lilou had to prise Eliot's fingers from her one by one when it was time to leave later that day.

'You're a liar! You said you'd stay with me!'

Lilou wished she could tell him that he might see his papa soon.

'It's only for nine days. That's a chapter a day of *The Little Prince*, up to chapter ten, where your special dragon chapter is. Then Kristian will be there, and he'll have the special pictures to help you remember, and find the hidden treasure that your papa left for you.'

Eliot's eyes lit up. 'Kristian!'

Marie-Madeleine looked at Lilou curiously. 'Quite the happy little family.'

'That's three hundred and ninety-six sunsets for *The Little Prince*,' said Eliot sulkily. 'A long time.'

Marie-Madeleine put her hand out awkwardly for Eliot. 'Come on, let Lilou go and you'll see her soon enough.'

Eliot looked unsure. The lad, Luc, from Sainte Roseline kicked a football for him, but it just bounced off his leg and fell to the ground.

'All right,' Luc said, 'what about you tell me the stories from your favourite book.'

'Only if you promise not to like me too much, I'm leaving soon,' he said seriously.

'Understood,' said Luc.

Eliot kissed Lilou solemnly on both cheeks and left silently. Another goodbye. As she picked her way back down the mountain, she knew that she was being stalked by the *maquisards*. They were good; a shadow the wrong side of a rock, a snap in the undergrowth, but never visible. As she reached the refuge, a change in the air told her the lads had melted away. *Don't let them die*, she whispered to whoever was listening. The worst of it was, some of them inevitably would.

Lilou found the key under the stone where they always left

it, and pushed open the door. Spiders made themselves scarce in the crevices behind pendulous webs, and damp moss was in danger of rotting the windows, but otherwise it was much the same as it always was when they arrived at the beginning of the season. The Mistral sheep would be in their pastures, subsumed into her neighbour's flock, so it was just her and the meadows. She flung open the windows, scraped off the moss, shook out the rugs and made up the bed with the fresh linen they stored with lavender. It was funny, living with it for so many years meant you could no longer smell it, but just the memory of its herbal sweetness, of better times, was enough to lift her spirits.

In the larder there were still jars of cassoulet – unimaginable luxury – pickled vegetables, pulses and Freddie's attempt at home-made wine. Combined with pickings from the overgrown vegetable patch, she'd have plenty to live on for nine days until her final mission with Eliot. Strange that, a year later, here she was in the place where she'd first encountered him.

She was alone here, but never lonely. She knew every rock, the meadows and pastures that surrounded the hut, the family of jays who owned the oak thicket, the boars who vied with her for the vegetable patch, the church bells that rang the hour in the distance from the medieval hilltop village. The last time she'd heard that bell ring was for Monsieur Pascal, the old man they'd shot for answering back at the *fête de transhumance*. It was hard to see where all this would end, easy to hate.

The evening fell slowly, no sign of war, just the mountains to admonish humans for their folly and to catch the sun to make her blush across them.

When darkness fell, she said a silent prayer for the abbé. He'd like that, though she hadn't prayed since Sunday school, and he knew it. How could such a big presence, as much a part of Vallon-Doux as the church building itself, just suddenly disappear? She remembered everything, from the day he'd come barrelling up the farm track through black clouds to anoint

Papa and comfort his grieving family, to the smashed Virgin Mary in the crypt when he'd found out that Eliot was caught. He expected as much from his God as he did from his parishioners. He'd been there at every turning point in Lilou's life. Gone.

She dozed off fitfully in the chair, and woke to knocking at the door.

She leapt up. Had she really heard it, or was it a dream? Creeping into the corner, she opened the rifle cupboard and prayed it was loaded, crept to the door, cocked it and opened.

There in the half-light was Kristian. He put his hands up. 'Don't shoot!'

Lilou laughed in relief. 'I'll shoot if you don't come in.'

He took the gun from her. 'Let me make this thing safe.'

He deployed the safety catch and gave it back. They searched each other's eyes for clues.

'Are you hungry?' she said.

'Starving.'

The air between them was heavy as a summer storm and Lilou wasn't sure who kissed who, but when he carried her to the bed and laid her on the cool linen sheets, she was already naked and the feel of him on her skin was everything in this whispering room, the air like velvet. There had been boys before this, but not like this, a call of the wild, a longing so sweet she cried with the shock and beauty and he kissed away her tears and explored her secret places like jewelled, quiet lakes in hidden depths. Outside, cicadas shimmered the night air with summer carols and the night folded them into its heart and they were lovers for countless times. In the morning, a shaft of sunlight danced in and found them tangled together in mellowed sleep.

When Lilou woke, he was already looking at her, a sleepy smile in his soft green eyes. She hid her head on his chest while he stroked her hair.

'Good morning,' he said. When he smiled, a faint dimple framed the corners of his lips.

She kissed him, and his hands slipped over her body and she was his, every part of her. She knew now it was inevitable, since the moment he'd taken Joseph's glasses and clicked in the lens with precise regret. A soft breeze blew the treetops, and Lilou prayed it wasn't the mistral wind. It always brought change, and Lilou wanted this burnished moment to last forever.

'How long can you stay?'

'I have eight days, until the thirtieth of July. After that, I'm assigned a major mission.'

'What kind of mission?'

He kissed her. 'I don't want to talk about it. We have eight whole days. That's two more than God had to create the whole world.'

In this world, in July 1944, he was right. They might be dead next week.

They raided the stores, ate cassoulet for breakfast in bed and talked till lunch. They told each other stories, compared notes on their favourite poets, sunbathed naked in the hidden kitchen garden and made love against the rough wall, then chased each other with buckets of water from the well, the sun catching the droplets in prisms. Never mind the glowering mountain cliffs in the distance that warned them not to get too close. What did they know? They would be there for millennia. Who knew how long Lilou and Kristian had?

So many rules were broken by the war and any that were left, they broke anyway. They danced in the fields with the moon frowning down disapprovingly. The morning dew woke them in time to sneak home before dawn, when they slept together in the meadow. They lit a fire and toasted last year's chestnuts and dipped them in honey and then fell asleep, naked on the sheepskins, after watching the fireflies in the lane on a moonless night. Lilou prepared feasts of pulses with meadow herbs, saucisson and cheese. She collected summer fruits, and they ate wild strawberries with home-made wine, lips stained and swollen. They sang each other songs from the dances they'd been to before the war, and tiptoed the dance steps, in secret caves filled with bats, old hiding places only Lilou knew.

They swapped knowledge and words like other lovers gave trinkets. The gilded hierarchy of bees, the Ring Nebula in Lyra in June, how long to wait for a newborn lamb to take its first breath before intervention, *Französin* and *Wanderfalke* – French girl and peregrine.

They didn't talk about the war. Kristian was a cocoon from all her troubles, and she was as light as a butterfly when she was with him. It wasn't real, and what they were doing was danger-ous, but that made it all the more magical and precious. Every-thing was heightened, each moment already filled with nostalgia and tinged with impending tragedy. The stars shined brighter, the wine was more heady, meagre dinners were feasts, while the world around them pulsed evil.

Lilou lost count of the days, refused to notice the setting of the sun, the rising again, another day gone, but every night Kris-tian studied the Eliot Papers, used his sextant, and wrote down figures, desperate to crack the secrets they held. One night, as they stared up at the waning moon, Kristian put his arm round her.

'Eliot's papa chose well,' he said.

'What do you mean?'

'It's in two days' time, and the moon won't rise till the morning on the thirtieth of July, so the stars will be bright. I think I've worked it out. With just a few pointers from Eliot, I think we can pinpoint the exact location. The constellation is Draco, and his eye, Eltanin, the orange one, is one of the fifty-eight navigable stars. Each of the pictures in the Eliot Papers refers to a picture in the dragon chapter, and all of them have numbers attached to them. The dragon has eleven spines, Eliot, his mother and father make three, the dragon's forked tongue has two points. It all makes sense. There's Draco, the Dragon constellation, the Dragon chapter in his book, and Draguignan, the town where I know the US troops are mustering.'

Night was falling on them, their last. The halcyon days when they had created their own world in nine days were over, and this moment was always going to come, but that didn't make it any easier. She couldn't tell him about the planned attack on German targets, about Operation Dragoon, which was the reason the US troops were arriving in such numbers. They had their own mission to complete, and then she might never see him again. Draco's eyes looked down, cold and indifferent, the starry tail glittering its icy glow.

'Draguignan, that's over forty kilometres from here. We'll have to leave tomorrow, and arrange to rendezvous with Eliot. How can something so perfect have to end in the name of something so wrong?'

He shushed her with a kiss. 'We have tonight, and a million stars.'

He took a sip of wine and passed it to her and they lay back on the blanket to watch them.

A shower of light passed across the night sky.

'The Perseid meteor shower, rocks smashing into the Earth's atmosphere,' said Kristian.

'Shepherds say they're tears, the sky weeping,' said Lilou.

'Not for us. Who gets to live a week like ours in their lifetime?'

'I would rather have the lifetime.'

'Maybe this is it,' said Kristian. 'Whatever happens, we met, and we loved. The Perseids come round every year, in July and August, so we'll never forget.'

'But they'll stop shining for me if you're not here.'

'We don't matter. They'll carry on regardless. That's the beauty, and the sadness.'

CHAPTER 21

HERE BE DRAGONS

DRAGUIGNAN, 30 JULY 1944

Lilou

Lilou, Kristian and Eliot huddled together in a vineyard set high above the town of Draguignan. The night was clear, zipped up by the Milky Way, the moon not yet risen. The vineyard was in the Domaine du Dragon. Eliot had been emphatic about that. The Dragon's domain. From Kristian's calculations, Draguignan was the general area, and with Eliot's intelligence the obvious place was the Domaine du Dragon. *Domaine* was the word for a vineyard business and they guessed the precise location would be somewhere within the grounds.

Kristian showed Eliot his papa's silk drawings, careful to hide the torch beam from prying eyes. Eliot sat between them, his head leaning on Kristian's shoulder while they studied together, one hand in Lilou's, hot despite the evening chill.

Kristian had tried to explain that the time was very important, and could be plotted against three elements with the use of a sextant – the precise location of Draco; a specific landmark;

and the moon. It was then to be cross-referenced with this year's navigational almanac and star charts. With a sextant, the general location was possible, but for precision other clues deciphered by Eliot would help.

'Do you think there's a time clue in here?' said Kristian. 'I think that will give us the key to the location, so think hard about what your papa said.'

Eliot was quiet as a kestrel, shimmering with focus.

'That's the picture of our house, number eleven rue Ferrachat, and right above it is the biggest star in the sky, the star of David, which has six points. So that makes it 05:00 GMT,' he said emphatically.

'Good. But it's very important that you're sure,' said Kristian. 'How do you know?'

'Because Papa taught me. The first clue is always the time.'

Lilou thanked Roman Stavinsky's lucky stars that he could be so prescient. No wonder this boy was so curiously clever.

Kristian noted down the time. 'That makes absolute sense. Without the time, we're lost, and everything has to refer back to Greenwich Mean Time. It'll still be dark at that time, though not far away from Civil Twilight.' He ran his finger down the chart. 'The moon will have risen by then, so we can use it to give us a position fix.'

Eliot didn't take his eyes off the silk drawings. 'The second line is a picture of flames from the dragon's mouth. You always step backwards from flames, and there are fourteen licks of flames on the drawing. Fourteen steps backwards!' he said.

Lilou's heart went out to this serious child so intent on fulfilling his father's wishes. 'Your papa would be so proud!'

'Maman wouldn't, she didn't like Papa giving me his secrets.'

Lilou shivered. His papa could predict the evil that was coming to the world, and the position of the stars, but not the precarious position he was placing his son in. Eliot's maman saw that, and now she was dead. Lilou hugged Eliot tight, but he shrugged her off, too deep in the pictures now.

Kristian moved the torch down to the next row of drawings – a row of triangles. Eliot counted them with his finger, just to make sure.

'Eleven dragon's spines, like stepping-stones. Eleven steps forward.' Eliot beamed at Kristian. Kristian ruffled his hair and wrote it down.

'You and your papa are quite the team. As a fellow astronomer, I'm impressed.' He bowed and Eliot giggled in husky delight.

Lilou crossed her fingers superstitiously – when numbers were this important, you should include a seven or it was bad luck. Kristian pointed to the next drawing, a dragon with a tail curving over like a scorpion's tail and a drawing of a book.

'How about this one?'

'That's the dragon, my special chapter, and my favourite animal,' said Eliot excitedly. Then more seriously, 'Even though they don't exist.'

'How do you know? This place is named after them,' said Lilou.

'There is no fossil evidence,' said Eliot, rolling his eyes.

Lilou silently admonished his papa. He could have let him believe.

'What do you think it means?' said Kristian.

Eliot took a moment to order his thoughts. 'It's chapter ten. The final clue is always a Roman numeral. Ten is X in Roman numerals, and X *always* marks the spot,' he said. 'And you can't go forwards and backwards without going sideways. That's our rule, so ten steps sideways.'

Kristian consulted his charts. 'All right, so if we use the sextant to measure the coordinates between the moon and the navigable star of Eltanin, which is Draco's brightest eye, then use the church as a fixed point, we can follow your papa's instructions and find the buried treasure. He must be a very clever man.'

Eliot nodded and folded his arms. 'Very.'

'You, too,' said Lilou.

Eliot searched the stars. 'I miss him. And Maman.'

'I know,' said Lilou. 'But you can talk to him through the stars. That's what you shared, isn't it?'

Eliot sighed. 'I'd rather just have him.'

Kristian and Lilou looked at each other. Neither of them could think of anything to say to comfort him, so they hugged him between them, an alliance for just one more night.

Kristian checked his chronometer: 03:48. Precisely one hour and twelve minutes more. After that, they'd follow Roman Stavinsky's instructions, by some miracle recover the blueprints, then part ways forever.

In the valley below them, in the town of Draguignan, US troops were mustering for Operation Dragoon alongside the French army. They both knew it; you couldn't miss the trucks and all the increased activity everywhere since D-Day. If Kristian was lucky, he would escape death, if not he'd be wiped off the face of the earth. Lilou had seen enough to know it was sickeningly random; no hand of God, no reprieve for good behaviour, no respite for families who might have already lost a son.

If there was such a thing as right, the Germans would lose, Eliot and his father would be reunited and Kristian would be cut down as he flew his jet under orders to kill.

But up here, just for another hour, they were allies, lovers, a little family, and the stars in the sky were their guide, their guards, their world. And they were beautiful, ringing a thousand carillon bells. Kristian held her hand and Eliot snuggled in against the cold.

To pass the time, they took it in turns to name the stars. Kristian gave them facts, Lilou recounted the myth of how

Draco arrived in the sky hurled there by the goddess Minerva, and Eliot guessed which of the stars were the planets referred to in his favourite book.

At 04:48 Kristian set up his sextant, using the vineyard wall as the fixed point, tracked the moon and Draco's eye against them, and at 05:00 on the chronometer marked down his position fix. From that point, Eliot paced his workings-out, fourteen steps backwards, eleven steps forwards, ten steps sideways, which took him to an old ruined church and a stone altarpiece still intact.

Kristian shone his torch all around the crumbling stones. Nothing. The sky changed almost imperceptibly from night to a tinge of day. Nothing really visible to the naked eye, just a change in the air, the birds stirring, the night giving way; and Lilou railed against the dawn and their parting. A part of her was glad they hadn't found the blueprints that promised such destruction. She'd seen enough for a lifetime.

Eliot sat on the tumbledown wall, head in his hands.

'Papa told me finding the blueprints was the most important thing I'd ever do, and we can't find them.'

Lilou took the torch from Kristian and skirted it over the stones. Behind the altar, the wall was still intact. But the stones weren't set quite right. Running from left to right, a rough dragon's head emerged within the stonework, and, where the eye would be, a faint X scratched into the sandstone.

Lilou shone the torch closer. 'This has to be it!'

Eliot jumped up and Kristian levered the stone out to reveal a cavity. Inside was a steel box.

'Here, you open it,' said Kristian.

Eliot put it on the ground, opened the lid, and pulled out a sheaf of papers in a brown paper envelope. Underneath, a sealed envelope, addressed to Eliot Stavinsky, Esq. Nobody spoke.

Eliot gave Lilou the blueprint, which she carefully opened.

In the burgeoning dawn, she scanned the incomprehensible set of diagrams, and when she looked up Kristian was eyeing it enviously. She turned away to shield them, and continued reading.

Particle Beam and Directed Energy Technology

The transmission of electrical energy without the need for wires, that may be used to destroy property and life. The plans for my prototype can in theory produce many thousands of horsepower, transmitted by a stream thinner than a hair, which is impossible to resist...

'Can I see?' said Kristian. Lilou was loath to let it get into his hands. Their last week together fell away. This was bigger than that.

'You still don't trust me, after everything? Give it to me, it's impossible for you to understand.'

Kristian held his hand out, jaw set in anger. Lilou imagined Marie-Madeleine's triumph when she delivered the precious document. All those sacrificed lives, the abbé, Joseph, Xavier...

Lilou squared up to Kristian. 'Marie-Madeleine is waiting for me to deliver them, and I never renege on a mission,' she said.

'Stop it!' yelled Eliot. He'd opened the envelope that was addressed to him, and tears were pouring down his face.

'Papa wants us to destroy it, and I agree. Kristian's eyes are all hard, and you look so mean. He says he called it the Peace Weapon, but if it's me that finds it and not him, it will destroy everything, and it's already happening, and I'm scared! You look like the soldiers who took Maman and Papa,' he sobbed.

Lilou grabbed Eliot and hugged him as he wept into her shoulder.

'It's all right, I'm so sorry.'

'Give the papers to Kristian to look at, then I'll know you're still in love.'

'I can't do that,' said Lilou.

Kristian's face twisted with hurt. 'Yes you can,' he said. 'Give them to me.'

Eliot dried his tears on Lilou's dress. 'He's telling the truth, I know he is. He's kind and good even though he's a bloody Kraut.'

A faint laugh washed over Kristian's eyes at that and his face softened.

'No, I don't need to see them. You're right, Eliot. No one needs to see them. We don't need any more evil in this war. The Allies are winning, and it's as it should be. You can tell Marie-Madeleine we never found the blueprints. There's always been scepticism as to whether they really existed, anyway.'

Eliot held out his hand formally, and Kristian shook it. 'Deal.'

'Here.' Eliot handed Lilou his papa's letter. 'You do it, he tells us how to.'

Lilou read Roman Stavinsky's letter to his boy.

Dear Eliot,

If you are reading this, I am not with you, and for that I am sorry, but I knew you would endure and that you are special. As I write, it gives me great comfort to know that on finding this you are alive, and have found a way to get to this place. You must take comfort too, from that.

Whoever you are with, and however you got here, you must destroy these documents. Underneath the false bottom in the steel box, you will find the means.

Know that wherever I am, I am with you in my heart. Be good, be brave, use your knowledge for good, and be happy, that is all I ask.

Your loving papa

Lilou lifted up the velvet divider in Eliot's box, and there was a box of matches, and another blueprint, identical to the first.

Using the bricks from the old wall, they made a firepit and scrunched each special piece of paper into a ball.

'Here, you light it,' said Lilou to Kristian.

'Gladly.'

The three watched the papers go up in smoke, cinders escaping and making a bid for the sky while the sun rose on a golden Provençal day, and chased away the stars that had led them here forever.

They waited till the embers glowed, then mixed the ashes with soil and covered them over to hide all traces.

By the time they'd finished, the sun was half above the horizon, bathing the vines in gold, amidst a joyous dawn chorus. Lilou didn't need Kristian's chronometer to know it was time to say goodbye.

'They're waiting for us,' she said.

'Likewise,' said Kristian.

'Will you come and find me when all this is over?'

'I won't need to.' He thumped his heart. 'You'll always be here.'

'He can find you with it,' said Eliot knowledgeably.

'I hate goodbyes.'

'Let's not, then.'

Kristian's eyes were the Bavarian forest, his smile the Provençal dawn, and he was gone, and the sun would never rise in the same way again, and the stars would stop shining for her.

'Don't cry,' said Eliot as they set off back through the vineyard to their rendezvous with Marie-Madeleine and Alliance.

'I'm not,' she said.

'Yes you are. You just don't know it,' said Eliot. 'Adults are so stupid.'

As they walked back to the troops mustering, to more bloodshed, to the abyss of lost loves, and weapons that hadn't even been invented yet, she couldn't argue with that.

CHAPTER 22

FLIGHT TO FREEDOM

LA MÔLE, NEAR SAINT-TROPEZ, 31 JULY

Marie-Madeleine

Marie-Madeleine sat dwarfed by the great dining hall, the radio crackling on the enormous empty table, a dishevelled Tonio by her side, hands still oily from his latest grapple with an aeroplane engine.

'Paris, this is Madame Hérrison. Do you read me?'

'Loud and clear.'

Marie-Madeleine still marvelled at the voice coming out of the little box, the chipper delivery of an agent who'd succeeded in their mission.

'And? Mission accomplished?'

'Affirmative.'

Tonio smiled his rogue's grin and punched the air.

'So the little man has his papa back? Not many who can boast that nowadays.'

Marie-Madeleine noted the tears in his eyes. Tonio had lost his own father at four years old.

'En route to Switzerland. Location fourteen.'

'Rendezvous and transport will be arranged. Confirm arrival tomorrow,' said Marie-Madeleine, beaming. This boy saved, and reunited with his papa, was for everyone who'd given up hope.

'Roger that.'

The radio clicked off.

'I've got the Lockheed primed and ready to fly at eight tomorrow morning. It's a short hop over the Alps and it will be an honour to have the little lad as my co-pilot, *patronne*.'

Marie-Madeleine regarded her old friend, the great aviator and author. Just being in his presence was like magic. If Lilou was the soul of Provence, he was the pride of France – dashing, eccentric, aesthetic, brave, even with his shirt buttons done up wrongly and engine oil on his forehead. A man of the sky and of dreams.

'And after that?'

'I'd like to die for my country. This body is an obsolete vessel nobody will miss. Too many crashes. You know what I've realised? For me, there's no breathless wishing for life to continue when I'm heading for the dirt at two hundred miles an hour. There's a strange kind of peacefulness, a resignation.'

'Don't talk like that. You'll go on forever, and it seems this war will not, thank goodness,' said Marie-Madeleine briskly.

'What about the beautiful mountain girl? Did she dutifully save the world for you as you ordered? No one dares to defy you, even when you ask the impossible, which we all know *is* possible with a little wit and daring.'

'In a way she did,' said Marie-Madeleine. 'I sent her into the wild with the maps, a German Luftwaffe pilot and a small boy, and after just over a week she came back and said she'd found nothing.'

'Does that mean the blueprints are still out there?'

'No – once the time had passed, the coordinates would be

impossible to find, so they're lost forever. But it doesn't really matter, because my instincts are that she found them and destroyed them.'

Tonio whistled. 'That girl's got more nous than even I gave her credit for. They build them tough in the mountains. How can you be sure?'

'We tracked them as far as we could. They disappeared into an old wine *domaine* near Draguignan, and in the early hours we spotted a fire. Careless of them to draw attention to themselves, or perhaps not where the blueprints are concerned. Goodness knows what nightmares were in those documents.'

'I hope you're right. If you know anything about celestial navigation, you could still use the coordinates to find the documents using the correct almanacs.'

'Not without the little lad and what's in his head.'

'The sooner we get him out of here the better, although Roman Stavinsky said he was developing a weapon that had the potential to end all wars.'

'There'll be others, and having witnessed the best and the worst humans can do I don't believe that's possible. There'll always be war, and God knows where all this destructive technology will take us.'

'Appropriate that the girl who represents the old France, the old ways, should destroy the blueprints.'

'She defied orders.'

'Good thing, too. The boys are buzzing about Operation Dragoon back at the airfield. We're on the home straight, I'm sure of it. Any news of Eagle?'

'Still missing in action.'

Marie-Madeleine stood up to indicate their interview was over.

'I'm sorry. He's strong and he knows you love him, if he's still out there. Don't shut me out with your show of efficiency.

Take a turn around the old gardens with me, I'll show you my childhood haunts.'

Tonio regaled her with stories of the boy he once was, with golden curls, who tore around these tropical gardens, falling out of trees, setting things on fire, never without some sort of injury. The same boy who built a flying bicycle with wicker-framed wings he persuaded the local carpenter to make, who grew up to fly the mail planes to South America, marvelling at the light above the clouds, the rivers scything through the land, the orange trees dotting the farms, the hallucinatory silence of the desert after a plane wreck.

With Tonio, life was a blast, a tragedy, a rhapsody. Drink deep, do right, never give up, and accept your fate when the time comes.

A rare peaceful morning passed in those gardens, Tonio's childhood home – a converted monastery with two medieval towers, tropical gardens, a wonderland planted when no one could have predicted the two world wars whose advancing technology could wipe out more and more innocent people, a world where greed and injustice had nevertheless always existed.

In the afternoon, Lilou and Eliot emerged from the rooms in the nursery wing where they'd been tucked up in fresh sheets and ordered to sleep.

Eliot had slept the minute his head touched the pillow, but Lilou lay staring at the ceiling, haunted by someone who wasn't there. Marie-Madeleine understood. Her German pilot. She'd seen them together at the rendezvous in Draguignan. She didn't need to tell her about the week they'd spent at her mountain hut in the Alps. It was clear in the way she looked like molten honey in his presence, in the way he glowed when she spoke, and in how Eliot stood between them, bathed in their happiness, despite the horror of his world. She missed Eagle, and she missed her own children, but for now she couldn't allow herself that.

Later, the two emerged, looking refreshed. How Lilou could still look like mountain dew after a few hours' sleep and a splash of water Marie-Madeleine would never know. Whatever it was, if she could bottle it and put it on the shelves of the Galeries Lafayette in Paris, she'd be rich.

The kid was like her shadow too, and who could blame him? She was fierce, beautiful and affectionate, every child's idea of a fairy godmother. She'd chosen well in his protector.

'My two best agents, all present and correct,' said Marie-Madeleine.

Eliot bowed formally, but Lilou looked far away. She'd been crying. Eliot looked shyly at his hero, Tonio, and he obliged with an ace of diamonds from behind his ear, which elicited a husky giggle.

'I have the best news for you, Agent Stavinsky,' said Marie-Madeleine.

'It's about time,' said Eliot gravely.

Strange, serious child. She pressed on. 'Yes it is. Your papa is waiting for you in Switzerland, and Tonio is going to fly you to meet him tomorrow morning.'

Eliot leapt and clapped his hands and wrapped his arms round her waist.

'He's escaped! I knew he would, especially after I remembered everything and followed his instructions so carefully at the Domaine du Dragon.'

She patted his head and peeled him away from her. A lovely moment, but it was easier to stay in control when people, even children, stayed at arm's length and kept their emotions in check.

Lilou knew what to do though. They danced a little circle, and Tonio made up a 'going home' song on the spot and found a king of hearts up his sleeve.

'Is Maman with him?' asked Eliot.

Marie-Madeleine looked desperately at Lilou for help, knowing she wouldn't say it right.

Lilou crouched down to his height.

'No, your maman isn't with him. She's in heaven, and watching over you, using the moon as a swing.'

Eliot froze and scrunched his fists. She'd never known a boy stand so still, almost disappear into himself. Watching him surrounded by relative strangers, and trying to be brave, was the loneliest thing Marie-Madeleine had ever seen. *Cry*, she willed him, but he didn't.

'You can't use the moon as a swing, it's cold in space, and Maman hates the cold,' he said, almost imperceptibly.

'I can draw her a nice warm shawl if that would help,' said Tonio.

'Yes please, she'd like that,' said Eliot, but Marie-Madeleine was unsure if he was just being kind to the adults who were so desperate to console him.

'I'm sorry,' whispered Lilou.

'I couldn't even say goodbye. She cried when they took her, but she told me not to so they wouldn't hear me,' said Eliot.

'I know, but she'd be glad to know that you and your papa can be together, and she would understand if you cried now.'

Eliot didn't reply, he was concentrating too hard on not crying.

Marie-Madeleine stood on the runway. In a world of uncertainty, double-crosses, acts of unbelievable bravery and inconceivable failures, this was a moment to savour. The little lad, only just tall enough to see over the cockpit, safely strapped in behind his hero, Tonio de Saint-Exupéry.

Of all the moments she'd stood on a makeshift airstrip over the past two years, this would be the one she'd be most proud of.

A small Jewish boy plucked from the talons of the Third Reich, his brilliant father saved, France's eminent aviator and beloved national institution at the helm. Beside her, determined, brave Lilou Mistral, her Provençal lucky charm.

Tonio saluted them, the sky behind him vast and blue, a morning breeze whipping off the sea full of promise.

'Perfect day for it. The ozone tastes of lemon and sugar on a fine day like this.' He winked at Eliot. 'It's your job to look out for angels. If you see one, wave, and think happy thoughts.'

Eliot blinked, thought for a moment, then waved at Lilou, closed his eyes to think happy thoughts. His own guardian angel.

Lilou waved back through tears. 'Say hello to your papa for me, and don't forget to say goodnight to me through our star every night.'

Eliot blew her a kiss. 'I love you more than all the stars in the sky.'

'All right, back to the home planet,' said Tonio, sliding the cockpit shut.

It was only then, when they stood back away from the roaring engines, that Marie-Madeleine noticed what Tonio and Eliot had spent the day doing: a dragon's jaw was painted on the plane's nose, breathing fire. The fuselage was daubed with dragon's spines, and the tail curled round the back, identical to the pictures in Eliot's extra chapter.

They watched the plane take off, Marie-Madeleine triumphant, Lilou sobbing her heart out as soon as they were gone.

Kristian strapped himself in, checked the dials. His first sortie since he'd said goodbye to Eliot and Lilou. Outside, Provence, the lavender fields a bruise of sweet perfume, deep gorges with turquoise rivers, sparkling seas, street cafés and restaurants, geranium-filled village squares, and Lilou, angular as the rocks and fierce and passionate as the sun. He had no choice but to be back flying for the Luftwaffe. Desertion would mean incarceration for his family back home. At least he'd be fighting air force targets, not civilians or Resistance, like Lilou and her friends. Please God the war would end soon.

In here, it was easier to forget, his co-pilot silent behind him. Just him in the driving seat, his Messerschmitt, the grey certainty of death, for him or his enemy. The instrument board to absorb his thoughts and banish any others, pointers that jumped to attention on engagement. Fuel counters, altimeter, airspeed indicator, hydraulic pressure, ammunition counter switch, check, check, check.

His co-pilot gave the thumbs up, and he took off. A moment to marvel at the thin blue sky, the ruddy cliffs against the sapphire water, a frill of lacy foam on the shore, a turn out across the bay, then there, directly in their sights, a lone reconnaissance plane, a Lockheed as far as he could make out. Room for two, pilot and co-pilot, French or American, probably around his age, his opposite numbers. He put the thought out of his mind, pulled higher, positioned himself for stealth, let the training kick in, the humanity kick out with the jet stream. He told himself he was working for good from the inside. He thought again of his family back home. He had no choices, did he?

'Shoot, shoot, before we're sighted!' screamed his co-pilot.

Kristian hesitated. The co-pilot leaned across and fired. The missiles flew, sleek as swifts. A split second before they engaged, the Lockheed cockpit snapped and ejected a figure, only one of the two, then a bloom of flame exploded the side of the plane, and it nosedived and split the water with a plume of foam.

It was only after he banked, and set his course back to base, the sun streaking at his eyes, that he knew. He'd been close enough to see the unusual red marking on the side of the plane, and it came into focus now in nightmare clarity. The dragon drawing from Eliot's book. It was unmistakable. He checked his watch, and the date. The thirty-first of July, the date of Eliot's transport out of France. He'd just shot down Eliot's escape plane.

CHAPTER 23

LOVES LOST

LA MÔLE, NEAR SAINT-TROPEZ, 31 JULY 1944

Lilou

Lilou stood next to Marie-Madeleine on the runway, watched as Eliot's plane banked over the bay, saw the Messerschmitt fall in line with Tonio's plane, shouted into the wind as it flew for a few seconds in his blind spot, then watched hopelessly as a streak of fire, angry as a dragon's breath, sent it plunging. She fell to her knees, convulsing, while Marie-Madeleine held her.

'It would have been quick, drowning can be a dreamlike death,' whispered Marie-Madeleine, her bony arms like a vice around her, holding tighter as Lilou's sobs convulsed her.

The grief was so hard she couldn't feel her legs. What if he was all alone in the deep sea, calling to her? What if there was a chance? In a frenzy she pushed Marie-Madeleine away, ignored her protests, ran across the scrub, and jumped into the swell beyond the airstrip. The shock of the cold paralysed her until she surfaced, Marie-Madeleine's calls at the water's edge whipped away on the sea. She was a good swimmer, but the seas were high here, the waves crashing over her head as she struggled to make progress against the deep pull, swallowing salt, screaming for Eliot. Impossible, useless; the heartless expanse stretched out in slate waves, vast and wild. Even if by some miracle she could power through, she'd never pinpoint where he was; the plane had already been a slim needle of light by the time they'd seen the downward trajectory, too far for any human to reach across the waves.

She hauled herself out, sea water blending with her tears, eyes fixed on the point she'd seen the plane go under. Nothing. Nothing but the sound of the sea, the pitiless sun beating down, and emptiness.

He'd looked so brave and excited when he took off, shining with the idea of seeing his papa, serious and awed to be with his hero Tonio, trying not to look sad at leaving her. She'd blown him a thousand kisses, trusted him to the skies, only to be cut down. Marie-Madeleine was wrong about drowning. He would have been terrified, known he was falling, horrified that no one was there to catch him.

Ever the fixer, Marie-Madeleine went back to try to muster a rescue mission, but Lilou knew it was useless. One little boy who'd served his purpose and a washed-out pilot wouldn't warrant valuable manpower in a war where so many sacrifices had been made, and resources were so scarce.

She stayed fixed to the shore all day, kept her eye on the exact place she thought the plane had hit the sea. Birds cried, white horses flew, clouds scudded. Nothing. Hope seeped away blood-red into the horizon with the setting sun, and Lilou remembered how her little astronaut had always grieved at sunset as he counted another day away from his family. Lilou knew this would be her fate every day for the rest of her life.

When night fell, she called his name over and over, in case he was afraid of the dark.

Marie-Madeleine appeared and put her hand gently on her shoulder. 'He's gone, Lilou, come inside.'

She submitted, and in her dreams Eliot cried out her name, begged her to catch his fall, wept as the terror of the waves overwhelmed him. Her eyes snapped awake. Better not to sleep than endure it.

At first light, she was back at the shore, calling, straining to see. No small boy with a cap of shining dark hair appeared to admonish her for her abject misunderstanding of the situation at hand. No hot fist in hers while he tried to hold back his tears. No more cartwheels in the hay meadow, or counting the sheep, or deciding which planet they'd live on when all this was over.

She stayed at La Môle, Tonio's old house near the airstrip, and the last place she'd been with Eliot. Going home was out of the question, even without hope of finding him again. The village would take care of Maman, as they had been doing. She couldn't leave when maybe somehow his presence was here.

Soldiers came and went, Marie-Madeleine went about her business. She was feverish with plans for Operation Dragoon, the D-Day style offensive planned for the southern French coast, and noisy preparations gathered around her at pace.

Every day Lilou went to the spot near the airstrip to watch for Eliot. Nearby, a patch of angelica attracted a brace of swallowtail butterflies who caught the breeze like dancers, as if Eliot had arranged the display for her. Provençal lore had it that souls came to say goodbye via butterflies. After this war, Lilou knew that such poetry wasn't possible. It was a wrong that could never be put right. Eliot was special, a bright, clever spirit, and he should have lived.

Days, maybe a week went by, and Lilou wandered the shoreline every day in a kind of daze. As she searched the horizon, Eliot came back to her in vivid colours: the moment he was lowered down the ladder in his neat corduroy trousers and entrusted to her, the first night he slept in the Alpine hut and used Scout as a pillow. Hiding from the Germans under the beehive and counting to infinity till she came; his husky giggle and exasperation at the stupidity of adults. She ached at the thought of his hero-worship of Tonio, his delight in Tonio's *Little Prince* book, which was the only place he could feel safe. She missed the way Eliot trusted in Kristian, the little family they created amongst the chaos, a dream that could never be.

After a week, Marie-Madeleine insisted Lilou go home. A grieving farm girl was ballast they couldn't afford with Operation Dragoon nearly upon them, and she was bad for morale with her haunting of the airstrip and the coast.

When she returned, Maman didn't even acknowledge her. Maybe, like Eliot, she felt it was safer not to love after so much heartache. She'd been away too long, and Maman had retreated further into whatever safe place she went to in her head. The village had ensured she'd eaten, and she was alive in body, but not in spirit. Everyone Lilou had ever loved had disappeared. Lilou stuck to the farm, couldn't face going to the village where the abbé and the Monteux should be, where half the lads who'd taken to the hills were gone.

For weeks, then months, she watched down the gravel drive for Kristian to return, but he never did. As her strength returned, she wondered how Tonio's plane, on a lone sortie outside of the battle zone, could have been shot down. She knew Kristian was on a mission on the same day. Had he somehow given them away, had she misjudged him? Or was he just another casualty?

Life carried on, and talk began to bubble that the boys like Freddie who'd been sent to forced labour camps might soon return. When autumn came, Draco closed his glittery eye and gave way to new constellations, and the heavens continued their processions regardless of the human folly below.

Lilou whispered a prayer to the sky every night, to Tonio and Eliot, to Joseph and his maman, and all who'd lost their lives to this war. The stars sang back to her in a chorus of beauty, diversity and joy for all the lives lived and loves lost, to the future and hope and peace. But as long as the world kept turning, and Lilou could watch from her little farm as the stars swept across the sky, she would never forget.

EPILOGUE

LA MÔLE, NEAR SAINT-TROPEZ, 1950

Lilou

Lilou stood with Marie-Madeleine on the tower at La Môle watching the fireworks. Every year since the war, the 14 July Bastille celebrations had grown more and more feverish, in defiance of the six years of horror. They weren't happy occasions, necessarily, more reckless and hedonistic. For Lilou, the place was full of ghosts, shapes where the people should be. The last time she was here overlooking the water, Tonio was gazing restlessly skywards, regaling them with tales of his night flights amidst the stars, and planning his escape with Eliot. His body was never found, but he died doing what he loved.

Marie-Madeleine's handsome lover, her brave deputy and strategist, the man who always escaped, ran out of luck. Eagle, Léon Faye, was executed after long incarceration in Bruchsal. Miraculously, Marie-Madeleine had found his last will and testament, and a letter he'd hidden behind the radiator in his cell. No one would ever know what was in the letter addressed to Marie-Madeleine, but in his will, written in a manacled hand, the hard-bitten colonel had simply wished for the world to enjoy peace again, to indulge in happiness, songs and flower-covered inns, to close the prisons and drive out the executioners.

Marie-Madeleine and Lilou chinked glasses. 'Amen to that.'

But they couldn't smile, not with so many missing. The abbé had written letters from his incarceration, offered passionate solace to fellow prisoners, but never returned, and Lilou had never stepped foot in the church again, not even to baptise her two sons, Antoine – Tonio for short – and Eliot.

Two years after she'd said goodbye to Kristian, she'd married Luc, the man who'd taken Eliot under his wing at the Resistance camp in the Var. He loved the farm, and he loved her. Now, six years later, they were a family. Their sons' favourite book was *The Little Prince*, and they had secret planets all around the farm, and a peaceful country childhood thanks to all the brave people she'd known.

One of the abbé's letters from the POW camp had found its way to her, with so many censored expletives about the Nazis it was barely intelligible. It made her laugh and cry, and miss him more than ever. At least he'd been himself right to the end. There was a sealed letter for her maman from him, too. It was obvious he'd always loved her from afar, and his note elicited a rare smile from Maman as she slipped it in her pocket. The next time she smiled was when Freddie came home. He'd left a boy, and came back a man, and with his return Maman came back to them, a clever, attentive grandma to Lilou's sons.

Freddie left again as soon as he could. The village was too small for him after what he'd seen, but the farm and village were Lilou's world. The farm, her bees, her sewing room, the fields and hills and rivers were dearer to her than she'd known before the war. The freedom of the land in all its harsh beauty was always enough for her.

In the roaring party in the ballroom below, the band struck

up, and that hurt. Joseph had played with this quartet before he was taken, and he had transcended everything when he played. He and his mother had been wrenched apart on the train platform, just as Kristian had told her, then transported and gassed. Their tailor's shop was still boarded up all these years later, a reminder of what many had stood aside for and allowed to happen.

Things had not ended well for Madame Aveline. After the war, the Resistance boys came back from their hiding places, brutalised by what they'd seen. Madame Aveline was shaved and paraded in the square for her collaboration, but Lilou had taken her in when they'd finished with her, and let her sob on her shoulder. She'd always been the fixer, and that was what she'd been doing, in her misguided way. She believed her when she said she had Lilou's best interests at heart in trying to stop her night-time missions. It didn't make what she did right, but surely they'd all learned that love and humanity was the only way out of this?

Oppenheimer's bomb finished the war where Roman Stavinsky's invention had failed. Foolish to think that anyone could halt the march of destruction. The world now had the means to destroy itself, and the only thing Lilou knew to do with that knowledge was to keep loving what she had.

And what she had even included Eliot Stavinsky, now finally safe with his papa in Switzerland, and a prolific letter-writer. He'd been ejected with a parachute, and picked up. Tonio had been scrupulous about that, strapping him up, telling him what to do should the eventuality arise. And it was so like Eliot to listen carefully, and to have the presence of mind to pull the ripcord. He was a survivor, that was for sure.

Two weeks after she'd returned, bereft, from the airstrip to the farm, Marie-Madeleine had found the time in the midst of Operation Dragoon to seek her out. A fisherman had seen the whole thing, and scooped Eliot from the waves. A good Resistance supporter, he'd worked out from what the traumatised child said that he was Marie-Madeleine's ward and had found her through the networks that operated along the coast. Marie-Madeleine had immediately spirited him across the border, and he'd been reunited with his papa.

Lilou had her faith restored in whatever was out there, her lucky stars, the inherent good in most people; sheer, wondrous, joyful serendipity. She'd even said a prayer to the abbé's God, and to Joseph's too, to everyone's. Her beautiful boy restored to the world, a wrong righted, and a curious angel who'd arrived from the sky was hers again, as much as he could give.

Marie-Madeleine gave her a letter from him.

Dear Lou-lou,

Mont Blanc is 4,808 metres high. That's very close to the sky, and me and Papa have an observatory in our house halfway up. It is part of a massif of eleven peaks, the same number of spines as my drawing of the dragon, so I know I am in the right place.

We can see the constellations very clearly from here, and I speak to you every night through our stars. Please ensure you do the same for me as you promised. I'm glad I let myself love you in the end even though I had to teach you quite a lot of things. I have done a drawing for you.

Yours faithfully,

Eliot Stavinsky

PS I love you to the moon and I think probably as far as infinity, if it exists.

Lilou had unfolded a crumpled drawing. A girl with a pixie

crop in dungarees, a tall man with high cheekbones and kind eyes holding a telescope. In between them, one of his hands in each of the adults', a small, frightened boy with a star of David above his head. Bigger than all of them, an oversized Patou with a lolling tongue and a big wet nose. The family that never was.

Eliot was fourteen now, an urbane young man, fierce about social justice and already a promising astronomer. He'd spent summers on the farm with her and the boys, and never ceased to remind her children how lucky they were to have her for a maman.

'You see that star?' Lilou said to Marie-Madeleine. It was summer, and Draco's eye was shining bright.

'There are hundreds, all indistinguishable, but I'll humour you,' teased Marie-Madeleine.

'It's Eltanin; mine and Eliot's star. We still wish each other goodnight on it every evening.'

'And what about your German, did you have a star, too?'

It still burned, that he hadn't come to find her after the war. Luc was a good man, but no one would ever make her feel like Kristian had. Up above the moonlit sea, five shooting stars wept their sparkling tears, tracking down the black sky in quick succession. It was July, the Perseid meteor shower. Her annual reminder of him.

'Not really,' she lied.

'You can't fool me, I'm an old hand at covering up the fact that you can only truly love one man. Eagle was that for me, and I know that German boy was yours.'

Dear Marie-Madeleine. The war had hardened many, but softened her. She'd remarried, adopted the son she'd had with Faye and subsumed him into her new family in her inimitable way. Her life was now devoted to the families of lost agents, to stamping the corridors of power with her demands for recognition, compensation for the Resistance, and tirelessly working to repatriate the bodies of her lost Ark agents.

'I'm not sure he felt the same about me in the end,' said Lilou.

Marie-Madeleine took a bitter sip of her champagne and held it up to the sky. 'I have a gift for you. Him. You know that Eliot was saved, and I told you that a fisherman had found him? It was unfeasible that he'd be lucky enough to be found in the middle of the deep sea, you said, and you were right. It was Kristian who piloted the plane that downed them, and Kristian who fixed the location and went back for Eliot. He had our radio codes from the abbé's original contact with him, and found me. He asked me not to tell you, he didn't want you to know that it was his plane that shot them down, though it was his co-pilot who released the bombs.'

Lilou had lain awake so many nights, watched down the gravel track for him so many lonely days that it hurt to even hear his name again.

'Where is he now?'

'He was one of ours, so I kept track. They court-martialled and executed him for insubordination. He already knew he was going back to give himself up, to save his family from being punished, and he knew what would happen. It's what he wanted, after shooting down his hero, the author of *The Little Prince*. He said he knew you'd never forgive him.'

'He was wrong,' muttered Lilou, the stars blurring with her tears.

'I know,' said Marie-Madeleine, 'but it could never have been.'

Marie-Madeleine crooked her arm for Lilou to take.

'Come on, let's go into the party and join the survivors. The stars will never shine as brightly for us, but they will again for our children, and we owe it to them, and to everyone who gave their lives, to never let them dim again.'

A LETTER FROM HELEN FRIPP

Dear reader,

I'm so delighted that you picked up The Girl from Provence, and I hope you enjoyed being dropped into Lilou's world, and joining the unlikely band of hopefuls who fought against all the odds. If you did enjoy it, and want to keep up to date with all my latest releases, just sign up at the following link. Your email address will never be shared and you can unsubscribe at any time.

www.bookouture.com/helen-fripp

There are so many incredible stories of hope, love and bravery from this turbulent period in our history. The Girl from Provence is an amalgam of real-life stories that I uncovered, but overall it's based on the spirit of resistance and resilience so many ordinary people found within themselves throughout the Second World War.

Marie-Madeleine Fourcade is inspired by the real woman who headed up Alliance, a branch of the French Resistance, with over 1,000 agents who communicated with the British Special Operations Executive, facilitating the exchange of information and people between France and Britain.

Madame Fourcade was a renowned society hostess before the war, with her own radio show and a penchant for flying. At a time when most men thought women incapable of such things, she led the movement, inspired men and women alike, and undertook amazing feats of bravery. The account of her incarceration in a Nazi jail and subsequent escape through the bars are based on real-life events, as are the stories of her disregard for her own safety, her brazen sangfroid when confronted with danger, her ability to absorb and order information, her love affair with her beloved Eagle, and her subsequent tireless mission to repatriate and fight for the rights of former Alliance agents after the war.

Antoine de Saint-Exupéry, author of Eliot's favourite book, was a wonderful writer and dashing aviator whose exploits on the mail planes from Europe to South America and Africa are well documented in his beautiful stories and autobiographical accounts. He died on 31 July 1944 while undertaking a reconnaissance flight for the French Air Force. Years later, in 1998, a fisherman found his silver identity bracelet in the sea to the south of Marseille, and in 2003 the wreckage of his aircraft was found. In the same year, a German Luftwaffe pilot became convinced that it was he who'd shot down Saint-Exupéry's plane all those years ago, and was devastated that it was he who was responsible for his favourite author's death. The idea fascinated me, and these uncorroborated events were the original spark and inspiration for The Girl from Provence.

The character of the abbé is inspired by the brave abbé at the village of Bargemon who is still remembered and revered as a Resistance leader in the region, but Lilou, Kristian, Eliot and all the other characters are entirely fictional. However, they represent a spirit, the best and worst of humanity, the wonderful people who refused to give up, and the realisation that every single person can make a difference when evil takes hold.

I really hope you enjoyed The Girl from Provence, and if you did I would love it if you could take the time to write a short review. Your words make such a difference in helping new readers discover my books, and it's wonderful to hear what my readers think.

If you'd like to get in touch directly, I read and try to answer every single message – you're what makes it all worthwhile! You can get in touch through my social media, or my website any time.

All best wishes,

Helen

www.helenfrippauthor.co.uk

 facebook.com/hfrippauthor
 x.com/helenfripp
 instagram.com/helenfrippauthor

REFERENCES

Atwood, Kathryn J., *Women Heroes of World War II,* Chicago Review Press, 2019

Bourhill, James, *The Killing Fields of Provence,* Pen and Sword Military, 2019

Bourne-Paterson, Major, *SOE in France,* Frontline Books, 2016

De Saint-Exupéry, Antoine, *Le Petit Prince,* Folio, 1999 (Éditions Gallimard, 1946)

De Saint-Exupéry, Antoine, *Letter to a Hostage,* 1943, translated by Cheryl Witchell, Babelcube Books, 2016

De Saint-Exupéry, Antoine, *Wind, Sand and Stars,* 1939, 'Written' by Evelyne Marotte, translated by Emma Lunt, 2016

De Saint-Exupéry, Antoine, *Night Flight,* 1931, translated by David Carter, Alma Classics, 2016

De Saint-Exupéry, Antoine, *Flight to Arras,* 1942 Reading Essentials

Dunlop, Storm and Tirion, Wil, 2023 *Guide to the Night Sky,* Collins, in association with Royal Museums Greenwich, 2022

Fourcade, Marie-Madeleine, *Noah's Ark,* Ballantine Books, 1974

Goldsmith, John, *Accidental Agent,* Pen and Sword Military, 2016

Goss, Chris, *Luftwaffe Training Aircraft,* Frontline Books, 2019

Kedward, Rod, *The French Resistance and Its Legacy*, Bloomsbury Academic, 2022

Maeterlinck, Maurice, *The Life of the Bee,* translated by Alfred Sutro, Digireads, 2004

McCairns, James Atterby, *Lysander Pilot Secret Operations with 161 Squadron,* Tangmere Military Aviation Museum, 2016

Olsen, Lynne, *Madame Fourcade's Secret War,* Scribe, 2019

Perrin, Nigel, *Spirit of Resistance,* Pen and Sword Military, 2008

Read, John A., *50 things to See with a (Small) Telescope,* Stellar Publishing, 2013, updated Sept 2019

Schiff, Stacy, *Saint-Exupéry,* Random House, 1994

Seaman, Mark, *Undercover Agent,* John Blake Publishing 2018

Sobel, Dava, *Longitude,* Harper Perennial, 2011

Torrie, Julia S., *German Soldiers and the Occupation of France 1940–44,* Cambridge University Press, 2018

Verity, Hugh, *We Landed by Moonlight,* Crécy Classics, 2000

Wake-Walker, Edward, *A House for Spies*, Sapere Books

OTHER REFERENCES:

L'Association Azuréenne des Amis du Musée de la Résistance Nationale, selected pamphlets and magazines

Dossiers from the archives, Musée-Galerie Camos, Bargemon

ACKNOWLEDGEMENTS

Thank you to my brilliant editor Ellen Gleeson whose insights are always razor sharp, and to Pierre Razet, Musée Camos, for access to his meticulous Resistance archives, fascinating discussions on Second World War social history and references to prominent figures and events in southern France. Thanks also to my agent Kiran Kataria for advice and support, to Katja Willemsen for edits, motivation and much-needed virtual cuppas, and to Claire Worthy for all the brainstorms and encouragement.

As always, to Nick, Tara, Charlie, Michael, Rosalie, Terry, all my extended family, and of course Jemima.

PUBLISHING TEAM

Turning a manuscript into a book requires the efforts of many people. The publishing team at Bookouture would like to acknowledge everyone who contributed to this publication.

Audio
Alba Proko
Sinead O'Connor
Melissa Tran

Commercial
Lauren Morrissette
Jil Thielen
Imogen Allport

Contracts
Peta Nightingale

Cover design
Debbie Clement

Data and analysis
Mark Alder
Mohamed Bussuri

Made in the USA
Las Vegas, NV
23 January 2024

84795743R00184